W9-DJP-525

FEB 2 4 2021

SEP 1 5 2021

Love in the Late Edition

Love in the Late Edition

By Reg Henry

Carmel, California

September 2020

Love in the Late Edition is an original novel by Reg Henry. The characters, events, and circumstances in this book were created completely out of his own fertile imagination.

Love in the Late Edition

All Rights Reserved
© 2020 by Reg Henry

No part of this book may be reproduced or transmitted in any form or by any means, electronic or mechanical, including photocopying, recording, or by any information storage and retrieval system, without written permission from the author.

ISBN-13: 978-1-7349057-4-8

Printed in the United States of America

Table of Contents

Love in the Late Edition

ACKNOWLEDGMENTS

A loyal crew of friends and relatives in the United States and Australia helped me along the way to finish this novel. My heartfelt thanks and appreciation go out to all those who read an early draft in full or part, and/or offered suggestions and encouragement. They include (and forgive me if I forget someone) Ted Smyth and Mary Breasted Smyth, Mike and Gail English, Gary Nelson, Toni Smart, Roslyn Smart, Julie Deall, Alison McLeod, Linda Bell, Linda Moody, Rick Manning, Katie Henry, John Mendelson, Kit and Mary Newton, Sheri Edmondson, Sandy Putnam, Paul Patek, Stefanie Kaku, Alan Cosseboom and (to protect the innocent with a degree of anonymity), Peter C. and Daniel L. I am also thankful for my excellent publisher, Tony Seton.

But my greatest thanks go to my blessedly breathing wife, Priscilla, and our children Allison Gilpin and Jimmy Henry, for inspiring me. Love always.

Reg Henry
September 2020

Love in the Late Edition

PUBLISHER'S NOTE

It's not always easy for a journalist to pick up the quill to write fiction. But Reg Henry was not only a serious journalist, but he was a very fine writer. The good news is that he brought his considerable talent to what is clearly a true love. He tells this story from the heart, and his delicious tale is sprinkled with epistemological gems.

Reg has written much more than a story that entertains, even captivates. He raises important points about how we live our lives. And these life-learned lessons have considerable value. For instance, if you are an infrequent public speaker – perhaps called to deliver a eulogy – here's what you might think about:

> *People in an audience don't want to feel embarrassed for the speaker. At the very outset, when they are prepared to cringe, the speaker must reassure them that they can rest easy. A speaker may be shaking in his boots but his words must be full of authority.*

Reg's advice comes not from reading books, though he has surely enriched his life in the pages of thousands. Rather, he has lived an important life, particularly as a journalist with an overarching, professional interest in who people are, how they think and behave, and why. Underscoring that interest, and the key to his success in recording his observations, is that he was willing to replace an earlier impression with an updated one. He was not one to let opinion stand in the way of facts.

Please know, however, that this is not an academic work. It is poignant with emotions – desire, outrage, hurt, and love – such that it demanded that I defer other tasks to stay with Alistair,

Linda, Phillip D. Jones III, and the others on the Estate stage. And there are countless laugh-out-loud moments that raised appreciation from the soul.

A last point...this is a novel. But it is so real – in its content and its writing – that it could be true. That's fine writing.

Tony Seton
Carmel, California

1 - THE NIGHTMARE

My baby just wrote me a letter -- The Box Tops, 1967

Dear Susan,

I am writing this letter because that is what we did long ago when things went wrong between us. I know you won't read it but what else can I do? My world has been shattered, because I woke up earlier today to start our new life together only to find that you had left me. After all these years, I can hardly believe it.

I know that the act of writing this letter is a symptom of a mind unhinged by shock and loss but for me it is desperate therapy borrowed from the past. I remember how in the early days, when we were young and newly a couple, back in Pittsburgh, we would sometimes leave each other notes in some handy place, on our bed or on the kitchen table, for the other to find later.

Those notes were usually written after some minor trouble, a spat or silly argument. I remember the ones you wrote. Once you put a note in my shoes for me to discover as I got dressed for work. It said: "I am very sorry for our fight but walk a mile in my shoes and you may understand. Love always, Susan. xxxx."

Another time you put a note in my underwear. I was in a rush and I didn't notice that my briefs contained a letter and somehow I didn't feel it either, at least not until later in the day when I went to the men's room and there it was. The guy standing next to me gave me a strange look when I pulled a piece of paper out of my underpants and started reading it. I don't remember what it said but our letters were always signed the same way, whichever one of us wrote them.

Love always xxxx.

Our notes were often apologies, and not I-said and you-said and this is why I am right and you are wrong. They were a stab at restoring communication after the sudden darkening of our sky – hello, I am over here, come and hug me and relieve the gloom. Whether they apologized or encouraged, they were really love letters.

It is a long time since I have written one of these notes to you. When we are grown old, we put away childish things, I suppose, but I think after a while we took each other for granted, at least I did. I wish we had never stopped writing to each other.

Maybe I should be angry at you. It was you who brought me here to this strange place to spend our retirement – against my better judgment – and then you left me on the very first night we were here. I woke up this morning alone in a place of strangers.

I feel numb and incomplete without you. Think fondly of me if you can. I have no place to leave this letter where you will find it. I can only rip it into tiny bits once I am done and then store its words in my heart and deliver them with my every fondest thought of you.

Love always,

Alistair xxxx.

2 - A STRANGER IN A STRANGE LAND

*Well, since my baby left me /Well, I found a new place to dwell/ Well,
it's down at the end of lonely street/ At Heartbreak Hotel*
-- Elvis Presley, 1956

My wife had died in the night. After the formal period of grieving was complete, after my grown-up children had returned to their own lives following the funeral, I was left alone in the Whispering Pines Estate for Community Living, a retirement community that I didn't particularly want to go to in the first place.

This is what little I knew about the Estate, which is what everybody called it.

I knew that meals were provided in a dining hall – excellent meals with lots of variety served by courteous staff members. Nobody expired because of starvation, although rich desserts might do a few of them in.

Games and activities were on the daily schedule and swimming pools and a gym had their devotees.

Shuttle buses were provided to town for medical appointments and church on Sunday (of course, some of the residents kept their own cars).

I knew you could be as active or as indolent as you liked. You could watch TV every day if you wanted, and some did, although the resident nurse might pay you a visit if you were never seen in public to make sure you still had a pulse.

You could garden if that was your hobby, although a team of professional gardeners kept the grounds blooming and immaculate.

You could join resident committees – the welcoming committee to conduct tours for prospective new residents, the hospitality committee to greet those recruited to become homeowners in the Estate, the public events committee to find speakers from the outside, the technology committee to make the computers, projectors and sound systems work for the visiting speakers. A thousand committees in the naked wrinkled city.

Without Susan, none of this had any appeal.

This was how the first regular day of the rest of my life was spent at the Estate: I didn't know what to do and I didn't know anybody to ask what I should do and in what order I should do it. I felt like a little kid on his first day of school, complete with the tears and fearfulness.

I found out later that a volunteer was supposed to be on hand to help. When new people arrive at the Estate, the welcoming committee sends another resident couple or a single person to greet them and tell them what they need to know. The members of the welcoming committee are known informally as the Howdy gang – as in "Howdy, stranger!" That corniness aside, the system generally works well.

By perverse chance, the single lady who was supposed to be our Howdy took ill on the very night Susan died and died herself a week later, not itself an unusual occurrence at the Estate. But in my case, it was a tragedy set upon a tragedy and nobody picked up on this snafu until two weeks later when I wasn't a complete stranger anymore and in no more need of a Howdy.

Left to my own devices, I struggled to adjust. I knew that some loose ends had to be attended to – the dismal process of disentangling the affairs of the living from the dead, including various people to be notified, paperwork to be completed, Susan's last will and testament to be found and shared bank accounts to be converted to one.

I made an appointment to see the manager, Mr. Higgins, to confirm that I would be staying here, not moving in with my daughter or son. And then he would tell me when I would be required to move from our double cabin to one suitable for a single mourner or monk. Since I hadn't even unpacked, I supposed the sooner the better for the second move, though this promised to be another source of sadness.

Not surprisingly, the numbing details settled on me like a fog and in my depression my concentration wasn't enough to face the smallest bureaucratic task on that first day. So I went to breakfast instead. That seemed to make the most sense. When in doubt, have breakfast – a maxim a man of any age can relate to. While I wasn't really hungry, eating bacon and eggs was surely better than talking to a lawyer or an insurance agent about my new situation.

I made the solitary trek over to the dining hall, a large, attractive building in the style of an old Spanish hacienda, only to find an argument going on outside in the area where residents leave their walkers. I was late arriving for breakfast and some of the diners were already coming out. These were the ones who were now yelling at each other over a dispute over who owned particular walkers.

Walkers can look pretty much the same standing together in a forest of legs. So for identification purposes, some of the residents decorate their walkers with colored ribbons, just as travelers do at the airport so they can pick out their bags on the carousel. At the Estate, some residents go a step further, adorning their walkers with stuffed animals tied to the holding bar – fluffy cats, cute puppies etc.

As I passed by, I heard one feisty old guy say to another, "Take your mitts off my walker! That's mine!"

"No, that's mine," said the other old fellow. "It has the purple hippo!"

"You are crazy! I have the purple hippo and I'll punch you in the snoot, buddy, if you don't let go"

At this moment, a small lady walked up – small but obviously with the large authority of a wife – and said to the guy laying first claim to the purple hippo, "Harold, you give the man back his walker. Your walker has the spotted giraffe."

I did not stop to see if her intervention resolved the dispute, but I doubt it came down to snoot punching, which might have knocked both gamecocks off their perches and led to walkers tumbling like dominoes, which would have been a sight to see. All I could say to myself was: Susan, what did you get me into?

Thankfully, drama did not follow me inside the dining hall. Though the serving staff was cordial, none of the residents said anything to me in the dining hall, nor did they yell at each other. I got a plate of something for myself from the breakfast buffet, filled a coffee mug and hunkered down at a distant table.

Social isolation has its good points early in the day whether you are recently bereaved or not – it is certainly better than artificial conviviality at that hour. I am not alone in thinking that heartiness should be against the law and that those found guilty of being excessively cheerful before noon should be sentenced to jail or at least community service in a monastery sworn to silence.

If I had met with jolly talk wishing me a good morning on that rotten morning, I might have felt sorrier for myself than I already did. Or I might have punched some guy in the snoot. But it didn't come to any of that. I was blessedly left alone. Misery doesn't always like company.

Susan would have called me a curmudgeon for these observations. "I love you all the time," she would often say, "but in the mornings not so much." Here I was remaining in character but with nobody to think well and bad of me at the same time.

I read once that at certain retirement communities a man who had lost his wife was thereafter visited by a species known as casserole ladies, who bring the poor man home-cooked dinners in order to insinuate themselves into his affections. But I was left completely unmolested by casserole bearers. While I had no desire for casseroles or unwanted attention, the chance of meeting legendary beings might have been interesting.

That this didn't occur was perhaps not surprising. No one knew me. For now, I was just another anonymous old guy with a mustache in the Land of a Thousand Mustaches, a look that seemingly every second guy sported in order to pay homage to his glory days in the '60s.

The breakfast revived me a bit. I thought then that I might make a start of the packing by shedding some of our stuff that barely fit into a cottage for two and would be too much for a single. A lot of the stuff was Susan's and I didn't have the courage in my fragile state to start throwing her clothes away but I could start on some of my own.

I remembered that the Estate had a secondhand store, where residents could donate possessions they no longer needed for resale to other residents, with the proceeds going to subsidize various activities such as providing the garden club with sufficient tulip bulbs. I supposed correctly that as residents passed on or went into full-time assisted care across the street the secondhand store would raise quite a bit of income.

It was called Secondhand Rose. After breakfast, I went back to my cottage and gathered a small number of items in a box. I thought I'd start small as a way to check out the store, which was only a short walk away.

When I arrived, box in hand, I found another customer already being served. He was a short man of uncertain antiquity and he had apparently wanted to donate a box full of second-hand underpants to Secondhand Rose.

The volunteer lady behind the counter was large and formidable. "We don't take underwear," she said brusquely.

"Why not?" he asked.

"Because it's gross, that's why."

"Well, you wash items of clothing don't you?"

"Of course we do but we don't have industrial-strength boilers with enough steam to handle used underwear. And even if we did, we don't have those tongs they have in nuclear power plants to lift the radioactive material. We don't have Haz-Mat suits either."

"So underpants are out?"

At this the lady gave the little man such a withering stare that it was lucky he did not immediately curl up. "OK," he said, and he meekly and wisely left.

"Next!" she bellowed, in a voice that a hog caller would be proud to have.

I stepped forward, feeling intimidated myself. Fortunately, my box was underpants-free and I was able to donate my items without further incident.

"Next!" The cry went up again. Another resident had slipped in behind me but he only had a question and he came out only a few yards behind me. I turned around to him on the walking path and said: "Boy, if that's Rose, she certainly has some thorns."

He was a tall guy, maybe a bit older than me, and he smiled and said: "A lot of people around here need to learn to relax."

"After that, I think I need to learn to relax too."

"You should come see one of our movies. Very relaxing. Many

in the crowd take a nap it's so relaxing. Thursday night at 7.30 pm. Full disclosure: I am the AV guy responsible for making the projecting equipment work and I feel better about the job when there's an audience actually awake." (AV stood for audio visual).

"OK," I said. "I promise to relax but not sleep. My name is Alistair, Alistair Brown," and I put out my hand. "Gavin Halsey," he said, shaking it.

So ended all the significant events of my first day. I did not know it then but I had made my first friend.

By Wednesday, after meeting with the manager, the Estate staff had hauled our furniture and other belongings into one of the single dwellings, which became so crammed with stuff that further visits to Secondhand Rose became a necessary routine. Underpants were given a decent burial elsewhere.

3 - THE SMOOTH-TALKING MAN

"Don't sit under the apple tree with anyone else but me"
–The Andrew Sisters, 1942

Once established in my new cottage, I soon met another in the Estate's cast of characters, Romeo Rawlings.

We were both walking along the path to the dining hall for dinner. At 5.30 pm every day, a bell would ring to summon the faithful to food. As we walked along in the golden part of the late afternoon, past the flower beds and the trees, other residents, mostly couples, were slowly coming out of their cottages.

What was remarkable in this corner of customarily casual California was how dressed up many of them were. The women wore pretty dresses and scarves, the men had slacks and button-down shirts, and some even wore coats and ties. The old social habit of dressing for dinner was still observed as if the Estate were an exclusive country club, which, given the cost of buying a berth here, I suppose it was.

By shabby comparison, I wasn't wearing jeans and I was reasonably pressed and cleaned but I still felt positively under-dressed, although it turned out the casual set had its own contingent. To be dressed up or to not to be dressed up? That was the question for any ancient Hamlet resident at the Estate.

Romeo and I fell into step. He apparently was a near neighbor in a part of the Estate where there were more single residences than doubles. Even by local standards, he was very nattily dressed. He wore white pants, a button-down light-blue shirt, a scarf in place of a necktie, a blue blazer and highly polished loafers.

He was about 5 feet 5 inches tall, had white teeth and a full head of grey hair slicked back and he sported a tan and the obligatory dashing mustache. If someone had tossed him a cane and a top hat, and he suddenly started tap-dancing, he might have passed as an aging Fred Astaire. This was Romeo, lover of the mature female form, as I soon discovered. I am still not sure of his age. It used to be said unkindly of older women that some were mutton dressed as lamb. Romeo was mutton dressed as ram.

"Hey, guy," he said, offering a well-manicured right hand for me to shake, "I haven't had the pleasure. My name is Bob, or in more formal settings, Robert Rawlings Jr." I didn't know then that everybody called him Romeo even though he didn't admit to the name. It made sense because he played the part to perfection. (When I later did learn this, I thought of the old Beatles song: "Her name was McGill, she called herself Lil and everybody knew her as Nancy.")

After I introduced myself, he said: "I don't remember meeting you before. Do you have a wife with you?" When I didn't reply immediately, confirming in his mind that I didn't, he further asked: "Did she go across the street?" I didn't understand this local expression then, and I suppose I just looked confused.

Romeo took my silent bafflement as the shame of a traditionalist who finds it hard to admit to a divorce, although this was a wrong assumption even if I had been divorced. Actually, I have nothing against divorce. While it is undesirable and often painful, my view is that parachutes should be available to those trapped together in a plummeting two-seater plane.

"Oh, don't worry about having split up. There's nothing to regret in ending a relationship. I know. I am an expert in that field." I did not doubt this.

And so the great misunderstanding began between Romeo and myself. He proceeded as if I were a confidant in his affairs – he being happily single and fancy free – and me, unbeknownst to him, unintentionally single and loaded with care. I could have corrected him at our first meeting but he hadn't actually used the word divorce and I figured that he and I weren't destined to be great buddies anyway. Most of my pals were not strutting roosters hoping to ruffle some feathers.

When we got to the dining hall, he found places for us at a table with a group of apparently single ladies. I soon discovered that where people sat in the dining room was dictated by how formal their clothes were. The coat-and-tie, frocks-and- pearls brigade sat at the best tables. The more casual diners sat in the cheap seats, near the heat and bustle of the kitchen. This sartorial class consciousness was later to become an issue that involved all of us, but that is a story for another day.

Romeo chose to sit down in the casual section, a bit surprising given his sartorial splendor. Looking back on it, I cannot tell whether he did this as a favor to me, the newcomer, or because of the location of the potential victims of his charm. Probably the latter.

In the meantime, I stopped to ask the maître d' about the chances of getting a glass of wine, then Romeo waved me over to where he was sitting. He had probably told the women his version of my history by the time I took my place. The result was that they didn't say much and viewed me with polite suspicion, perhaps on the reasonable theory that any single friend of Romeo's wasn't necessarily bound to be a friend of theirs.

Only later did the women find out the story of Susan's passing on our first night and sympathy and friendship replaced caution and aloofness. I was amazed that they had not heard anything about the guy whose wife died so soon. But, of course, the Estate management had plenty of practice in being discreet and the sight of a hearse in that community was sadly not all that unusual given the clientele. Say not for whom the bell tolls, it is probably for the guy two cabins up the street.

Romeo held forth that night in full geriatric flirt. A bottle of wine was produced and that served as a prop for his spiel. While feigned suaveness continued on one side of the table and nervous giggling on the other, I sat there quietly trying to control my mental nausea. The food was not the problem. The food at the Estate was unfailingly good. No, mental nausea is what happens when you hear things that no sane mind can digest without involuntary brain convulsions.

At one point, I remember one lady said that she wasn't very good at tennis, to which Romeo quipped, "Well, sweetheart, it's like all things, you just need experience." He lingered over the word experience, extenuated it, buttered it with innuendo and complemented it with a smarmy look. No doubt he hoped this crude pantomime would come off as a twinkle in his eye but it could not help being seen as the common leer it was. More giggles came from the end of the table, but not from the hapless tennis player, who looked slightly aghast. If she weren't so ladylike, she might have looked completely horrified.

My brain went into spasm. And so it went on until I could flee the premises at the first moment that did not seem impolite.

I happened to see Romeo again the next morning. "Hey, guy, great to see you last night at dinner. Cute gals, eh?" (Had he forgotten my name was Alistair or did he divide the world up into guys and sweethearts?)

"You can do all right for yourself around here if you dress right and let them know you are in the game." To which I said, "Frankly, I am surprised there is a game. I would have thought growing old was nature's way of discouraging romance."

Romeo did not take this as a witticism. "Say, how is your Viagra supply?" he asked, solicitously. "I know a supplier in Canada that can send it here cheap."

"Viagra?"

"Yes, you know, the little blue pill… it puts lead in your pencil."

"Thanks," I said in an unthankful voice, "but my pencil is sufficiently leaded for the moment."

Once again, I sent a thought to Susan: What sort of place am I in?

4 - THE VICTORY LAP

And we've got to get ourselves back to the garden
– Joni Mitchell, 1970

I was not interested in the sort of love Romeo Rawlings was peddling. I had experienced a real romance, a relationship of love always, not love when convenient.

Susan and I met on the Greek island of Spetses. We were in our twenties and neither of us was Greek. There I was, an Australian fresh out of Australia and living in England. There Susan was, an American fresh out of college and also then living in England. We both happened to be visiting Greece. The year was 1973 and that summer all the youth of the Western world seemed to be on the road.

On the June day we first saw each other, she was sitting like a mermaid on a rock at the edge of the sea and I was a passing voyager clueless to conspiring fate. She wore what then passed as a tiny green bikini – this being before the use of dental floss in the construction of young women's bathing suits. She didn't have a tail like a mermaid but that didn't matter because the effect was the same. The sky was blue, the sun was on the waves, her blonde hair glistened and I was dead in the water the moment I saw her.

As a flirtatious way to make myself look useful, I offered to go buy her a Coke at the taverna near the beach and bring it back to her on the rock. I figured that Coke would be sort of a love potion for an American girl, a species I hardly knew except from the movies. This was a ridiculous idea – how stupid can a young guy be! On the other hand, it worked. Maybe the caffeine jolted her affections.

That evening back in town, after having dinner together, we finally kissed with the moonlight now doing the romantic work of shining on the water. In that moment my life was set on a new road.

Ever since that day, my advice to young people has always been the same: Watch out who you kiss in this life. If not, you might to your surprise end up celebrating a holiday called Thanksgiving, as I did, surrounded by strange relatives who thought my accent was cute to the extent they could understand it.

Until I met Susan, I had never expected to live in America but we moved there just two years after we were married. And, yes, this being a fairy tale come true, we lived happily ever after, although ever turned out not to mean forever and happily in the traditional marital script meant grumpiness and disagreement interspersed with the love and affection so life would never become boring.

I never thought that the mermaid on the rock had lured me to my doom. Embracing her siren song as my anthem, I loved her and my new country both. Of course, any mermaid who climbs off a rock and moves to a conventional house will find her terrestrial husband irritating, and I was told that I was more irritating than most, for which I was apologetic. This happens to a lot of husbands even if they haven't married mermaids.

In due course, two children arrived – as I say, kissing can have its consequences – and our son and daughter made our days brighter still. The calamity was still many years in the future, unimagined, waiting for us to come to this place. I gloss over the story of most of our marriage years because it is painful now to think back on them. It is enough to say we looked ahead with optimism and confidence as the current of the years carried us along.

As different as we were, Susan and I were of one mind when it came to our expectations. We were both from the Baby Boomer generation and we believed that if we worked hard and saved our money, and we met with a little luck in health and circumstances, we could look forward to a happy retirement. Before we knew it, the kids grew up and left home and we began to think the empty nest seemed too empty and perhaps it was time for us to move on too.

My idea of what retirement might look like was less inspired than Susan's. I was happy to settle for getting up late, playing some golf or tennis, spending long afternoons with a good book on a chaise lounge, drinking a little wine in the evening and smiling at our grandchildren.

Susan did not look forward to a retirement like that; in fact, she thought there should be another word for retirement. "Retirement sounds like you are retiring from life," she would say.

"Isn't that sort of accurate?" I'd say. "Definitely not," she'd say. "I think it's a whole new chapter of our lives, something we have earned through hard work and perseverance, a chance to direct our accumulated wisdom to a new purpose. I think it should be called the Victory Lap." She made it clear that the late breakfast and the easy chair were not going to figure in our Victory Lap/retirement, no matter how much my accumulated wisdom begged to differ.

But when would this Victory Lap begin? The timing naturally suggested itself. I was in the twilight of a long career as a writer for a newspaper and, more sadly by my reckoning, the newspaper business itself was in the twilight of its existence.

For the past 20 years, I had worked at a morning paper in Pittsburgh and I finally came to realize that I was writing on the same subjects over and over. My life began to resemble the film "Groundhog Day" only with the growing suspicion that I might be the groundhog and my cubicle was the burrow. Important people in figurative top hats paid attention to my pronounce-ments but nothing I wrote changed anything.

Worse yet, the staff seemed to be getting younger and younger as I was getting older and older. I could see that I had come to be regarded as an institution. This was not flattering. The word institution for me conjured up images of mental asylums, penitentiaries and the Reserve Bank. The young reporters started to call me Mr. Brown when before I was simply Alistair.

One night I came home from work shivering in the cold of the Pittsburgh winter and knew that I had had enough.

"Susan, it's time for me to quit the paper and go somewhere sunny with you," I said, brushing the snow off my coat. "It's time to retire." That R word again. She blanched at the mention of it. "Take our Victory Lap, you mean"

As it happened, she had left her job in the office of a private school six months before, and she was now trotting through life in Victory Lap style.

But where would we go? We did agree that our old bones needed some warming up. "Florida?" I suggested helpfully. "Only old people go to Florida," she declared. I made a little ironic cough that went unnoticed.

"Alistair," she said, with barely a pause, "what was the most beautiful place with the best weather we lived in during your career?"

"Well, that's easy: Carmelito."

5 - THE TOUR

You are my sunshine, my only sunshine
– Pine Ridge Boys 1939

How did we end up at the Estate? We took a tour, which you might say was an absurdly pedestrian way to start a rendezvous with fate. Looking for a place to retire, we moved from Pittsburgh and returned to Carmelito, California, where years earlier I had been the editor of the local newspaper. We tried to buy a house but none turned out to be suitable. So we found ourselves at the Whispering Pines Estate for Community Living nestled on the slopes of a picturesque valley.

We had heard this was a final oasis on the long trek into the sunset. People said that this was no nursing home, no warehouse for the feeble old, this was something like a hotel for the fortunate few. And as the pine trees did their whispering, and we walked about on our first visit, we saw that the residents indeed seemed to revel in the luxury of being in a nice place among others of roughly the same age and condition and now at ease in California's version of a Mediterranean climate.

Yet despite the beauty of the surroundings, the Estate filled me with a special horror the more the tour went on. One of the best arguments for moving here was that we would never be a burden to our two adult children and nothing I saw destroyed that notion. Yet to me, something about nice didn't seem so nice.

Maybe I sensed that this was where personal independence ended and collective dependency began. The feeling was hard to explain. It felt more like an instinct throbbing at the edge of my consciousness.

Elderly emissaries of the recruitment committee led us on the tour and all the while I was sending Susan telepathic signals that this was not for us. One of the benefits of a long marriage is the ability to send thought messages to your spouse but on that day her brain was not in receiving mode. She was too busy being impressed by the flowers and the croquet lawn –"and, look, they have a tennis court and pickleball too, and you love pickleball."

Later I still struggled to find the right words. "Susan, this is a community of elderly people."

"Alistair, some are as young as 60 and you are only as old as you feel."

"If those women feel so young, how come some have strangely colored hair?"

"You have no hair and no standing to criticize the choices of people who do."

"But no children live here, no teens or other young people."

"They can visit and even stay with us and we can visit them."

"But," I said, only half joking, "I prefer a community that is not just seniors. I want to be able to rail about today's popular music. I want to look disapprovingly at some kid with his hair in a bun. I want to bitch and moan about ridiculous social trends. Darn it, I want to exercise the traditional prerogatives of a grumpy old man in the company of the clueless young."

"Ah, you will always find something to complain about," she said. (It was hard to argue with that but I tried.)

"In my head, I still think of myself as 25."

"Time to grow up," she said.

What she said did make some sense. I was in my early 70s and she was north of 65 and it would be convenient to live in a place where we had the illusion of independent living without the sharp edges and inconveniences that are the lot of the truly independent. To keep my lingering misgivings at bay, I repeated a mantra in my head: Our children will never have to worry about us. Never worry, never worry.

There was, of course, the cost to think about. We would have to buy into the Estate, and then sell half our possessions as well because they would not fit into the smaller space of our new residence. And, I was right, we would never be able to leave this to our children. The money would pay for our assisted care when we became too feeble to live on our own. In addition, we would have to pay a monthly allowance to the Estate to pay for the general expenses of living.

While it was rare for residents to die on their first night, death was no stranger to the premises, meaning euphemisms ruled and people always passed and never died. As much as a person's final retirement from this life was avoided as a subject of polite conversation, it was the reality of another euphemism that was most feared: Crossing the street.

The Estate was of two parts: The independent living part for those residents who could manage on their own and the full life-care, assisted-living part, which was literally across the street. When a resident said that someone had gone "across the street," the phrase was freighted with dread. Nobody wanted to go there. As far as the residents were concerned, the place across the street might as well have a gate with a sign saying: "Abandon Hope All Ye Who Enter Here."

My only consolation in Susan's death was that she had passed peacefully. But later on people would say to me: "Well, at least she didn't have to cross the street."

Before you cross the street, you start out living in a cottage among others like yourself, mentally alert folks still in the bloom of good health. That was the plan anyway, upset by Susan's terrible luck and mine.

When you come to the Estate, the official expectation is that you will be able to live independently in a cottage for at least four years. The math doesn't work for the facility if you need extensive care before that. The interest of the Estate was to recruit the active and the fit, not the halt and the lame.

Given the legal sensitivity around the issue of disability discrimination, I wondered if the tour guides secretly checked out how limber prospective new residents like us appeared to be. Maybe a geezer checklist was consulted. Do they walk up the stairs with a swagger or look like snails on their tedious rounds? Do they need canes or do they leap past every obstacle like Ginger Rogers and Fred Astaire? Must they stop for great gulps of air or do they look like they might resume a marathon at any moment? Are they, in short, four-year prospects to stay in the pink? If so, they are to be encouraged. If not, well ....

We did not fall down on the tour and we weren't visibly incontinent. This was presumably good for our prospects. We passed muster and we found ourselves a few days later in the office of the manager, Mr. Higgins. Yes, a cottage would be available in about two months, allowing time for the Estate to renovate the property prior to us moving in.

Susan and I signed the papers. We embraced the future and trusted to our luck.

When the day came to move in, the job of unpacking our stuff took until 8 pm – too late to go to the dinner hall for the first time. So we ordered pizza to be delivered to the cottage and opened a bottle of red wine.

"Well, here we are," Susan said, lifting her glass, "here's a toast to our California dream, slightly amended. ... To our first night of living happily ever after."

This may have been the very moment that upset the surly gods responsible for putting banana peels under the feet of overly optimistic mortals. So much for the Victory Lap.

6 - A NIGHT AT THE MOVIES

You must remember this/ A kiss is still a kiss
– Dooley Wilson, Casablanca, 1942

On the Thursday I was supposed to go to movie night I bumped into Gavin at lunch and he invited me to come over to his cottage that evening for a pre-movie glass of wine. As the AV man, he would work the projection equipment and I would try and not fall asleep. This might be more of challenge than I thought as Paddington was the movie scheduled that night, which I understood to be aimed at a mostly children's audience. His cottage turned out to be not too far from mine.

When I arrived, his wife Trish, a sprightly elf of a person whose blue eyes scanned the world with a natural curiosity, opened the door to greet me. She was in the act of going out but not to the movie. "I do my sleeping at home," she said happily as she left to meet lady friends for some undisclosed purpose beyond the required knowledge of men.

I found Gavin was in the midst of writing his obituary. "Are you feeling poorly, Gavin?" I asked.

"Not at all," he said, "I am just feeling elderly. Everybody our age should write their obituary. I think it is part of the Grim Reaper greeting kit – you know, bank accounts squared away, trusts and wills ready, funeral arrangements pre-paid, that sort of thing. A pre-written obituary helps survivors too sad to write down what you did."

"You are right, Gavin, I should do that myself." I said this all too knowingly. It was very fresh in my memory that I had been required to sit down and write an obituary for my dear Susan, which was an added burden in the midst of my grief.

I did not mention Susan to Gavin right then – he would find out soon enough – but I told him a little about my previous career in newspapers and how writing obituaries was sometimes a part of the job. "Oh, you must take a look at this," he said. He gave me a sheet of paper and then poured us both a glass of a nice local Pinot Noir.

He had written only one paragraph.

"Gavin Halsey, aged xxx (place figure here after his toes curl up), died yesterday of institutional boredom at the Whispering Pines Estate for Community Living in Carmelito, CA. Beloved by all as a scholar and a gentleman, philanthropist and entrepreneur, Mr. Halsey was internationally renowned as the greatest scientist in the field of gases never to have won the Nobel Prize. To the scientific community and at the Estate, he was known as the Father of Gas."

"Hmm," I said. Gavin clearly didn't know that real journalists, despite popular prejudice, have a fondness for facts. "This is very amusing and there's nothing that says an obituary can't be funny," I said diplomatically. "But I am sure you are an accomplished man who doesn't need to gild the lily or the gas."

"Too much gas and not enough reality?" he said. "I did say that I never won the Nobel Prize."

"That was wise but I think it would be wiser still if you toned down the flippancy a little. This, after all, will be the official history of your life and you don't want to come off sounding like a deceased Bozo the Clown. I am happy to help you with this."

Though looking a little disappointed, he took it quite well. "Good point," he said, "and I'll take you up on your offer."

In subsequent weeks, we did work together on producing a professional obit. And, as I expected, Gavin turned out to be an accomplished person. He was a graduate of Stanford University with a Masters in chemical engineering and later the founder of a prosperous company specializing in industrial gases. He had won various awards, although the Nobel was never likely. He was known as the Father of Gas, but only among a few of his male pals. At that time, he was 77 years old, and I ruefully remembered his remark about people "our age." Being only 71 myself, I wondered whether mourning had aged me.

Half an hour before the scheduled start of the movie, we walked over together.

"Did you choose Paddington for the featured movie?" I asked.

"Oh no," said Gavin. "There's a committee for that. You will discover there's a committee for everything at the Estate."

"And what do they want in a movie?"

"It's what they don't want. No sex, drugs, excessive violence, except wars and football of course, foul language...all of that stuff is out."

"I am thinking a movie about Paddington Bear doesn't have much of that."

"Yes. That makes Paddington the perfect movie for the Estate."

"What is the committee afraid of? I would think that most of the residents would be familiar with sex and violence at some stage of their lives, may have even participated in it."

"Yes, of course, but seniors can be the victims of their own stereotypes. Or else, a lot of these old folks ran naked through the streets when younger but now wish to forget it ever happened."

"Must be hard to pick a perfect movie for the Estate when so many movies of today have items on the no-go list."

"Yes, that's why there is a committee. Many of the movies we play are ancient, suitable for ancient audiences. Maybe the studios should add a classification to the PG and Adults Only group...Ancient Adults Only."

When we reached the hall, I helped Gavin move the audio visual equipment into position. He gave it a trial. It didn't work. He then proceeded to swear in language that stevedores and Marine drill sergeants would be familiar with but was shocking to hear in this place.

"Can I help?" I asked, not that I knew anything about how the equipment worked but I just wanted to be helpful.

"You can help me cuss," Gavin said.

So I did. "You bloody mangy mongrel, bastard piece of dag, don't come the raw prawn with us, you stupid galah."

Then the machine worked. "What language was that?" said Gavin in wonder.

"Australian," I said. "I came to the U.S. from Australia 45 years ago. That's why I have an accent. The speech therapists say they can't do anything for me."

"I think I need to learn Australian."

"I think Japanese or Korean might work better on this equipment. It probably comes from there."

I understood later that this swearing routine was common practice for Gavin, except that it was restricted to indecent American English. Some people complained about the foul language but got used to it and then forgot. It struck me as rather funny that the movie committee was keeping bad language out of the movies but the AV man showing them was busy filling the vacuum.

Mr. Higgins had appointed him to the job on the basis of his scientific background. On paper, he looked good but his expertise was in gases. Unfortunately, the AV equipment was not gas operated. In the dining hall where movies and lectures were held, he was in the dark as much as anyone else. But no other AV man or AV lady was available and Gavin, as gruff as he could be to machines, was too kind to refuse the offer.

Gavin's idea of audio and visual equipment was the traditional one: He would rather speak in a loud voice and point to things written in chalk on the blackboard. But he was not left to his own devices; the devices of the modern age were now his responsibility. If trouble were encountered, his preferred method was to swear and/or hit it with a stick. He might then deign to check whether the leads were properly plugged in.

Visiting speakers were his biggest challenge. If the movie stopped, the audience could leave or keep on napping and nobody was left embarrassed. But a live guest speaker couldn't be left with a PowerPoint presentation without the power. A good night for Gavin was getting the speaker happily through his lecture without interruption. But lectures were sometimes punctuated by Gavin's frantic cries of "What the heck?" and "I thought I'd fixed that!" He usually shamed the equipment enough that it eventually worked for him but this took a toll. "I am going to die of stress in a non-paying job," he'd often say later.

I liked Gavin from the first time I met him outside Secondhand Rose and my regard for him only grew. He was a selfless man driving himself crazy for the sake of his little community. His unfailing but sorely tried good nature became an inspiration to me to find a job that was useful – although not one like his that involved so much perspiration.

This night the movie equipment behaved itself after its initial rebellion. Against all expectations, I liked the Paddington Bear movie, which was made in Britain and was witty enough for adults. It was ironic to watch it in the midst of an audience snoring their heads off as if impersonating bears hibernating in a large cave.

I decided that night that in my quest to find something meaningful to do, I would not be joining the movie committee. I would then feel an obligation to attend more movie nights. It was fun this once but it wasn't for me.

7 - THE NEED TO KEEP BUSY

Just whistle while you work
– Snow White and the Seven Dwarfs, 1937

The trick to being retired is to stay busy, or so busy retired people say. For some reason, those seniors who are not busy and sit around and drink themselves into the sunset are not usually asked for retirement tips.

Yet in my first few months of grief, my inclination was to join the drinkers on the porch. However, my conscience still took instruction from my dearly departed Susan, so I set out to find something to do. The mental note to myself was written in large letters: Must Keep Active.

Because I was among other lonely people seeking a purpose, I gradually made friends. One of them, of course, was Gavin Halsey, the AV man whose friendship and example was to have a lasting effect on my time at the Estate.

The opportunities to stay busy at the Estate were as numerous as the chances to do nothing. Gavin had told me that committees existed for everything and he was right; the number of committees and sub-committees rivaled that of the government. Those speakers that Gavin assisted were first invited by volunteers who met to discuss possible candidates. The movies he showed were picked by volunteers. And Susan and I had met volunteers whose job it was to show prospective residents around. But none of those jobs appealed to me.

Maybe an activity was better than a job. As if these were not enough committees, various clubs convened to banish idleness from the residents' lives altogether.

Perhaps I could join the gardening club. Every morning I saw small groups of people in floppy hats trudge out to their designated plots to till the soil with trowels and shovels. They chatted a lot. I think they chatted up the seeds from the soil.

I love plants and I was tempted to join the garrulous gardeners, and I was only stopped by my lifetime aversion to getting my hands dirty and my knees muddy. The petunias would have to spring forth from the ground without my assistance, ditto the carrots.

Perhaps I could learn to play bridge by joining the bridge club. I understand that bridge is among the mental pursuits that help keep the aging brain active and alert. But the thought of spending many hours indoors studying cards while the sun was shining outdoors was not appealing. My view is that gray matter is best stimulated by activities pursued under a blue sky.

I did play tennis with a bunch of guys on the Estate's courts – we were all dressed in traditional white according to the prevailing stuffy rule. But a person can play only so much tennis and a further disappointment was that our games tended to be unsatisfying. Clearly, a few of the players had been quite good in their youth – their strokes showed the residual traces of expensive tennis lessons – but nobody now was very athletic. Unable to run, they lobbed and used drop shots to decrepit opponents in a game dedicated to the art of creative immobility. You could pull a drop shot on a 90-year-old who normally used a walker and nobody thought this was unsporting.

When not trying to return shameful drop shots or lobs so high they were a danger to low-flying aircraft, I went to the gym. Staffed by friendly and enthusiastic trainers, mostly young women, the gym was well equipped and offered a variety of classes, mostly low-impact calisthenics.

I chose instead to work out by myself almost every day, hoping that the young women trainers would not think that the

10-pound weights were all I could manage. I also hopped on a stationary bike and pedaled furiously, fighting the thought that this was a metaphor for my life – all that pedaling and still going nowhere.

But these activities weren't as good as a real job. I envied some of the residents who had found themselves volunteer jobs outside the Estate. Martha Evans was one of these. In her previous life, she had been a school teacher, which turned out to be an ideal credential when she applied to become a volunteer at a local nature reserve.

Martha was an enthusiastic person who needed to have a job to keep busy. She was a Girl Scout grown to full maturity and she didn't have a cynical bone in her body, which meant that she didn't have a whole lot in common with me. She wouldn't have made much of a drinking companion if we had both decided on a retirement of laziness and drinking.

I had met her in the dining hall one night and the subject happened to turn to volunteer opportunities. "There's about half a dozen of us here at the Estate who volunteer at the Carmelito Nature Park. We take turns doing shifts at the visitor center, go on trail walks and help visitors understand what they are seeing. Would you like to shadow me on one of my shifts?"

I would. What was there to lose? So two days later she drove me out to the Carmelito park in her little car, only a 20-minute trip away. The park is famous for its beautiful natural coastline. The sea beats against rocky promontories, stony coves, and sandy beaches, and the tourists walk its trails in hope of seeing sea lions, seals, and otters. It is all stunningly picturesque, every vista offering its own iteration of a magical picture.

This beauty is extravagantly described in the world's tourist guidebooks. One edition of such a book is said to rate the park second only to Disneyland among the most desirable places in California to visit. For some visitors then, the imagination moves from seeing a giant mouse in clothes and large shoes to a seal on a rock in its natural state.

To help interpret and digest these disparate experiences, the volunteer corps stands at the ready. The hundred or so of them are well-trained and seasoned, and when I say seasoned, I mean mostly getting on a bit in years. Cynics might say – and, of course, Martha would not be one of them – this is really a program to keep the elderly off the streets.

But the volunteers are needed. Thanks largely to those guide-books, the tourists come in droves, more numerous than the anchovy swarms the seals chase. Even at nine in the morning on the weekday we went, the tourists were starting to stream in. For the next two hours, Martha was in charge of the visitor center. She took the job for the chance to tell the visitors about how the otters use a tool – a stone – to open the abalone shells for their dinner or that the sea lions on the rock were mostly male, because the females had the good sense not to put up with them more than was necessary for the propagation of the species.

But the most frequently asked nature question was about the call of nature – "Where's the nearest bathroom?" (Behind the center.) They also asked: "Can I buy a snack here?" (No.), and "How do I get back to the road?" (The trail is over there.) Perhaps the park with the giant mouse in shirt and shoes does it better.

Still, a job is a job and I could point out the bathrooms as well as anyone. In fact, better than most anyone, as I am an older person and we keep careful track of bathroom locations. But what decided me finally against being a nature volunteer was something that happened near the end of Martha's shift.

Members of the public visiting the Carmelito park can borrow binoculars from the visitor center for free. All they have to do is leave their car keys as a surety to guarantee their return. A group of four young overseas visitors – three boys and a girl, all in their early twenties – decided they needed to borrow binoculars and duly handed over their keys. They didn't walk very far in the parking lot before they decided to reconsider the deal. They discussed the matter at length in some language I could not identify. I imagined they were asking themselves whether they needed binoculars to see a giant mouse.

But no. They came back to Martha and the young man who was evidently their spokesman said in accented English: "We don't want to leave our car keys. Can we leave the girl instead?" For her part, the girl said nothing and showed no emotion. For all I know, this happens in her culture all the time.

Martha was firm but polite. She took back the binoculars and went to retrieve their keys. She did not explicitly say that the park's policy was not to take human hostages in exchange for binoculars. That's where I would have failed the test. I would not make an unfailingly polite volunteer. I had lived a straight-for-ward, argumentative life. My diplomatic skills had atrophied and weren't likely to be reinvigorated in retirement. Clearly, a nature volunteer's life was not for me.

I gave some thought to becoming an auxiliary volunteer at our local hospital in Carmelito. When I went to visit a resident who had been moved to the hospital from the Estate clinic for an operation, the person who looked up the room number for me at the front desk was a volunteer. But did I really want to work in a hospital? No matter how bright and cheery as our local one is, hospitals are depressing places. That's no surprise. They are filled with sick people and their concerned relatives and friends.

Anyway, I figured I would probably be seeing enough of hospitals as I grew older.

A few of the residents I met at the Estate used their professional skills from their former lives as accountants or lawyers to help their neighbors and other elderly people in the greater community. This obviously was a worthy service. But I can't do tax forms for other people when I have always had an accountant do my own. And my knowledge of the law is pretty much restricted to the laws of libel, the occupational hazard of journalists.

Some of the boys from the tennis group – I use the term boys loosely – invited me to clean up litter on a nearby highway on Sunday mornings once a month. They had adopted a stretch to clean up under a state-sponsored plan. A permanent sign by the road identified what group had the responsibility for picking up this area – the Racketeers. "You will find lots of interesting items. You might even find some cash," they said. "And we all go and have a big breakfast at the golf club later."

That sounded good. So I went out with them, put on my mandated orange vest and flexed my tongs. Each of us walked for a mile or so against the flow of traffic, which at eight on a Sunday morning was not too bad, and filled up trash bags, one pincer-full at a time. I found no interesting items or cash. All I found was gross garbage that had been thrown from passing cars.

The sense of community service I was expecting from this experience soon gave way to a feeling of disgust and anger at the wanton carelessness of the litterers. I began imagining ways that offenders could be punished if caught. Fines and imprisonment were too good for these despoilers of the environment. I thought some torture involving tongs applied to delicate body parts might be a deterrent. So as I walked along picking up the trash, the side of the road became cleaner but the inside of my soul became murkier and my contentment level lower.

It was another detour on the road to finding some pleasing activity. However, I did enjoy the big breakfast at the golf club later.

What had my life equipped me to do? I was lately a professional husband but was now unemployed in that line of work. For the moment, I was busy just trying to figure out how to stay busy. If only Susan were here to tell me what to do. And to think I once resented her for giving me instructions.

8 - MICROPHONE MIKE

Over there, over there, send the word,
send the word over there that the Yanks are coming
– Over There, George M. Cohan, 1917

It was Memorial Day – my first at the Estate – and it became memorable for the wrong reason.

For all the lip service about veterans and the ultimate sacrifice some pay, Memorial Day is often too much about the holiday and the start of summer and too little about the commemoration. A committee at the Estate existed to make sure that at least in this little corner of the world the proper meaning of the day would be honored. Of course, in the home of multiple committees, such a committee was bound to exist. And, of course, many of its members had trim mustaches, a uniform of sorts for men at the Estate.

I have a natural aversion to committees. As wags sometimes observe, it was a committee that designed the camel, but at least the camel is a useful animal, which is more than can be said for the handiwork of most committees.

However, the work of the Memorial Day committee had my full support. I am a veteran, although not of the usual American variety. Having grown up in Australia, I was drafted into the Australian Army in 1969 and spent the next year in Saigon, South Vietnam. My dad and many male relatives had served, so family tradition made this seem like a good idea at the time.

Well-meaning people who never served tend to view all veterans through the same gauzy light of noble sentimentality. While that is nice, those who did serve know a little better. They recognize that some vets are undeniably heroes and the others are best described by the line from the poet John Milton, "They also serve who only stand and wait."

I was in the latter group. I had been a trainee journalist in civilian life and, by an uncommon stroke of luck, because militaries everywhere are notorious for putting square pegs in round holes, I was assigned to a small unit of army reporters. My role in Vietnam was unheroic. The only thing of heroic proportions about me was my beer consumption. I say this with no pride. In my defense, I can only note that Australian beer, the nectar of the gods, was 10 cents a can in our billet and a man could hardly afford not to drink

In between beers, I wrote stories for the army newspaper and did other duties that did not require me to fire a shot in anger (or any other emotion). I did venture out into the bush sometimes and I will never forget the fear-laced excitement of those patrols. But the Viet Cong never had the decency to shoot at me after all the training I had done to be ready.

In short, I was in combat situations but never was actually in combat. This ambiguity extended to my view of the Vietnam War in general. Like most people, I think the United States and its allies made a tragic mistake in fighting that war but I am still proud I served. At age 21, I felt mine was not to reason why, and besides, the Domino Theory of communist aggression looked more reasonable if you lived in Australia, the last domino. Not that I had much choice in the matter. My number was called in the random lottery of life.

I do not hold anything against those who reasoned that is was folly and didn't go. What I do not tolerate so well are today's political hawks who had the same conservative outlook then but sought deferments to avoid having the courage of their convictions.

But Memorial Day is no occasion for reviving the bitter divide of my generation. The Estate had other veterans of foreign wars, including one or two vets from World War II, now in honorable antiquity and so old and bowed that the very weight of their medals seemed about to topple them over. A few more had been in the Korean War and they were followed by representatives of other conflicts, mine included, and still others who had served but never were sent overseas.

Some in the crowd simply came along out of a feeling of patriotic duty to thank the vets for their service. We were all out on the lawn seated on folding chairs shaded by the pines, about 50 of us men and women, some wearing medals, many not. The time was 11 am and, under a clear sky, the day was warming up after the usual morning chill.

The committee had arranged for a local brass band to play a selection of marches and patriotic numbers, but first a troop of Boy Scouts marched in the colors. Then a bugler in the band stepped up to play Taps, which he did skillfully, the haunting notes setting the appropriate somber tone.

But, as the horn sounded its melancholy alarm, I couldn't help being mentally transported back to my old high school in Australia, the Brisbane Boys Academy. Some of the boys, me included, signed up to join a company of army cadets that drilled once a week at the school, something like an ROTC unit over here.

About 15 of the boys in the company made up the cadet marching band, which was notable for marching badly and playing their instruments even more badly. Perhaps the boys who played in the band had expressed some vague interest in music and that was enough to be picked but somehow the need for talent was overlooked. As would-be-soldier musicians, the band appeared to be practicing for a war against tunes. It was enough to arouse the dead to laughter.

This had memorable consequences. When we had a memorial assembly at school, a cadet from the band would play the British Commonwealth version of Taps – the Last Post, similar but somewhat different. From the first off-key note to the last, the solemnity of the occasion was completely subverted. You stood stock still out of respect and then you would hear the bugler being a one-man firing squad for the music and inevitably you began to shudder trying to suppress the laughter. It was wrong to laugh, you knew, but you couldn't help yourself. Everywhere boys were convulsing with secret laughter and trying to hide this fact from their unforgiving teachers, who I am sure were also swallowing laughs mid-throat.

So I heard Taps at the Estate and I kept a respectful face but my memories were plotting to make me howl in a disrespectful mirth that only I could understand. Thankfully, the speeches came along soon enough to restore my inner respectfulness. The small parade of speakers who trooped to the podium one by one proceeded to say the right words for the right occasion – unremarkable but well-intentioned words but too familiar to be long remembered.

At one stage, a speaker asked all veterans to stand and be recognized. This put me in a familiar quandary. Should I stand or stay seated? I was a veteran of a foreign war but in the service of a foreign government, which, however, was an ally of the United States. As the speaker's idea of veterans was probably exclusively American veterans, I did not rise on this occasion. Someday I might.

A tall, thin man came up to speak. He looked out of place. He wore no medals and he did not have what could pass as a residual military bearing. He sort of slouched, his gray hair was longish and his voice had a high pitch to it. An unknown lady turned to me with an anguished expression and muttered, "Heaven help us, it's Microphone Mike."

I never found out his real name. But as I came to learn later, he was a well-known figure who everybody simply called Microphone Mike, or sometimes Mic Mike for short. He was notorious for never meeting a microphone he didn't want to speak into. He was in love with his own voice and the microphone was the instrument of choice in consummating his desire. If you didn't know him well, you might put this down to the eccentricity of a colorful character. But characters are interesting and Microphone Mike in full vocal flight was a long-winded bore. I was soon to get a full dose.

For 15 minutes he spoke in that high-pitched whine that began to sound like metal rubbing against stone. He seemed to take no noticeable breaths but kept up his monotonous and grating patter as if he had a snorkel hidden in his hair. Most bizarre of all, he offered very little reason for why he was speaking on this occasion.

His spoke not so much about Memorial Day but on the subject he knew best – himself – and the veterans seemed almost an afterthought. As he said with a great show of regret, he was not a veteran but he had always wanted to serve. Unfortunately, his draft number had not come up and then, he said, he couldn't decide whether he wanted to enlist or not, but now he was sorry he hadn't, because veterans are universally wonderful people, really angels in disguise, and he could have been one of them, but he was in spirit, and nobody loves them like he did, and, well, etc. and etc.

In the final agonizing moments of the speech, he lavished veterans with such sentimentally sweet and syrupy praise that if they weren't already diabetics, they would soon be in danger of becoming so. I just wanted to get up and shout a note of reality, "Hey, pal, you are only 50 years too late with this support." But I had no standing to say anything, being a veteran of another army.

The crowd grew restive. The lady next to me whispered, "I pray I will outlive this guy so he won't speak at my funeral."

Finally, the chairman of the committee had to get up and hover nearby to shut him up. He returned to his seat looking highly pleased with himself. The realization suddenly came to me that Microphone Mike had done to this solemn occasion what the Brisbane Boys Academy army cadet band had achieved long ago: His off-note performance had made the proceedings ridiculous.

The band struck up a Sousa march to put us in a better humor. But for all their good efforts, I am not sure the combined brass managed to produce as much wind as Microphone Mike had achieved in his orgy of oration.

After the proceedings ended, and the old soldiers faded away, I went to the picnic lunch being served outside the dining hall. I was glad to see Gavin there. I had missed him at the official commemoration. "Gavin, I thought you might be at the big event to handle the AV equipment."

"I sent a substitute. Did the microphone and speakers work OK?"

"Perfectly."

"Typical," he said. "They wait until I am not there to do their job."

"Well, the equipment certainly got its patience tested today. There was one guy there who could talk the legs off a piano."

"Yeah, I bet it was Microphone Mike. That's why I got a substitute. An AV man can only stand so much."

"You have encountered him before?"

"Numerous times. The man is a microphone junkie. There's hardly a public meeting where he won't leave the microphone unmolested. He turns up at funerals, bar mitzvahs, you name it. You should see him at residents' meetings. He asks convoluted questions that are almost impossible to follow. When someone makes the mistake of asking what his point is, he takes that as an excuse to talk longer and longer."

"Can't the meeting chairman cut him off?"

"Yes, but the guy will be heard whether anybody wants to hear him or not. Somewhere there is a pile of smashed gavels broken in the cause of trying to bring Mic Mike to order. And he also joins the cast of our amateur theatrical productions in order to have more opportunities to speak and sing."

"He sings too?"

"Well, he couldn't carry a tune in a suitcase but around here just an ability to remember the words makes you a star."

I went off and had a hot dog and chewed on the possibility that we might have gotten off relatively easily. At least he didn't sing.

9 - ALL BENT OUT OF SHAPE

*Puff the Magic Dragon/ Lived by the sea/ And frolicked
in the autumn mist/ in a land called Honalee
– Peter, Paul and Mary, 1963*

I was finally moved to do some activity other than tennis, even though I have always loved playing the game. However, as I observed earlier, playing tennis at the Estate is a unique experience. It is a ballet of immobile statues and the tempo is much different. So is the scoring.

What motivated me to seek a change from tennis was a particular incident. I was playing with the boys and the following scene unfolded.

Brian was serving. He lost the first two points. "What's the score?" he asked the rest of us. "Thirty-love?"

"No, Brian," I said, "it's love-thirty."

"OK, thirty-all."

"No, love-thirty."

"Got it, thirty-forty."

We rolled our eyes, Brian served, perhaps when the receiver was still rolling his eyes because the guy receiving the ball hit it into the net.

"Forty-fifteen," Brian said happily.

Yes, I clearly needed something else in the way of exercise.

Susan had always encouraged me to do yoga with her. I resisted on the theory that yoga can make a person too darn flexible. I used to say this to her as a joke, of course, but a part of me was not joking.

"Besides," I would say, "I would commit an offense against public decency if I were to be seen wearing yoga pants in mixed company."

"You flatter yourself," she would say. "You haven't got enough in your pants to be anything but a curiosity."

"Well, thanks a lot." Another reason for me not doing yoga was likely being the only man in a group of women. I would feel like a spy in an opposing camp. That could lead to another embarrassment.

"Susan, what if I stood on a frog in the middle of class?" I'd say.

"Lots of people pass wind in yoga classes. Nobody bats an eyelid."

She did not mention any batting of nostrils.

So yoga did not then become part of my routine, despite Susan's frequent speeches about the need to exercise as we get older to stay healthy and live a longer life – a view that was to hold a terrible and unfair irony, because I was to be the one left living.

And it wasn't until Susan died, and I was left casting about for something to do, that I decided to give yoga a new look. Susan had gone but her commands had not. From far away in the ether, or perhaps from the middle of my skull, came the words I knew so well: "Be active, be active." I decided to try yoga to put her spirit to rest. Maybe an old dog can learn some new downward dog tricks after all.

Putting my old prejudices in storage, I signed up for a beginners' class in the gym. The instructor's name was Molly and she was petite, perky, pretty, and perpetually in motion. My initial impression was that the young woman needed a healthy dose of inertia to make her tolerable.

As expected, I was the only man in the class and everybody

including Molly was wearing yoga pants except me. With my dread of yoga pants still operational, I wore sweat pants. I reasoned that I wore them every other place on the Estate so why not here. We started out by bowing and saying "Namaste" with our palms closed. We were told that "Namaste" is a respectful greeting. It wasn't fully translated for us but I suppose it means, "Yo dude, your butt is pleasing enough for sticking in the air." Mine wasn't but we soon did this anyway.

As an aside, I must say the obvious: Age does terrible things to the human posterior, reducing it to a skinny and bony replica of its former gloriously round and padded self. Those who live a sedentary, middle-class lifestyle eventually fall victim to the chairs in corporate meetings or civic forums. Those hot seats rub away the glutinous maximus to an inglorious minimus.

After furniture has done its worse, the last thing people our age need to be doing is thrusting their butts in the air as if presenting their posteriors to the world as their best feature.

But I found that putting your butt in the air is easier said than done. What the class taught me was that yoga is very hard. Usually, it is my tongue that gets caught up in knots, either in embarrassing situations or speaking a foreign language, but now my whole body was twisted into strange positions. Molly tried to be encouraging but in my case it was like trying to bend a stiff board. Some of the ladies were no better than I was but they seemed to enjoy it more. That's not saying much. I enjoyed it not at all. I felt like a beached whale with its flukes in a twist.

Flexibility was apparently not my thing. And if I were to further heed Susan's call to stay active, I realized that yoga would soon put me in traction.

Limping back to my cottage after the class, mumbling "Namaste phooey," I passed by a swimming pool and had another thought: Maybe some aquatic exercise might be low-impact enough not to be actually dangerous. The water would cover our contortions and everybody would be wearing swimsuits, which, unlike yoga pants, could have enough material to cover the unlovely body in a tent-like shroud.

The Estate had a couple of nice heated swimming pools, including one large one that stood in an oasis of umbrellas on a big expanse of lawn.

That looked inviting. As a little boy growing up in Australia, I spent countless hours in the water, either in pools or in the ocean. But one of the great differences between the young and old is the ability to entertain yourself swimming. A kid can jump in a pool and never tire of it, making games of diving, holding long breaths, doing somersaults, playing Marco Polo, or having races. An adult jumps into a pool and thinks, "This is very pleasant, now what do I do?"

Some adults swim laps, of course, but the lap swimmer is left alone with his thoughts and my thoughts lately tended to be miserable. I thought that a regimen of boring repetition, up and down the pool, was unlikely to improve my depression.

The gym staff conducted water aerobics classes in the big pool. So at 10 am one day, I put on my bathing suit under my sweatpants and joined a class.

Once more, all the other participants were women, which again I found a little intimidating. Most wore old-fashioned bathing caps and suits with little skirts on them. Our instructor was none other than Molly from the yoga class, apparently an amphibian at home on land or in water. Not that she conducted the class in the water. Still dressed in stretch pants, she directed us from the water's edge. She was probably 50 years younger than most of us in the class so I think we were on our own when it came to rescues, as management apparently did not pay her enough to get wet.

We were first equipped with flexible Styrofoam tubes about

4-feet long – noodles – and Molly started the class by putting her noodle behind her back and saying: "OK, form a circle and grab your partner's noodle" – a remark that in any other setting might have seemed indelicate but here nobody had the slightest hint of a smile.

Molly started a pounding song on her little music player, and we went through our noodling routine, each of us according to our own ability. I knew that the exercise would be low impact suited to an older group and I wouldn't be swimming the equivalent of the English Channel. What I didn't imagine was that it would have no impact at all. Jumping to conclusions and running up bills would have been better exercise.

When we finally finished 30 minutes later, I was left thinking that the people who stayed dry in their cottages and had simply gotten out of their beds had now as much exercise as I had gotten here. But the ladies seemed to love it. As I was toweling, feeling rather stupid, one of them said to me: "Some workout, eh?"

There was no way of answering this honestly without seeming a jerk, so I said: "Yes, some."

She introduced herself as Deidre Williams. "My friends call me Dear Me Williams." She added after a moment: "That's a little joke."

I did not immediately get it, not having a dry microscope handy for the inspection of little jokes. Besides, it was still morning and in the mornings I move like an old tortoise hiding under my carapace lest hearty conversation assail me.

"Alistair," I said, "Alistair Brown. Pleased to meet you," and I offered an unenthusiastic hand representative of my unpleased mood. "Oh, you have a British accent," she beamed. "How wonderful. I love Masterpiece Theatre."

With not a pause to allow digestion of non sequiturs, the interrogation briskly proceeded, and never mind that she was wearing a vivid orange bathing suit that made her look like a popsicle, and I was in decrepit, salt-stained board shorts that made me look like a log washed up at high tide.

"What brought you here, Alistair?" I was tempted to say: "Oh, I just needed some place to curl up and die like an old bull elephant at the community pachyderm graveyard." But Deidre was too eager to get the facts to wait for me to respond. She said bluntly: "Are you married?"

"I was – but now I am a widower." This was the first time I had spoken that word in public. A sense of sadness seemed to animate the very breath I used.

"Then you need a partner," she declared chirpily anyway. I had a fair suspicion whom she was suggesting as a possible candidate for partnership.

"You mean partners like Laurel and Hardy? Abbot and Costello?" This was my own little joke to divert her troubling line of thought. It did not work.

"No, silly," Deidre said. "Not like that. Men and women can be partners. We have lots of them here at the Estate. Folks don't worry about getting married at our age. They just team up and look out for each other."

At this, I began to wonder whether I had at last met the mythical casserole lady, but I soon discovered I was wrong again about judging a woman's intentions. Deidre was not a cook of casseroles or anything else and she wasn't looking for a partner for herself. The only casserole Deidre would be delivering was for Meals on Wheels.

Nevertheless, the talk of partners looking out for each other mildly astonished the vestigial social conservative in me. This was California, of course, and partners of various stripes are thick on the ground. But, while I was again not sure what age Deidre was referring to when she said "folks at our age," I was pretty sure that she and I were brought up in a generation that officially frowned upon "living in sin."

As I came to learn in living at the Estate, all sorts of behavior frowned upon in the past had become acceptable in people of advanced years. While some clung to the old standards, others were too old to care about social conventions. It seemed that a senior discount was available on personal behavior. Well, I suppose there has to be some compensation for the general withering.

Thankfully, my meeting with Deidre did not last long, as I told her I had an important appointment. She did not have to know that it was another trip to Secondhand Rose. Still, she made me nervous that the joys of partnership would recur as a subject in the coming weeks with others I met.

To paraphrase Oliver Hardy's frequent lament to Stan Laurel, this was a fine mess I had gotten myself into. I did not want a partner. What I wanted was a job, an occupation, an activity, something to fill up my time and keep grief at bay. I wanted Susan back.

10 - AT THE TABLE OF WISDOM

Oh my pa-pa, to me he was so wonderful
– Eddie Fisher, 1954

All across the nation old guys meet in the mornings to discuss the state of the world. They discuss all manner of things – they discuss politics and religion, farm prices and TV, sports and women – and sometimes, make that oftentimes, they become nostalgic.

The old guys meet in Dairy Queens, they meet in coffee shops, and on park benches. These gatherings constitute so many Tables of Wisdom, although the old guys will tell you that what is spoken is less wisdom and more the fertilizer that falls out of the back of livestock. At the Estate, the old guys gather in a shaded portico outside the dining hall with easy access to a large pot of coffee. They shoot the breeze and the breeze is impervious to their best shots.

I was there with my new friend, Gavin, one morning when we got on the subject of stereotypes.

"Gavin, do you know Brian Cooper, the tennis playing guy?"

"Sure I do, an attorney, I think."

"Right, he is very successful, even today. But the guy is an old tennis player in caricature. He is immobile and deaf as a door-nail. He can't remember the score from one game to the other, heck, one point to the other.

"But off the court, Brian is still practicing law part-time and winning large judgments. Not everything is what it appears. Of course, tennis is trivial but in the important things of life Brian still has a good grip and what he doesn't hear is not as important as what he does hear."

"Yes, Alistair, but what is your point?"

"Well, in my time at the Estate, I have seen a lot of people who seem like stereotypes but then they surprise you. Young people may think of them as old codgers, and old they are, but the term codgers doesn't do them justice."

"The human need to put labels on the various types of humanity will never disappear," Gavin said. "It serves a useful purpose for some part of the population. It sorts people out for them, so they don't have to think."

"Right," I said. "I am a senior citizen in the eyes of the world. But I ask you: Are there junior citizens? Are there young codgers? No. When you are younger, you are just a citizen and a person, free of labels. I would argue that I am just a citizen and a person too – a naturalized one in my case but that doesn't matter. I am a senior citizen, or more often, a senior, only because people wish to think of me in a different way even if I don't care to be thought of as different."

"Exactly," said Gavin. "And in comprehending your senior status, people trundle out a number of well-worn stereotypes. You could be a kindly old person, bathed in golden light as you sit on the rocking chair on the porch, the sort of dear old person who is kind to children and animals and never smoked pot at a Grateful Dead concert. Come Thanksgiving, this is the person that family members ride over the hills to grandmother's house to see."

"Yes, I said, "But if that wonderful old soul shrugs off the shawl of humility for just a second, and stops to give visitors the finger, then another stereotype must be quickly deployed. Why, that old man is a curmudgeon or she is a witch or a mad woman."

"Actually, you are a curmudgeon," Gavin said.

"True," I said, "and my wife used to tell me that all the time. But is there no curmudgeonly behavior among the younger generation? Of course there is. Bad manners, offensive attitudes, you name it and some younger people have it. Yet some others of them are the epitome of sweetness. As it goes for the old, so it goes for the young, but the old are mostly the ones to get the labels. Unless they are teenagers – and that lot deserves it."

Gavin thought for a moment and said: "Some labels describe the undeniable physical decline associated with aging. Your buddy Brian is an example. It is true that old ears are among the first body accessories to deteriorate. But that process starts young and the young leave rock concerts with their eardrums still rocking and with hearing aids rolling into their future.

"It is also true that older people like Brian forget stuff. Brian may forget the score but off the court I bet he can relate the history of the Supreme Court. He will tell you details of life during the Eisenhower administration. A younger person might never have heard of Ike. To forget you first have had to remember."

Gavin was running with the ball now. "The human brain is a great absorbent mop of useless information accumulated over a lifetime," he said. "Aside from dementia and senility, the average elderly person is bound to forget lots of things because he or she has learned a lot of things, and the valuable knowledge must compete with ancient baseball lineups committed to memory, the words to random pop songs, and all the other details of modern living. In simpler times, you just had to remember how to milk a cow. And if you did forget, all you had to do was walk around the back of the cow to remember."

After a pause to absorb this, I said: "I think the wonder is not that most elderly people forget stuff but that they remember as much as they do. Other cultures look to the old as the keepers of wisdom. In our world, the elderly are patronized when they are not being ignored."

"True," Gavin said. "As for always talking about their health problems, another stereotype of the elderly, most people's conversations are based upon the daily experience of their lives. Old people go to doctors a lot...no surprise there. People are like automobiles, the older the model the more the maintenance. So older people have pains in places they previously didn't know they had places. To be an old man is to be stiff in every part of your body except where it might be useful. So guess what old guys naturally talk about?"

"Sure," I said, "they talk about their health problems. And if people go fishing, they talk about boats and bait and the ones that got away. If they watch sports on TV every day, they think watching the NFL draft is actually normal entertainment worthy of discussion.

"I guess stereotypes retain sway on the popular imagination because they usually contain a grain of truth that obscures the general absurdity. Australians, for example, are known to like their beer and it's true for most, even if some of them don't. Stereotypes are one size fits all, which is the problem. What I have learned at the Estate is that the usual labels often can't stick when life is being lived. There are no senior citizens, just citizens who may be old."

"Well said," Gavin said.

"Young man take a look at my life, I'm a lot like you." Here I was quoting the lyrics of Neil Young and in a retirement community to boot.

The Table of Wisdom had once again explained the workings of the world. Later, as I walked back to my cottage, better for the company and the caffeine, I got to thinking about the role of chance in our lives and how all sorts of planets had to align to bring me to this strange place at this strange time.

I thought: What a crazy, chance-ridden, coincidence-racked,

lottery, lucky dip, human horse race, tumbling poker machine, mathematical freaky, blind bingo, miss-and-near-miss game our lives really are. And it's not only peculiar events on one day, it's the sequence of them over the years.

Even the most seemingly ordered and settled of us is not immune to the flying numbers that defy probability and expectation. A person can grow up methodically treading a succession of familiar pathways hewed by family and class to the respectable heights of accountancy, and never dream that it was dumb luck that should get most of the credit.

The very milieu in which a person is plucked down at birth is sheer dumb luck. That accountant could very well have been born a naked mole rat. (I think this possibility is more likely for newspaper editors or lawyers.) He could have been born Swedish, which is a much better outcome but involves eating a lot of herrings. We are shaped by our DNA but what DNA we get is dictated by what cosmic betting ticket is randomly chosen for us.

When the stork delivers the baby, the kid growing up must still run an unpredictable gauntlet to adult success. School administrators may or may not overlook a foolish transgression deserving of expulsion, cars may swerve and miss, grave diseases may afflict others but not him or her, unsuitable romantic partners may come and go, mean bosses may be transferred to other departments. The various planets must align.

I think I am stating the obvious here but it appears that the obvious has gone out of fashion. As evidence, I refer you here to some of the flagrantly flawed politicians the public elects to high office.

The random nature of the universe should caution all of us against excessive pride. The truth is that those who wish to be pleased with themselves – who wish to ascribe their success solely to their own wonderful actions – will resist any notion that subverts their high opinion of their self-presumed success.

Others, with more sincerity and modesty, will see instead the hand of fate, kismet, or divine intervention in the workings of the world. They may discern a divine purpose in the trajectory of their lives. Good for them. It may be so. Nobody this side of the breathing or breathless divide can say for certain. I guess we will find out when we die. After all, there has to be something to look forward to.

As for me, I am not sure that I am special enough to warrant my own ascribed purpose. I will concede that the Lord may move in mysterious ways, His wonders to perform. But too much has happened to me in my life to think any of it makes any sort of sense. The Almighty may know the flight of a single sparrow but I am inclined to think there's a bureaucracy in heaven that takes care of the details. If you had a heaven full of angels, archangels, cherubim, seraphim, and newly arrived saints, you might want to give them something to do other than singing hosannas. And in heaven as in Washington D.C., departmental mistakes are made.

Oh I am not saying that the Lord does not touch someone with His long finger to make him Mozart, or intervene in a crucial battle at a timely moment to seal Hitler's doom, but these interventions are not the norm. The whole point of the universe is that it is random and people must make the best of it, or so I believe.

This amateur theology of mine may be questionable but it does explain why bad events – famines, earthquakes, the defeat of a favorite football team – are allowed to happen. Don't blame the Almighty. Blame the divine bureaucrats who take an eternity to do anything.

All of this was obviously a subject for the Table of Wisdom and a fresh pot of coffee on another day.

For now I had to go on grappling with my own unfathomable situation: Talk about a crazy, chance-ridden, coincidence-racked, lottery, lucky dip, human horse race, tumbling poker machine, mathematical freaky, blind bingo, miss-and-near-miss game.

The death of my dear wife from a heart attack on the first night at a retirement community was the least of the improbability. People die unexpectedly and sometimes when you least expect it. No, the strangeness was being retired in California at all. In a million years, this was not what I would have guessed back there as a boy in faraway Australia. I have crossed the wide world over to be in this situation and all the time it could have so easily gone another way. As I say to young people, watch out who you kiss in this life – it can change everything.

That was enough thinking for one day.

11 - SISTER, CAN YOU SPARE A JOB?

Que sera sera/ Whatever will be will be
– Doris Day, 1964

The thought occurred to me that what I needed was not only a volunteer job but one that also provided some peace and quiet. Surely that is what retirement is supposed to be about. I did not need to help Gavin yell any more at the audio visual equipment as he obviously had that task well in hand. And I did not feel like telling visitors at a nature park where the nearest restroom was located.

But what sort of job would provide a haven from the everyday distractions of the world? Why, a library job. Although I was yet to pay a visit, I knew the Estate had a little library tucked away behind the main administrative office. What better place for a writer, as I was for many years and still am with this journal, than in a depository for stories? While I knew nothing about library science, I was a friend of books and perhaps I could help other friends of books in a quiet and studious atmosphere.

As I soon discovered, the library already had a volunteer librarian, a resident of the Estate who had been a professional librarian in her former life. I confess that even before I met this person I trembled before the librarian stereotype. She would surely be a formidable character, perhaps with bifocals balancing on the edge of her superior nose, someone who patrolled the stacks in her sensible shoes and fussed to keep everything in order, stopping only to cast an accusing stare at anyone who broke silence or needed a timely "Shush, please" if the hint were not taken.

Of course, like most stereotypes, this assumption turned out to be nonsense, except perhaps the strong character part of it. She did have a presence about her, not stern but naturally dignified.

Her very appearance spoke of calm, grace, and intelligence. She was tall – about five feet-ten – and she was thin but athletic. I found out later that she had been a runner all her life. Her hair, cut fairly short, was white and her eyes were pale blue. No bifocals. When we first met, she was dressed in tidy summer clothing; a green skirt, white blouse, and trailing her long elegant neck was a white scarf adorned with red and blue flowers. She was not young but she was not old; well, at least old enough to live at the Estate where everyone was old.

I am not a particularly observant person and I do not normally take inventory of what women wear and how they appear, and that was especially so now, four months into the lamented state of being a widower. It seemed almost unfaithful to Susan's memory to take note of such details and to think the thought I instinctively tried to suppress the moment it formed: "My, my, this woman is striking. Why did I not notice her before?"

I found myself uncharacteristically flustered and at a loss for words.

"Hello...I, I was wondering...."

She looked up from whatever little task she was doing and fixed me with a look of mild curiosity and friendly amusement.

"How can I stop you wondering, I wonder," she said.

"It's about the library job."

"What job would that be? I am the only one who works here."

"Yes, I know," I said in a way that suggested that I didn't know and that it was news to me. "I was wondering if you needed any help from a volunteer."

"That depends. You are the first person to ask and I have not considered this possibility before. It is a small library as you can see." She gracefully waved her arm in a small circle to illustrate this, and together we surveyed the main room and the little office adjoining. Indeed small. Book cases, tables, chairs, a few computers for the use of patrons. If ten people came in, it would seem crowded but there seemed little chance of that. She and I were the only ones there this morning.

"I am sorry," she said, "I think we have not met. I am Linda MacDonald." She offered me her hand to shake formally, which I did, matching her light but sure grip.

"Oh," I said. "I am Alistair Brown," further embarrassed that I had forgotten to introduce myself immediately. If this conversation were a tennis game, she would already be up 40-love. Maybe I could forget the score in the traditional local way.

"Mr. Brown, do you know the Dewey system used in libraries?"

"I know of Admiral Dewey, hero of the Battle of Manila Bay, but I don't suppose he invented the system."

"No, I think he was more for navigating around oceans rather than stacks of books but I commend your historical knowledge. Do you read much?"

"Yes, all the time."

"What was the last book you read?"

I couldn't think of anything. Of course I couldn't. All those books I had read suddenly seemed to be flying away like birds, their pages being used as wings, taking their titles away with them. Panic seized me. "I read....newspapers."

"Newspapers?" I couldn't tell by her expression whether newspapers were too low brow for her tastes or whether she was just puzzled by my lack of responsiveness to her original question.

"Yes, newspapers." Pause. "And histories." Pause. "And novels." I thought my attempts to suggest that I was a complete idiot were now complete.

"We have all those," she said, not unkindly. "I would be delighted if you came in and regularly chose some to read. But, in all honesty, Mr. Brown, I really don't think I need any help here. Besides, I am sure you don't want to be spending your retirement in these little rooms when you could be outside enjoying the sunshine."

"I suppose you are right, Miss MacDonald. I do like to get out and about, but for the moment I don't have a pastime to engage me." I immediately regretted this remark, thinking that it was laden with self-pity, which it was.

"I am sure you will find something," she said and smiled warmly. "If you will excuse me...Please help yourself to some coffee." She now had another customer to attend to and clearly my job interview was over.

My first instinct was to flee the premises dragging my self-confidence after me. After all, there is nothing more demoralizing than being knocked back for a non-paying job.

But I did stick around and I did have a cup of coffee. I needed to collect my thoughts and consider my options. The truth is that I would make a lousy librarian. Peace and quiet is all very well but my life had been lived in noise and strife. What does an old warhorse feel like when he is finally put out to pasture? Bored, I would think.

I needed to stay in the fray, mixing with lots of people with no thought of keeping my voice down. The librarian had read me like a book.

It was a shame, though. I have always regarded libraries as temples of civilization, fortresses of wisdom built by bricks of words, epicenters of communal knowledge. I would have liked to help them in their holy work, but the only service I can ever do for them is to keep reading books, even if I can't remember their names when put on the spot.

A few more patrons had trickled in and Miss MacDonald was busy answering their questions and generally directing them. I marveled at her kindness and efficiency. Busy as she was, she understandably gave me no sideways glance. For her, the peculiar man had come and gone like an insignificant character in a novel. I was sure that by tonight she would not remember my name and this was somewhat reassuring, given that my meeting with her had been totally awkward.

My gaze fell upon the notice board. A number of jobs were advertised there. The welcoming committee was seeking volunteers to show prospective residents around the site, just as Susan and I had once been guided. This had not appealed to me at first but now I reconsidered. The job would at least get me out to meet people. But I was held back by the realization that in my current state I would not be much of an ambassador for the Estate. "Oh, you are single? You should definitely come here to live – the food is great, accommodations are wonderful and you will die of boredom if the loneliness doesn't get you first. Or maybe you can get a partner and decay together."

No, not a good idea. Unfortunately, all the opportunities for volunteering listed on the board were still unappealing to me. I would have to look elsewhere for a purpose in life. What a strange predicament to find myself in. Our youth is the time when we are supposed to find ourselves and here I was doing it all over again decades later. It was déjà vu with a side order of irony.

Susan, I thought, why I am so lost? I can't even make a routine inquiry without getting my lines tangled like a sailboat wallowing in the sea. I can't even go to a swimming pool class without being thought of as someone who needs to be rescued by a partner.

I walked out in the sunshine with no better immediate plan than to play some tennis with the boys again. It was either that or water aerobics.

12- WINE, CHEESE AND INFORMATION

Some enchanted evening
You may see a stranger
Across a crowded room
– South Pacific, 1949

Apparently Romeo Rawlings, the Estate's resident Lothario, had a polar opposite in this small cooling world of passion – Betty Bosworth, or as I thought of her at first, Betty Boop, that character from the long-ago cartoon with the big eyes, the pouting lips and the short, tight dresses. To my jaundiced eye, Romeo and Betty seemed to be counterparts, although not partners. Perhaps they both recognized that no thrill of conquest was to be had in wooing the flagrantly available.

I met Betty at a little wine and cheese gathering hosted one evening by a tennis playing buddy and his wife – Bill and Diane Gibson. Many of the guests were Bill's tennis playing friends taking their ease after a hard day of making drop shots on stationary opponents.

Their off-court partners were invited, too, but Betty was not there with a partner. She was by herself and appeared dressed to kill in the event that live prospects were to materialize. In my vanity, I shuddered to think that I might qualify as a prospect.

Betty was a woman of perhaps 70 going on 45 after lots of cosmetic reconstruction. She had the big goo-goo eyes (check), the inviting red lips (check), the well-coiffed and dyed black hair (check), the tight skirt (check) and, it must be said, an abundant bust (check) that was either defying the laws of gravity or was held aloft by heroic corsetry. (Or this alternative explanation, perhaps she had a welcoming casserole strapped to her chest.)

Like Romeo, Betty left the initial impression of someone putting on a residual mating display, inviting all comers to a dizzying waltz around the senses in the lengthening shadows. I was fascinated but not tempted. In my mind, single and in mourning, I was a prospect for nothing more than a lonely life. The last thing I wanted was to get into a new relationship with a woman with a casserole on her chest and eyes inviting me to take a taste.

When she walked across the room to meet me, these thoughts of mine seemed confirmed. I was the only single man there that night. Although other single ladies had been invited too, they showed no interest in me, a testament no doubt to their good taste. As I was to discover, women always outnumbered men at the Estate's social gatherings, bearing witness to the demographic fact that they live longer than men.

Betty definitely wasn't one to wait for proper introductions. "I haven't seen you before," she said. "Are you a new resident?"

"Yes, allow me to introduce myself. I'm Alistair."

"Alistair, I'm Betty," she said, extending a small, delicate hand to shake gently.

"Where's your wife tonight, Alistair?"

"She recently passed away."

"That's sad," she said, looking not particularly sad. "We have seen a lot of folks pass lately. That's what happens at the Estate. You can only stand it by holding your friends tight. Love the one you're with."

It seemed to me that Betty freighted this remark with just a hint of innuendo, like a wisp of perfume dabbed strategically behind an ear or on a wrist. (Actually, perfume was banned at the Estate due to allergies, so eau de innuendo would have to do.) The thought occurred to me that when Stephen Stills sang "Love the one you're with," he was not thinking of a retirement community.

"I see you have Dupuytren's contracture."

Oh great! One slight handshake and she felt intimate enough to start exploring my physical shortcomings. Dupuytren's contracture is a genetic condition that men – mostly men, but not exclusively – can contract if they have northern European ancestry. Over time it makes fingers curl up. I have the affliction in my right hand and it has defied previous medical treatment. As handicaps go, it is not as horrible as some. So far I have been little inconvenienced and it does help me keep a tight grip on my tennis racket.

I hid my slight embarrassment – or maybe annoyance. "Yes, how did you know? Were you a physical therapist or a nurse?"

"No, I just notice things. You also have a British accent."

It didn't take much talent to notice my accent but I remained polite. "Yes, I grew up in Australia but I lived in England as a small child and later as an adult. So I have a sort-of British accent."

"I love British accents. They are adorably sexy."

In my American life, I had heard many variations of this compliment concerning British accents and I always wondered whether English women were similarly taken with American accents in men. But Betty's added word "sexy" sounded like a warning to me.

In the pause that I needed to digest the perilous turn in the conversation, Bette returned to her previous thought. "Somebody once told me that men who have a hand curl up with Dupuytren's also suffer from a curling in another part of their anatomy. Is that true?"

"Excuse me?"

"Does, you know, your...curl up? Have a bend in it?"

"You mean...?"

"Yes, I mean...I just want to satisfy my curiosity."

"Well," I said, "I can't say one way or the other. But if it's good enough to stand up, I don't mind if it takes a bow."

Betty smiled just enough to suggest she had a sense of humor without confirming this outright. She went on with her social inquiries, although thankfully without straying again into territory that made me uncomfortable.

It was not a one-way conversation. By nature and professional practice, I relish finding out people's stories. I want to know what they did, where they were born, what schools they attended, military service if any, parents' situation, jobs current and past, clubs, hobbies, views, politics, and why they thought what they thought and what series of events brought them to this place.

This thorough interrogation no doubt marked me as a bore with some people but most seemed to be flattered by the attention. They took it as a sign that I was interested in them, which, of course, I was to some extent. But mostly my questions were seeking an answer to a larger question: How on earth do our lives work exactly?

What I found out about Betty was that she had been married a couple of times, one husband divorced and the other lost to mortality, had no children, was originally from the East Coast, and had gone to private schools and college back there; that she had lived in Chicago where she had worked in the advertising game, first as a copywriter and later as an account manager, and that she came out West with her second husband quite late in her life and very late in his.

I found out something else as well: Everything I had assumed about her was wrong. This was no ditzy Betty Boop. She was smart. She was not looking for a partner, at least not overtly; she was just social and inquisitive and liked to look attractive. All my assumptions about her turned out to be more about my male chauvinism than her character.

Because she was smart, she would have sensed that I wasn't ready to be anybody's partner anyway, even if she had been interested. We had a nice chat and then she went off, leaving me surprisingly impressed, to see if our hosts could fix her up with another Chardonnay.

Gavin Halsey walked over and shook my hand. Now at least I knew someone at the party other than a tennis player. "What's up, Gavin?" I said. "Do they need audio and visual assistance?"

"Well, actually they do. They have slides of their vacation in France and want to project them up onto the wall. An AV man's work is never done. I am on the job even when I am not on the job."

As Gavin went on his way to have possible harsh words with the computer, I started chatting with Diane Gibson, our hostess on this evening. She had the look of an artist, someone who in her younger days had lived in lofts and worn her hair in long braids and had hung out with friends in dimly lit coffee bars with bearded men in sandals and jeans and women in flowing silk dresses. On the other hand, she may have gone to accountancy school. Looks are deceiving, as I had so recently been reminded, and a bored imagination recruits deceptions for itself and invites stereotypes to flourish.

Maybe I had imagined an early hippy life for her because her manner was in such stark contrast to that of her husband, Bill, who was large, loud, irritatingly cheerful, and full of lame tennis banter ("One set to the good guys" "I'll call the ball in but only because I want you to owe me"). He was some sort a business-man in his career but he was the sort of fellow that made a business of selling his personality, such as it was, even when he was relaxing.

As it turned out, Diane was an artist but not with paint or brush or clay. She was a photographer, a good one as I found out.

Large photographs of the Carmelito Nature Park decorated the Gibsons' cottage. Portraits of grandchildren, unusually sensitive portraits, were displayed atop book cases and tables.

"Did you take these?" I asked.

"Yes," she said, "photography has been my hobby since college."

"They look good enough to be professional. Did you ever work as a photographer?"

"Sort of but never full-time. I helped Bill in his insurance business back in Indiana – running the office, doing the books, that sort of thing. But we needed some promotional shots for advertising and I thought, 'I can do that.' "

"Did that lead to anything else?"

"Not back then. But lately I have been shooting pictures here at the Estate for our little weekly in-house magazine, actually more like a newsletter."

I was only vaguely aware of the newsletter. I had seen it lying about in the dining hall but had never bothered to read it, perhaps because Susan's passing had robbed me of the ability to focus much on anything. But I was interested enough now to make a mental note that I should check it out.

What a strange script our lives follow. Seemingly inconsequential events at the time can have larger effects in the future. So it was with this one random cocktail party, the contacts made there and the nuggets of information imparted. Because of this, my story was soon destined to become richer and more complicated.

13 - EMPLOYED AT LAST

I sell the morning paper, sir, my name is Jimmy Brown

– Flatt and Scruggs, 1931

Mr. Ronald Higgins, the Estate manager, could not see me immediately the day I paid him another visit. His assistant, a prim, neatly dressed middle-aged woman with brown hair in a bun, told me that a crisis had occurred that required his immediate attention. Well, fair enough. I sat down and read the National Geographic magazines in the waiting area outside his office.

The night before I had read the Estate's house newsletter and wasn't impressed. This wasn't necessarily a disappointment. After first learning of the publication's existence at the wine and cheese party a week earlier, my initial thought was that I might lend my skills to improve it – and after close inspection that possibility now seemed more plausible. Clearly, the magazine needed help and I needed some sort of volunteer job. I was coming to see Mr. Higgins to ask about my chances of part-time employment.

The newsletter – named The Pine Nut – was only six pages measuring eight by ten inches. The layout was designed haphazardly and the content was beyond bland – the stories sat like congealed oatmeal spilled on the page. Most of the content was announcements from the Estate office; like the date of the bingo night, the next speaker to give a talk to residents, the menus at the dining room for the next week, that sort of thing. The only signed column was by a Goofy Gopher, complete with a little line drawing of a rodent with big teeth. Unfortunately, Mr. Gopher wasn't the greatest writer and didn't get out of his hole enough to gather interesting material.

The designer of the newsletter – if design isn't too fancy a word for plopping the copy carelessly down in the space – had the unfortunate tendency to make the headlines italic or in a bizarre font in a doomed attempt to make the magazine seem jazzier. The only good feature was the few photographs by Diane Gibson, my new acquaintance from the cocktail party. No wonder I hadn't heard about the magazine. It was never going to be the talk of the community in its current form.

After ten minutes or so, a harried Mr. Higgins came through the front door from his urgent task outside. He greeted me and escorted me back to his office. "Terribly sorry to keep you waiting, Mr. Brown," he said.

"No problem. I am sorry to interrupt you in the midst of a crisis."

"We ran out of pickleball balls."

"Excuse me?"

"The balls for pickleball. They went missing and some of the residents were agitated."

"I see. You were in more of a pickle than a crisis."

"Yes, but then the plant watering system came on and wet the pickleball players searching for spare balls in the bushes. It was a mess but it's all sorted out now."

"I hope they saw the funny side to it."

"They are still searching, Mr. Brown, not for the balls but their sense of humor."

"That's too bad. By the way, please call me Alistair."

"Thank you, Alistair. And you may call me Ronald. I believe you are the gentleman whose wife passed away on the first night here. Am I right? Ah yes, terrible business. What has it been now? Four months? Six months? Can I help with anything? Your new cottage is working out OK?"

"Everything is fine on that front, thank you. I actually came to speak to you about The Pine Nut."

"The Pine Nut?" He looked puzzled. "Pine Nut?" He had apparently forgotten the name of his own newsletter.

"Yes, your weekly newsletter for the residents."

"Oh, that Pine Nut, of course! Our little newsletter! A very fine publication indeed. What about it?"

"I was a journalist for 40 years and the editor of a paper. I was wondering if I could help with its production. Can you put me in touch with the current editor?"

Mr. Higgins visibly brightened. "Of course, that would be great. We don't actually have an editor at the moment and, in fact, I don't think we have ever had one. I and my assistant, Marge, over there, just get the material and take it to the printer. I would be the first to admit that the current system is not working. The publication could stand a lot of improvement."

"I certainly think it has a lot of potential and I'd be happy to help with that."

"That's just fabulous. You are the editor from now on. Start tomorrow; no, start today. I have all the menus for next week and the announcements ready to send you. I'll do that immediately. The magazine must be ready to be sent to the printer Friday morning. Can you do that?"

I nodded. "Sure!"

"Good. To tell the truth, the work has been a real burden and distraction for me. Marge and I don't have any special literary skills. We are good at dealing with crises with the residents as they come up, one lost pickleball at a time. Magazines are not the reason we got into retirement home management."

He paused as a concern suddenly occurred to him. "One thing:

I assume you will do this as a volunteer. We have a strict budget for everything and the magazine is no exception. It is not going to cost any more money is it?"

Mr. Higgins was an unwilling amateur publisher by his own admission but this question showed he could act like a publisher of many decades standing. Quality was fine but containing costs came first.

"Yes, a volunteer. And I hope not to spend any more money. I want more space for exciting things I have planned but I can talk to the printer about how much that will cost. I don't actually mind making up the difference from my own pocket. And maybe we can talk about having some advertising."

"Advertising? That's a revolutionary idea, I mean, for around here. And your editorial changes, they don't include having pictures of the female residents in bikinis posing beside the pool, do they?"

"I can't think why but the thought hadn't occurred to me," I replied, not knowing whether he was joking or not. "But there is one thing I wanted to ask you. Who is the Goofy Gopher who writes the column?"

"Her name is Emily Watson, or rather, was. Sadly, she passed just last week, not a surprise really, she was 86 and ailing, but her absence will leave a hole that needs to be filled."

So Mr. Gopher was actually Mrs. or Ms. or Miss Gopher and that reference to the hole that needed to be filled once again left me wondering whether Mr. Higgins was joking. He was either the most subtly droll person within 100 miles or he was totally devoid of irony and wit. Marge, who sat in an office within earshot when the door was open, offered no clues. All efficiency and concentration, she pecked at her computer with no telling giggles.

"I might let Goofy Gopher go gently to her rest without recruiting another to take over the job. Call me old-fashioned, but I don't want gophers writing for the newsletter." I did not say that her death was a fortunate coincidence for me and that a potential political problem had solved itself. Now I did not have to tell a well-meaning gopher that her services were no longer required.

Mr. Higgins had no complaint. "Yes, well, that makes sense. It was a pretty awful column anyway. Nobody will miss it."

So that is how I became editor of The Pine Nut on that cloudless day in July. No searching questions, no call for my résumé and or great interest in my background, no real inquiries about what I wanted to do editorially, no laying down the law that The Pine Nut was the voice of the Whispering Pines Estate for Community Living and that all changes had to be cleared through head office, no real concerns other than that more money might have to be spent and old ladies in bikinis might be made playmate of the week.

Instead, the joy of being unexpectedly liberated from an unwanted task had put to flight any concerns Mr. Higgins might have had. To Mr. Higgins, opportunity had knocked on his door. His weekly problem had become someone else's. Or so euphoria had deluded him into temporarily thinking.

Of course, the magazine would have to answer to management on matters of taste and controversy, even if Mr. Higgins did not trouble himself to illuminate the boundaries immediately. That would surely occur to him later, as it would for anyone ultimately responsible for a house organ. For the moment, it was a beaming smile and a hearty handshake – "Thank you, thank you, Mr. Brown" – and the deal was sealed.

I walked out of his office, past the unflappable Marge and into the sunshine, feeling relieved and more than a little surprised, all the while thinking: That was easy, now comes the hard part.

My first task was just down the garden path. Lunchtime had almost arrived and the residents were coming out and making their slow progress to the dining hall. I stopped in my little cottage, grabbed paper and pen, and proceeded to write in large capital letters in my best penmanship:

WANT TO WORK FOR OUR NEWSLETTER?

THE PINE NUT NEEDS YOUR HELP. NO EXPERIENCE NECESSARY.

CAN YOU WRITE, SHOOT PICTURES, DRAW OR DE-SIGN, MARKET OR PROMOTE?

NEW EDITOR HAS PLANS FOR THE ESTATE'S PUBLI-CATION.

MISSED YOUR JOURNALISTIC CALLING?

COME TO A MEETING 3 PM SUNDAY IN THE DINING HALL

OR CONTACT ALISTAIR BROWN AT SUITE 403

I took this down to the dining hall, and after asking and receiving permission to borrow the space Sunday afternoon, I tacked it up on the bulletin board. An editor needs a staff and sometimes he has to advertise. But he also has to personally recruit – and that was my food for thought at lunch that day. I had made a few friends in my few months at the estate, none of them particularly close, except maybe Gavin, but I hadn't given a thought to their possible literary or artistic talents. If enough people didn't come to the meeting, I would have to start asking some for help.

It was already Monday. The magazine came out Friday. In this short span and with no advance warning, I would have to produce this week's edition by myself.

This week's edition would inevitably be a lot like last week's – and that wasn't a bad thing. In my past life as a newspaper editor, my philosophy was to make changes gradually so that would-be critics might not even notice at first.

The biggest change would be in the layout. I would go to the printers, do it myself and make it respectable. In addition, I would write a column, filling the space left by the departed gopher. This piece would explain my new role as editor and invite residents to come to Sunday's meeting. Between the note on the bulletin board and the mention in The Pine Nut, maybe a few people would actually attend my recruitment pitch.

After lunch, I would call on Diane Gibson to see if she had any pictures we could use this week. A picture is said to be worth a thousand words, which is especially valuable when nobody else is available to write a thousand words.

As I finished up the last of my soup and sandwich, Martha Evans, former school teacher, current nature guide and perpetual ball of enthusiasm, appeared with her tray and sat down beside me. She had already seen my note. "Congratulations on your appointment," she said cheerily. "Count me in. I will be at next Sunday's meeting."

Her reaction immediately encouraged me. While I found Martha's manner a little grating, it suddenly occurred to me: What do teachers and nature guides do? Why, they lay out facts for an audience, they tell stories. With her bounding bunny of a personality, Martha might just have the makings of a decent reporter.

"Martha," I said, "I am happy to hire you on the spot. How would you like your first assignment?"

14 - THE FIRST EDITION

I did it my way
– Frank Sinatra, 1966

Although preparation time was short, my first edition of the newsletter went surprisingly well. The content was sparse but Diane Gibson came through with a few good photographs and I wrote a column that explained my hopes for the publication and encouraged attendance at Sunday's meeting for those who would like to contribute.

Most encouragingly, Martha Evans did a competent job in her first assignment, confirming my hunch that she had the makings of a solid reporter. She did a profile of the newsletter's only previous columnist, Emily Watson, or as she was known to the publication's few readers, Goofy Gopher. As no reader knew that the refined Miss Watson was the Goofy Gopher, I thought it might be interesting to tell the story of the dignified woman with the rodent pen name.

Happily for this hunch, Emily's story turned out to be quite extraordinary and nobody at the Estate was still around to remember it being told before. In recent years, 86-year-old Emily had stayed mostly in her cottage when she wasn't on her solitary nature walks and most of her friends had already gone down the road to eternity's retirement community. Emily may have burrowed out of sight like a gopher but nothing goofy was suggested by her life.

As several of her relatives told Martha in her role as The Pine Nut's first budding reporter, Emily was among the rare women in the first half of the 20th century who had earned a college engineering degree. During World War II, she had joined the illustrious band of women aviators who flew aircraft from factories for delivery to the Army Air Forces. Later, she had a career in middle management at Pan American Airways, only the glass ceiling of the era limiting her reach for the sky. She married and had five children, most of whom were still alive and delighted that someone cared enough to give her public recognition at long last.

Could we do this every week? People died at the Estate regularly and often their friends would hold a remembrance in the meeting hall. These events were noted in the newsletter in the calendar section but without any details of their lives. In a community where the deaths of residents were described with euphemisms, one got the sense that death was thought of as unseemly, and too depressing to be dwelt upon by those not directly affected. As in, perhaps if everybody ignored death it would go away.

Of course, the actuarial tables begged to differ. While it might be uncomfortable for Mr. Higgins and the owners of the Estate to be reminded that death is always with us, which admittedly is not a great marketing slogan, I decided that celebrating people's lives should be a part of the newsletter's business. And yes, while it was a newsletter, it was a little newspaper to me. And what does a good newspaper have? It has a good obituary section, which illuminates forgotten and overlooked lives and in so doing serves common humanity.

Could we do this every week? Sure we could and we would. And residents of the Estate would turn first to the obituary section just as older readers used to do when newspapers were kings in the realm of information. Readers of the newsletter might be saddened but they would be gladdened and enlightened, too. The Estate was full of people who had interesting lives. Not all of them would be a Goofy Gopher with a surprising past but even humble lives can make an absorbing story. And if that were not enough, some readers of The Pine Nut would turn to this new section, in the time honored way, to confirm they were still alive.

Just the same, I figured Mr. Higgins probably wouldn't like it: All those depressing funerals were bad for PR. But whatever reservations he had were soon swept away when he received a highly complimentary letter – copied to me – from one of Emily's daughter's. "What a wonderful tribute to our mother. Nobody did a better job of capturing her life story. Your publication is a credit to your organization." I never did hear anything from Mr. Higgins.

That is not to say that all was sweetness and light and that I bathed in popular acclaim. Of course not. Journalism is journalism no matter what the scale and it is impossible to make everybody happy. Minnie Miller was one of those who were not happy.

Happiness was an unknown emotion to Minnie Miller. She was notorious as the biggest complainer at the Estate. Known curmudgeons would see her in sullen action and remark, "That woman refutes the theory that only old guys like us can be chronic complainers. She has turned grouchiness into a fine art." They said this with obvious admiration, and appreciation for sharing the heat.

Minnie wrote a letter to me, not an email but an old-fashioned letter decorated with bunnies and flowers at the top of the stationery, always a sign of trouble. It was hand-delivered to my mailbox on Saturday, the day after the newsletter appeared and the day before my scheduled newsletter meeting.

She said that it was a terrible thing to reveal the true identity of the Goofy Gopher. "I think that when someone writes anonymously they should not be identified because of the unfortunate occurrence of their passing. We all wondered who the Goofy Gopher was and for you to unmask her now betrays a sacred trust. I loved that column and felt that I was taking a walk through nature with the gopher, not Miss Watson, whom I never had the pleasure of meeting. You people in the media will do anything to increase circulation via sensationalism. Shame on you. Yours in disappointment, Mildred Miller."

So we were considered the media now. This unwitting compliment was progress – and never mind that the complaint was silly. Nobody had wondered who the Goofy Gopher was because nobody was particularly interested except Minnie. Her letter also proved a principle I had come to recognize over 45 years in journalism. When someone said you should be ashamed for some piece you had written or edited, you probably should not be ashamed because you were just doing your job.

This was not my first encounter with the dyspeptic Minnie, who also happened to look the part. Her slight body seemed stiffened by resentment and the scowl on her face was so true to her character that you got the impression that if she smiled her face would crack.

I had first seen her in the gym complaining to the assistants about the loud rock and roll music – she wanted to exercise to show tunes – and then later I saw her in the cafeteria berating the staff about the food, the one feature that was the source of universal kudos from other residents. But nothing pleased Minnie. It was her life's work to be severely dissatisfied. If she died and went to heaven, she would complain about having to play the harp.

Why she was such a grouch I could only guess. What had soured her on life? Was she always miserable from childhood on or did some misfortune lay its unhappy imprint on her later in life?

I wanted to say to her: "Minnie, we have it good here. It is a warm and beautiful place, with attentive staff, and we are blessed to be able to live like this. Ours is not the common situation of many older people in this country or in the world for that matter. Some seniors are isolated, live in squalor and must resort to eating cat food because they are poor. We are the fortunate few who are able to afford this luxurious living in the company of others our own age similarly privileged. And yet all you can do is complain about petty annoyances."

Ah, yes, those words would have made her mad. And that is why I kept my mouth shut. There's no point in stirring the pot for people determined to stew in their own juices.

The other complainer was Sam Hudson, retired contractor and full-time patriot. His disgruntlement was easier to guess at, because he was representative of an unhappy class of people abroad in the land: The political malcontent, as opposed to the social malcontent that was Minnie (although sourness no doubted tinged her political outlook too).

Sam also hand-delivered a letter to my mailbox, but his had American flags at the top. "I was shocked and appalled that the newsletter that you boast about in your column continues to be a bland source of blind, boring drivel that ignores the real issues confronting this great country and our own beloved Estate.

"I looked in vain for an article about the threat to seniors posed by radical Muslim terrorists that makes many of us fear going into the town of Carmelito without armed escort. And how about something on taxes, which are wringing the life out of us on fixed incomes? I don't know why I expected anything better of the allegedly new and improved newsletter when I know that you were for years a member of the liberal media elite that wants only to provide biased information aimed at bringing socialism and sharia law to this country. Very best wishes, Sam Hudson."

I had not met Sam but my initial impression was that he was a guy like so many others in his generation who had fallen into the habit of listening to talk radio all through the day and come night turned on the TV for political commentary. When not doing this, he would likely troll the Internet to find sites that specialized in outrageous fake news for readers like himself who were disposed to believe it. What a way to make yourself miserable, spoil your life, and vex your friends and relations.

I do understand that some people think the mainstream media is an engine of fake news. But in my career in newspapers, every story that was wrong or misleading was subject to having a correction/clarification printed and a record of this was put in the writer's file. Do the talk radio hosts admit their mistakes? Until they do, I'll take their claims with a grain of salt if not bags full of it.

As for bias, I am jaded about that accusation too. Sure, it happens that some writers are biased, but most of these claims are simply a matter of having presented a reader with uncomfortable facts. I was once accused of having anti-Swiss bias. I can't remember why but maybe because I noted that Swiss cheese had holes in it.

So forgive me for defending a profession I love and through which experience I formed my definition of a journalist: A writer routinely accused of bias by people far more biased than he is.

People are entitled to their political views but I wish older guys like Sam would figure out that they have tapped into a grievance industry that was consciously set up solely for the purpose of reinforcing their worst assumptions and instincts. Old guys, in the last flush of testosterone, make an easy target for purveyors of such political propaganda.

The Sams of the world are presented with pleasingly tough talk, villains and heroes operating in a black-and-white world as simple to understand as a cartoon, and a whole language and attitude to equip them to harangue their assumed enemies. All this was writ large in Sam's letter. Sharia law in America? Islamic terrorists in our own little neighboring town of Carmelito? Possible, I suppose, but highly unlikely. A person was more likely to be inflicted by terminal quaintness in that tourist destination or else pay too much for a T-shirt.

I answered both letters immediately on personal stationery that

Susan had bought me long ago for Christmas. I was polite, made no argument or apology, but promised to print their complaints as letters to the editor in the next edition. That would surprise them. I wondered whether this would become a new source of complaint for Minnie. How dare I be so solicitous?

When I put down paper and pen, I felt a forgotten emotion – something like contentment. I realized then that my new project had shoved aside my grief for the first time in many months. I was now engaged in an enterprise greater than myself. Then I felt guilty for forgetting my dear Susan, if only briefly. As I held the box of stationery she had given to me as a gift, I reminded myself that she would want me to be happy. I repeated this thought over and over to myself, as an antidote to my sadness and guilt.

15 - THE NEED FOR COOKIES

Reach out and touch somebody's hand
– Diana Ross 1970

Promptly at 3 pm Sunday, an hour that allowed the residents time to go first to church and then lunch, I walked into the dining hall, somewhat fearing the worst, to begin my newsletter recruitment meeting. Would anybody come or would most succumb to the temptation of an afternoon nap? If this didn't work out, I planned to go back to my cottage and take one myself.

About a dozen people were waiting for me, which I took to be a good sign. With a population of maybe 250 residents, a dozen residents was not a huge turnout and did not constitute a great show of interest but it was enough for my purposes. If I could give jobs to four or five, that should be sufficient.

I scanned the audience quickly and then launched into my presentation before anybody had second thoughts.

"Good afternoon, my name is Alistair Brown and I am the new editor of The Pine Nut." Just saying this out loud almost made me burst out laughing but I pressed on with as much seriousness as I could muster. "Thank you for coming, it is much appreciated. I am here to explain my plans for the newsletter and hope to interest some of you to help me."

Immediately someone put up a hand to ask a question. It was an elderly lady, of course elderly, there being no other type. I did not recognize this particular lady. "Yes, ma'am," I said, fighting back mild irritation at the early interruption. "Do you have a question?"

She slowly stood up and said: "Are there going to be cookies?"

"Cookies?" I said, completely unprepared for this.

"Yes, cookies. Are there going to be any?"

"Er, no. Sorry." She was visibly disappointed and was about to slump back in her chair when a voice at the back of the hall suddenly contradicted me.

"I brought cookies," a woman said. It was Deidre Williams, not a casserole lady but a cookie lady apparently. She happily distributed her store-bought supply and looked at me in a vaguely triumphant way.

"Thank you, Deidre." Lord, help me, I had even remembered her name.

The woman who had asked for cookies was also happy and slowly sat down again to munch on them. A minute or two later her sugar high had passed and she fell asleep in her chair. I understood and sympathized. No point in staying up if the cookies are all gone. I think I taught my kids that in the long ago.

As it turned out, I knew most of the people in attendance, which was not surprising given that my few new friends and acquaintances might be expected to be among those wishing to help. Even so, some of those interested could not have been predicted by me in my wildest dreams. Sam Hudson, who had drunk too much from the partisan political bottle, was there – notwithstanding he had written the letter blaming the media for everything and suggesting The Pine Nut was part of the vast liberal conspiracy, a flattering notion but unhelpful.

Minnie Miller, the social complainer locally infamous for out-curmudgeoning the resident male curmudgeons, was sitting next to Sam, presumably by chance, although perhaps misery really does love company. Why Minnie came baffled me. All I could think was that – as a professional malcontent – she wanted her complaining to be better informed. Microphone Mike was there too, his presence threatening trouble come question time.

Mostly, I recognized friendlier faces. Gavin, the sorely tried audio visual volunteer, was in the third row. I could not guess if he had any writing skills but if a computer needed some good abuse Gavin was the man for the job. Diane Gibson, the talented amateur photographer and her tennis playing husband, the hearty Bill, were off to the left in the second row. Martha Evans, school teacher, nature guide and lately cub reporter, was front row in the middle, beaming the happy smile of the Girl Scout she was born to be. Betty was there, too – in the back, as always dressed to kill or at least inflict palpitations in the hearts of older gentlemen.

"Again, thank you all for coming. Thank you, Deidre, for bringing cookies, which have already given more enjoyment than I can possibly deliver with my presentation." At the mention of cookies, the lady who had first requested them appeared to stir in her slumbers, but perhaps remembering that there were no more, she subconsciously deduced that it was a false alarm and slept on.

"In my working life, I was a newspaper editor, as some of you may know. Twenty-five years ago, I was the editor of the local newspaper in this area but I spent most of my career in Pittsburgh, Pennsylvania, and before that in Australia, where I grew up.

"Ever since my wife died unexpectedly when I first became a resident here at the Estates six months ago," I paused briefly here as a low murmuring of sympathy and surprise arose now from the small audience – apparently most did not know my story, "ever since, I have been casting about for something to do. I have looked at the various offerings at the Estate, and nothing against them, they weren't really for me. I like a fine basket as much as the next person but I don't want to weave one in an arts and crafts class. Nor do I need to play bridge. Good luck to those of you who do but my old brain can't learn new tricks. Garden Club is not for me either; the plants have done nothing to deserve me as their gardener.

"Then I became aware of this opportunity. Being the editor of this little publication" – I could not quite bring myself to say The Pine Nut again – "is a way for me to go back to what I know and what I do best. For you, I hope, it will be a way to learn something new and have some fun along with me as we do it." I paused again to see if anyone was having fun yet and, optimism disappointed, I went on.

"There are, of course, major differences between a weekly publication and a daily newspaper. For one thing, we are going to be producing copy for something more like a newsletter or magazine, which requires a different style. We are also doing this at a time when newspapers – and magazines – are in full retreat, thanks to the internet in large part. But you and I are of the generation that prized their newspapers, liked to feel paper in their hands with their morning coffee, and I think we can recapture some of the old interest.

"We have a great little community here but we rely on information about it from notices posted in the dining hall or library or sent as emails from management. A good newspaper or newsletter can be a beacon to a community, like a church or a library, and it can be an engine of consensus and a force for good. It is a place where minds meet.

"In producing a publication worthy of our little corner of the world, we need to strive to be fair and impartial in the old-fashioned way, but also provide information that illuminates rather than clouds the interests of the community. Are you up for this?"

"Yes!" came the answer. It wasn't a full-throated roar that would greet a politician on the make. It was a demure and reserved sound of agreement but it was enough. "I miss my old newspaper," somebody said. "I don't enjoy reading things on the internet. I like the feel of paper." Polite noises of approval greeted these statements.

Then Sam piped up. "Papers died because the public realized they were so politically biased, and good riddance to them."

"And where do you get your information now, sir? "I asked.

"Well, the TV and radio talk shows I like."

"And they are not biased?"

"Of course not. I agree with every word they say."

"Ah," I said, momentarily confounded by this logic, "in your view, is fairness an impossible goal in reporting the news?"

"Well, depends what you write."

"It does. And I think you can rest easy on that score. The divisions that confound Washington look pretty silly from where we live down here at the Estate. They are removed from us. We are far away from that. It doesn't matter whether someone here is of one party or another, a conservative or a liberal. It matters only if they are good neighbors. Our issues are things like the availability of pickle tennis balls, swimming pool hours, and the varieties of wine available at dinner.

"Oh, I suppose, the national debate about immigration may impact whether the Estate can hire sufficient workers and we might take note of that, but generally we are in the thick of the grassroots and our subjects are to be found no higher than the lawn."

"You are going to make it a gardening newsletter?" The cookie lady had woken up again.

"No, that's not what I mean. I just meant that the subjects are going to be everyday things."

She yawned and went back to her nap.

"Alistair, what sort of subjects exactly do you think The Pine Nut will cover?" Gavin asked.

"Well, we are not The New York Times..."

"Thank gawd for that," said Sam.

"And we are the official voice of the Estate management, so we are somewhat limited in what we can cover. However, when I met Mr. Higgins in the front office, his only worry was that we might run pictures of ladies in bikinis around the swimming pool."

"I am in favor of that," Sam said. "So am I," said Betty in the back, her casserole-sized chest thrust forward.

"Well, I was actually thinking of feature stories on some of the residents here who have lived incredibly interesting lives. If you saw this week's Pine Nut (there, I had said it), you would have been charmed by Martha's story of the lady who wrote nature notes under the pen name Goofy Gopher. Martha did that as an obituary – and I think that is something we need to do more of – but we also should do profiles of the living as well as the dead.

"Lots of people have activities here that deserve stories. Martha is a volunteer nature guide and other people are in clubs. Maybe we can have a gardening column. Maybe a baking column." I confess that I said this out of curiosity to see if the cookie lady might stir again but she did not. The old trout was not going to rise for just any old lure.

"I also think we should have a society column," I said. "Not that there are too many swank masked balls around here, but people do have their little parties and would doubtless appreciate some coverage. We have got to get the residents talking about the newsletter."

"What about sports coverage?" Sam said, his first sensible remark of the afternoon.

"Very good idea, sir," I said. "We have plenty of tennis players, pickleballers, bocce players, and lawn bowlers. We could fill the pages with their lobs and muffed shots."

"Are you going to have an editorial page?" Sam asked as a follow-up.

(Ah, yes, I bet he would like to contribute his political thoughts to that but I would have to disappoint him.) "Unless Mr. Higgins wants to write an editorial on management policy every week, I don't think we will have editorials and therefore no need for an editorial page," I said.

Sam looked crestfallen.

"But I could see us having a commentary section that accepted essays from residents on suitable topics and letters to the editor responding to articles appearing in The Pine Nut," I said.

Sam brightened up.

"Those topics would be about local subjects; they would not be about national issues."

Sam went back to looking disappointed.

As an afterthought, I added: "However, I don't know what local issues would require commentary."

Microphone Mike now saw his chance to treat the crowd to the benefit of his vocal chords. He launched into a seven- or eight-minute question that was mostly about how he felt about newspapers. He told us that he wanted to have a newspaper delivery route when he was a kid, but his mom wouldn't let him, but he wished he had done it, but he had read newspapers all his life, except when he was in Seattle for ten years after college, etc., but newspapers weren't the same anymore, and etc. and etc. and so on and so on. Finally, as everybody in the small crowd was now in full fidget, he got to the point. "So, do you think anybody who writes anything can be trusted given all the negative publicity, all the fake news horror stories that leave people so confused, coming out of the political arena?"

"Yes," I said simply. Having seen him in operation before, there was no way I was going to get in a long debate.

He looked disappointed, like a kid who was not going to get his promised ice cream cone after all. "Yes? Is that all you have to say?"

"Yes," I said. "Yes is the answer to your first question and your second. Brevity is the soul of wit is what I believe. Thank you for coming today. Any other questions?" I looked around the hall and Bill, my tennis player buddy, asked: "Will you have advertising?"

"That's an interesting idea, Bill, but I am not sure. I will have to think some more about that. For the moment, we just need to get some content in the newsletter that would make it worth advertising in."

Before the meeting broke up, a familiar-looking woman I had inexplicably not noticed sooner – had she come in late somehow? – asked an excellent question: "Mr. Brown, you have ambitious plans for our little newsletter but how will you fit all these stories in when they are written? The Pine Nut currently has only six pages."

I explained that during my visit to the printer last week I learned that The Pine Nut was only using half its allotted newsprint due to a shortage of articles. We could double the space at no extra charge.

She smiled and I recognized her at last. I believe you are officially old when you fail to remember an attractive member of the opposite sex. She was wearing slacks now and her hair was done differently and she was out of context for me but it was her. The librarian.

From this small bunch of people, a staff for The Pine Nut emerged. Not everybody volunteered at the end of the day – curiosity rather than desire had brought some to the meeting – but enough came forward that we had a staff in place for my second edition next week. It was not a moment too soon. News was about to break.

16 - DRESSED FOR DINNER

A white sports coat and a pink carnation
– Marty Robbins, 1957

Romeo Rawlings broke the news with all the urgency of a pedestrian Paul Revere. A little group of us were chatting on a pathway after lunch the next day when he suddenly appeared in a high state of agitation. What could it be? A sudden outbreak of chastity among the mature objects of his affection?

He could hardly sputter out the words: "Did you hear what management is trying to do?...It's outrageous. So much for upholding the civilized standards of our community."

Well, that prospect seemed shocking enough, but the news when it was properly explained to me came as another sort of revelation. When I said at the meeting that some local issues might provide commentary topics for the newsletter, I had no idea how true that was. Now, confronted by the apoplectic Romeo, my casual comment suddenly looked like a fulfilled prophesy, although no prophet could have predicted this particular tempest in a teacup with its passions stirring at gale force.

"They are thinking about changing the dress code," he said, looking at each of us to see if we fully comprehended the nature of the outrage.

If you lived somewhere else, you wouldn't understand the calamity, because at first I didn't either. Romeo's idea of calamity takes a little explanation.

As you may recall, it was the rule at the Estate for people to dress up for dinner. For men, that meant a coat and tie and for women it was something more formal than slacks. It is true that nobody was turned away from the dining hall if they failed to meet the proper sartorial standards – the serving staff was not paid enough to be fashion police – but social pressure was nevertheless strong.

Men in coats and ties with their well-dressed partners tended to eat in one part of the dining room. Men wearing no ties or just Hawaiian shirts with khaki slacks together with their informal female friends sat down in another.

Where the actual boundary was between the tie wearers and the free-throated I was never able to figure out, but at every dinner hour the division appeared. The two groups were about the same size and even among the informal no one turned up in jeans and T-shirts for dinner. To that extent, a semblance of formality pertained.

In some parts of the country, this would not seem strange. Fifty or 60 years ago, dressing up for dinner was the prevailing social custom. Although the habit has since retreated, the East Coast still has its redoubts of formality in a few tradition-minded companies, boardrooms, country clubs, and stuffy restaurants. On the West Coast, at least in our little corner of it, most people are largely unbuttoned. That is one reason I like it so much.

As a person who had sworn off ties after 45 years of wearing them at a newspaper office, I ate my dinners at the Estate with the great unwashed, or at least the great untied. I had always thought that neckties were a corporate invention to throttle the life out of the hapless employees, a mark of their servitude that served no practical purpose other than being a barrier to spilled soup.

In the whole of the Carmelito area, with its many hotels and restaurants, I could not think of one where a man would feel uncomfortable by not wearing a coat and tie. In fact, you might feel the odd man out if you were more traditionally dressed. You could be on a local jury without a coat and tie – as I was – and convict a casually dressed defendant – as we did – and the only people in the courtroom with neckties might be the judge and the attorneys.

Yet here we were at the Estate with its archaic dress code for dinner, a custom entirely at odds with this Californian place and the informal nature of the times. It made no sense to me. My only conclusion was that many residents had come here from somewhere else, including the East Coast, and 50 or 60 years was almost yesterday for many of them. They dressed up because they always had and had never thought to stop. It seemed like the natural order of things, except it wasn't anymore.

The outraged Romeo was not quite right in his initial statement. This was not the work of management, in the person of Mr. Higgins, but was a motion agreed upon by the 10-person management advisory committee at their meeting that morning.

The residents on the committee had agreed only to call a meeting of residents to discuss the issue and perhaps take a vote. If the residents voted to recommend a change in the rule on appropriate dress, Mr. Higgins would consider it and make a decision.

Mr. Higgins was not bound to take the committee's advice but the last thing he wanted was for a large number of wealthy, elderly people to think he was a dictator. He had enough to worry about with keeping the pickleballs stocked and making sure that people got a sufficient range of desserts at lunch and dinner. Now he had to worry about a proposal that had the potential to make everyone mad. Whatever a majority of the residents decided, that would probably be all right with him.

After Romeo went on his way doing his Paul Revere impersonation – "The informality is coming! The informality is coming!" – it struck me that he was an unlikely candidate to be outraged by a weakening of the dinnertime dress code. After all, he was not a great champion of propriety. If anything, he was an advocate of impropriety, even if it was of a different sort.

True, he was always nattily dressed with coat and well- pressed pants but he mostly wore an ascot rather than a necktie. I suppose that pretentious rig qualifies as a throat strangler by any other name, but the overall effect was to make him look more like an elegant pimp than a respectable gentleman. And wasn't that the final goal of all stuffy dress rules – to turn all of us into respectable-looking ladies and gentlemen fit for polite society? Alas, my duds were never up to the task even when I tried.

My theory is that Romeo Rawlings was heavily invested in the antique adage that clothes maketh the man. If loose standards of dress applied, then men would have to make themselves desirable with their own physique and bearing – and here Romeo was at a disadvantage. He was really a puffed up little rooster who feared that without his fine feathers he would not make the same impression in the henhouse. Well, that's my amateur psychology on the matter – and, remember, when advice is free you always get your money's worth.

The only person I knew on the residents' advisory committee was none other than Martha Evans, amateur cub reporter and volunteer extraordinaire. Once more she was filling a role that came naturally to her. It was she who properly explained to me where the initiative had come from.

"It was some of the younger people who came up with the idea," she said.

"Younger?" I said with an eyebrow in the upright and shocked position.

"Yes, I know. We are all seniors here but among the seniors there are junior seniors and senior seniors and some who are middling seniors. It is all relative. The one or two on the committee in their late sixties brought it up and they got support from the group in their early to mid-seventies. The ones in their eighties and above were against it, so the discussion was generational.

"What surprised me was that the older ones eventually did agree that it could be brought up at a general meeting of the residents. The vote for that was unanimous. I suppose that the senior seniors don't really care much anymore about dressing up – oh, they pay lip service to the idea but they have more important things to worry about. Tradition is always a strong pull, but I think that secretly some would just like to go to dinner in their nightgowns and slippers."

Hmm, I thought to myself, maybe there is a better argument for a dress code than I imagined. The sight of some of the old gals in their nightgowns might put me off my supper and, if they wore fluffy bunny slippers with their nighties, this might force me to take my meals in my cottage.

All that afternoon residents could be seen in little groups around the grounds discussing the matter. You would hear snippets of conversation rising on voices of fury or approval. "Never heard of such a thing!" "Best idea this place has ever had!" "What next? We can come naked to dinner if we want?" "The tide of progress comes in slowly but it reaches even the Estate." That the residents were split on the issue was obvious.

Later that long day, after all the molehills had been piled up as mountains by the indignant spadework of overwrought discussion, it came time for all sides to troop to dinner. When I say troop, I mean it was a parade the like of which had never been seen at the Estate.

On that evening, those who wanted the formal clothing rule for the dinner hour came out as formally dressed as they could. Many of the ladies wore long dresses; many of the men had put aside their blue blazers and put on dark suits that you would not expect to see on them this side of occupying their coffins. One old gentleman was wearing a tuxedo. As for Romeo, he had decided that the ascot was too frivolous for the occasion and he was wearing a polka-dot bow tie.

The company of the informal were taken a little aback by this show of formal sartorial force. They had not been prepared for this. Some went back to their cottages quickly to change their clothes and they got the word to neighbors who had not yet come over. In the end, the informal people came out looking like hippies at Woodstock. They had jeans and tie-dyed T-shirts and sandals and blouses from India. One peace symbol was spotted on a lady who had put flowers in her gray hair.

Members of the Crips and the Bloods, if they ever live long enough to become geriatric residents of a retirement home, could not put on a better display of showing their colors.

To my history-besotted mind, the residents looked more like 18th century soldiers in their respective uniforms, perhaps the British redcoats and the American rebels at Concord, Massachusetts, where one musket spark ignited the Revolutionary War. The British were the formal ones, dressed in their regimental uniforms to uphold the cause of the royal standard and the status quo. The American rebels were the militiamen, looking like the farmers they were suddenly called from the plow.

The skirmishing at the Estate was postponed for dinner. The two sides faced each other across the now dramatically plain divide while they had their soup or salad. Baleful glares were exchanged. The singing started when most of the diners were eating their main course. The old hippies, outflanked by the first arrival of the splendidly dressed, now counterattacked by taking up John Lennon's old anthem, "All we are saying/Is give peace a chance." They now sang: "All we are saying/Is give jeans a chance."

Soon the formal forces countered with: "All we are saying is give ties a chance." So they sang at each other, each trying to outdo the other until it was time for dessert.

Nobody ever knew who threw that first chocolate éclair after dessert was served. Both sides blamed each other for what later became known in Estate lore as the "Confection Heard Round the Hall." By the time I looked up from my rice pudding, the fusillade of éclairs, pies, left-over bread rolls, and ice cream scoops was hailing down on both sides. Old ladies screeched, old men said: "Take that, you son of a bitch!" For a brief moment, food-fight pandemonium reigned and people were 20 years old again, back in their college dining hall behaving badly.

What saved this mad encounter from getting completely out of hand was that soon everybody ran out of ammunition. It was near the end of the dinner hour and the tables were largely empty of food and indeed some residents had already left the hall. Microphone Mike had found his way from the formally dressed seating area and was now on the public address system appealing for calm. Everybody ignored him.

Frightened ladies stumbled out of the hall crying softly and wiping their frocks with dainty handkerchiefs. Fortunately, no one fell down on the slippery floor or suffered a heart attack, although the lady with flowers in her hair had been deflowered by apple pie a la mode.

Though clothing would require large dry cleaning bills, the casualties were actually minimal. Romeo Rawlings had suffered a direct hit on his bow tie, custard blending in with the polka dots, but he looked happier than he had been all day. Sam Hudson also came out of the melee from the formal side covered with cream. He was beaming. "Wasn't that great?" he said.

At the back of the dining hall, the serving staff looked on bewildered and appalled. They would be cleaning up this mess. As editor of The Pine Nut, I smiled an uneasy smile. Here was grist for our mill.

17 - THE HANGOVER

Would you like to swing on a star
Carry moonbeams home in a jar....
Or would you rather be a mule
– Bing Crosby, 1944

The following day, a Tuesday, was another of those classic California days of golden sun shining in a flawless blue sky and not a hint of fog or cloud to pale the beauty. But an insidious mental mist hung over the Estate as if the residents were all suffering from a collective hangover. With the gentle breeze off the sea, the pines themselves seemed to be whispering our little community's unspoken thoughts of remorse, recrimination and plain embarrassment. The previous night's events were the shadows of the new day.

A false heartiness prevailed at breakfast. No one mentioned last night but nobody could stop thinking about it. People made a point of greeting each other with a contrived bonhomie but at the base of it lurked a consensus: People had gone too far. People had behaved badly. They had forgotten their manners. They had acted like children.

The women, being members of the civilizing gender, the ones who many generations ago first put curtains in the cavemen's caves – well, if not that, spruced them up by taking the mammoth bones outside – realized the folly of the fight before the men did. The men were still inclined to congratulate themselves for having rediscovered their wanton youth, however briefly, thanks to flying food items. But hell hath no fury like a woman and her pretty dress adorned by scoops of ice cream.

As the day advanced, men everywhere retreated in the face of their wives' and partners' unhappiness. "Oh, we were just having fun," a man would say. "Fun for 10-year-olds maybe," an unhappy partner would counter, "you should know better at your age." "Disgraceful!" "What a mess! It's a wonder nobody slipped and broke a hip on the slippery floor."

And so it went. All across the Estate, women met in their usual haunts and deplored the situation. It was the talk of the bridge club, the gardening club, and the yoga class. Soon apology cards were being written and distributed and flowers were ordered and sent to those parties assumed to be offended. Sometimes different ladies would apologize and send flowers simultaneously to each other. In the midst of this polite activity, the men mostly had the good sense to shut up, as years of marriage had trained them to do.

Everybody waited for Mr. Higgins' response. That he would hear about the bad behavior in the dining hall was taken as a given. Most residents assumed that the general meeting called for by the residents' committee for the following Tuesday would be postponed, perhaps indefinitely. Others thought that such an outcome would only reward one side – in this case, those who wanted to keep the dress standards – when both sides had taken part and arguably bore joint responsibility.

But as the day wore on, nothing was heard from the manager's office. Perhaps Mr. Higgins was sitting in there carefully considering his options as if he were King Solomon of a retirement community.

Actually, nobody had seen Mr. Higgins or his assistant, Marge Johnson, in a while. Perhaps they were away at a life care seminar somewhere, learning about cutting costs by buying pickleballs in bulk and that sort of thing. Alternatively, if they had heard about Monday night's uproar, maybe they were talking to other managers about how to discourage food fights by limiting the number of missiles available. Surely the Estate was not the only facility in the history of retirement homes to have seen a chocolate éclair thrown in anger.

Finally, two days later, an answer of sorts came. Residents arriving in the dinner hall at 5 pm were surprised to find an official-looking statement pinned up on the notice board. It was by the chairman of the Board of Trustees of the Estate, an official body hitherto unknown to most of the residents, some of whom never imagined that a Board of Trustees existed.

Typed on official-looking stationery, it read: "Effective immediately, the day-to-day management of the Whispering Pines Estate for Community Living will be the responsibility of Catering Manager Pedro Rodrigues, until such time when the Board of Trustees finds experienced replacements for Mr. Ronald Higgins and Ms. Margaret Johnson, manager and assistant manager respectively, who have resigned to pursue other opportunities. The board will conduct its search as promptly as possible and expects no disruption to the provision of services to residents or in the orderly life of the facility."

These 82 words were chewed over and digested more than the dinner that evening. Before that close parsing occurred, various residents went into the kitchen to find out what Pedro knew. The answer was very little. Pedro, an amiable man who wasn't a cook but usually wore an apron to help when needed, was just as surprised by his temporary promotion as everyone else. "A representative of the board showed me the note half an hour before you walked in," he said.

Did he know why Mr. Higgins and Marge left? "No," he said, "I never spoke to them. In fact, I haven't seen either of them since last Friday."

Did he think the Board of Trustees found out about the food fight? "Don't know. I never met anyone on the board before. I think most of them live out of town."

What was he going to do as temporary manager? "Same as I always do," he said smiling. That made some sense. The board had probably figured out that if it kept the residents fed, everything would be fine until new managers were found. Indeed, grumbling stomachs might cause grumbling residents.

When Pedro was fully interrogated to everybody's satisfaction, residents bore in on the cryptic news of the announcement. The usual division of the formally dressed and the casually dressed actually broke down as various people crossed over to talk in the hopes of making sense of what had happened. The general bewilderment served to dissipate whatever ill feelings remained.

Bill Gibson, my tennis playing pal, still wondered whether the food fight was the real reason the managers had resigned, or as seemed likely, had been fired.

"I don't think the trustees knew about that," I said.

"How so?" he asked.

"Look at the last bit of the statement. There will be no disruption to 'the orderly life of the facility.' After Monday night's mass outbreak of disorder in the dining hall, nobody in his right mind could assume that an orderly life existed. I don't think they knew about it."

"But did Mr. Higgins and Marge know?" Bill said. "Maybe they heard about that and said, 'to heck with it!' "

"That's plausible, Bill, but none of us has heard anything from them in a week, not even Pedro. It looks like they left town and nobody knew where they were to tell them."

It was a mystery and, as Agatha Christie had not located Miss Marple to do detective work at the Estate, it was not solved immediately. But solved it was, sort of, by the end of dinner. The Estate is a small community and everybody knows somebody and Betty Bosworth, formerly Betty Boop, knew everybody. It turned out that she had seen Mr. Higgins and his assistant, Marge Johnson, in a restaurant down in the village of Carmelito a week or so before. He was holding her hand over the cold salmon and kale and almond salad (Betty had an eye for detail).

As she explained to a group of us still lingering in the dinner hall, "They were making goo-goo eyes at each other," she said.

Now there was an expression I hadn't heard in 40 years.

"You mean, they were having an….?"

"It looked that way," she said. "They didn't look up and they never saw me, but I'd say that Mr. Higgins and his assistant were assisting each other in ways that went beyond the pickleball inventory."

"Well, I never," said Bill. "They must have been the only people in the Estate having a steamy romance," I added.

"You'd be surprised," said Betty, with a knowing look that for me conjured up some disturbing thoughts.

Betty's story soon became the official version of events as far as the residents were concerned, there being no other narrative available. The story of love blooming in a small office was unconfirmed and based on not much – the time-honored way rumors are known to start – but any doubts never mattered to the residents. The moral clucking started immediately although some of this may have masked a secret envy. I mean no disrespect to my fellow residents. There is no fun being old if you can't disapprove of something, and sometimes it is enough to make a show of disapproval to reconfirm your cranky credentials.

Mr. Higgins and his lover, if such she was, were never seen again, although the little office they shared took on a certain notoriety, somewhere between a hot-sheet motel and the balcony where Juliet shone the light for her lover.

With only half the story left to chew on, my old journalistic appetite was left disturbed by the unanswered questions. Did the board of directors somehow discover the couple's secret and fire them or did they really resign? Were they off on a Mexican beach somewhere, feeling young in their middle-age, not only because of the flush of love but because they were no longer surrounded by people 80 years old?

Not to spoil a good story, but I wondered if they were lovers at all. Could not Betty have mistaken the reason Mr. Higgins had taken his assistant's hand? Perhaps her pet cat had died. Maybe he was just consoling her over lunch and there was more boo-boo in their eyes than goo-goo. "Oh, Marge, I am so sorry about Fluffy. He was such a good pussy." "Thank you, Ronald, you are so kind." Then a gentle squeeze of the hand such as the pope himself could not object to.

Of course, they did leave their jobs at the same time but maybe the Estate just wore them down, as it does some of the residents. Whatever the reason, their departure was both an opportunity and a challenge for The Pine Nut.

Sam Hudson channeled his usual dark assumptions about the media, coming up to me with obvious glee: "Hey, Alistair. You sure have some material for your newsletter, eh? How about Mr. Higgins getting it on with Marge and the pair of them running away together for a bigger love nest? And how about that food fight? Great stuff for you, eh?

"Well, Sam, we don't know if they were getting it on, as you put it. We can't confirm why they left and where they went. Besides, they weren't public officials, just private individuals, and if The Pine Nut started printing salacious details about private individuals nobody would be safe here." (This wasn't quite true, as I thought sadly even as I said it. I would be safe, not because I was the editor but because my lonely single life was completely free of salacious details, notwithstanding a fondness for a few drinks.)

Sam seemed disappointed that we weren't going to take a sensationalistic approach, the very thing he regularly denounced bigger media outlets for doing. Nevertheless, he had a half a point. These were events we couldn't ignore in a newsletter edited by someone who fancied it a newspaper.

Martha, the ever dependable, volunteered to write a brief story about the departure of Mr. Higgins and his assistant Marge. She quoted the official statement in full and managed to reach the board chairman who lived in Boston. He wasn't very forthcoming but he did wish the two employees well, which is more than the original statement did. He also described what the board was looking for in a new manager – experienced, dependable, etc. Together with a few details of how long Mr. Higgins and Ms. Johnson had worked at the Estate, the story was concise and respectful and went no further than the established facts. In short, no hint of bodice ripping.

The story about the dress code was picked up by my friend Gavin, who welcomed it as a chance not to have to deal with uncooperative audio visual equipment for once. Even if she didn't have the other story, Martha couldn't do this one because she was on the committee that had taken the vote. He limited himself mostly to quoting committee members and the leading groups of the contending factions. As part of the overall story, he mentioned in passing how emotions had got the better of some people in the dining hall and various people were quoted deploring this.

Linda MacDonald, the librarian, took over the task of commentary editor and she solicited columns on the pros and cons of the dining hall dress code to supplement the main story.

The Pine Nut was coming together, even as the Estate seemed to be in danger of falling apart.

18 - FORMALITY'S LAST STAND

Let's go where they keep on wearing'
Those frills and flowers and buttons and bows
– Dinah Shore, 1947

There was still the matter of whether to go ahead with the residents meeting on the dinner hour dress code. While passions had calmed after the flurry of polite notes from ladies apologizing about their partners, wisdom suggested at least some postponement in the interest of not encouraging further embarrassment. The departure of Mr. Higgins had complicated this decision as it was the Estate manager who would have to accept or reject the residents' recommendation.

In the absence of a new manager, how should we proceed? Some people thought that the residents should wait to have their meeting until a new manager was appointed but there was no telling when that might be.

Others said that the meeting should be held in a month. If a new manager had not been chosen by then, so be it. The acting manager, Pedro Rodrigues, could act, because acting was supposedly what he was there for. That Pedro was the catering manager made this idea seem a little more attractive. The dress code in the dining room was arguably in his sphere of responsibility. An added benefit was that Pedro would be more likely to side with a majority decision of the residents than would a newly arrived outsider. Surely a catering manager would know on which side his bread was buttered.

As with all things in life, a small proportion of the residents did not like any of the sensible options. Minnie Miller, the inveterate complainer whose position on the dress code issue was for once not clear, was nevertheless drawn to the peevish dissenters who began to argue arcane questions about whether an acting manager was ethically permitted to make permanent decisions that a replacement would be bound to uphold.

Over the next few weeks, this group conducted a debate that seemed at times a parody of academic discussion on the finer points of constitutional law. Some of this played out in the letters to The Pine Nut, which was now accepting such letters to the editor under the supervision of Linda MacDonald, librarian turned commentary editor. Most residents rolled their eyes when reading these overwrought arguments but it was good for the newsletter. Slowly but surely, it was becoming the commons where people went to discuss community issues.

It fell to the chairman of the residents committee, Jimmy Devine, to decide whether to postpone the meeting and for how long. He was a round, red-faced, amiable character who seemed every inch a natural small-town politician except for one failing. Unlike almost every other politician in the world, he couldn't remember people's names. That might explain why he had not scaled any other political heights except this, the head of a strictly advisory committee in an old people's home.

But Jimmy was a straight-forward, practical soul and so he disgusted Minnie and her difficult pals by choosing the sensible option. The residents meeting would be held in a month. As he explained it to me, "Ronald, this is not rocket science. We are discussing whether guys have to wear a coat and tie to dinner. That's for the residents to decide and screw the trustees if they think we can wait around forever. They could take months to pick another manager. Besides, a month should give everybody a chance to cool down."

"Alistair," I said, correcting him. "That's my name. Otherwise it is all good."

"Right, Allan. As I was saying, as soon as people unknot their underpants, then I think we get on with this without any further jaw-boning."

Ronald, the name he had initially used for me, was Mr. Higgins first name, and it occurred to me that because Mr. Higgins was previously in charge of The Pine Nut in the absence of anyone else at the time, he put Mr. Higgins and me in the same category according to his own cockeyed logic. I did not take it as a flattering comparison. After all, I had yet to run away with any assistants. But the next time we met, my theory was confounded. He called me John. The time after that I was Tim. The man never heard a name that he could get right.

Martha told me that the committee meetings he chaired were inevitably a riot of misidentification. Jimmy called her Mabel in the board meetings but sometimes it was Mary. He apparently remembered that her name started with an M but just couldn't remember the rest of it.

She said it was the same for all the board members. "Hey, Bill, give us the figures for the new pool house improvement," he would say, and Bob would give him the figures. "Jane, that's a very interesting point," he'd say, and Jody would look pleased. The confusion wasn't restricted to prompts linked to letters. Dimitri, originally from Russia, was always called Alexander by Jimmy. Perhaps he though all Russians were czars.

Yet it would be wrong to think that Jimmy was suffering aged-related mental lapses. In every other respect, his brain was as sharp as a tack, as he had proved in making the right decision on the meeting postponement. His wife, whom I got to know socially, told me that he had always forgotten people's names, at least as long as they had been married. She herself was spared the fate of the misnamed others. He always referred to her as "Management." As in, "I don't like to wear neckties but Management told me I had to." I suspect that she would rather be called Edith, which was her real name.

Some people got so used to Jimmy's unreliability with names that they never complained about being called Bill when their name was Bob. They even seemed to enjoy being cast as a character named Bob as this suggested a life of new possibilities.

His habit of mangling names was especially interesting to me because, I confess, I have never been good at remembering names either. However, no sense of charm attaches to my cluelessness. I only remember Jimmy's wife's name because I had an Aunt Edith growing up. Otherwise, it would just be another awkward pause when I saw her.

At least, I have an excuse, one that also has nothing to do with elderly forgetfulness. I grew up in Australia where everybody is called mate, at least the men. In Australia, I suspect old guys who are forgetful don't forget actual names, they forget to call their mates mate.

Growing up in Australia is not good practice for remembering names. Although women Down Under sometimes call each other mate, it is essentially a male bonding phenomenon and generally men do not call women mate. The traditional understanding is that a mate is a friend whom you will not mate with. Of course, Australians have names and they use them, but mate is acceptable in all social situations that men find themselves in, for example, drinking beer, which is the main one.

If Jimmy Devine had been born in Australia, I reckon he would then have the complete set of political skills and would by now have risen to be prime minister on the strength of knowing what to call a large segment of the population. Mate.

Jimmy's acumen extended to one other decision associated with the resident's meeting. Everybody assumed he would chair the meeting but he decided to turn that responsibility over to another person not even on his committee.

"What next month's meeting needs is someone in charge who is completely unassociated with any of the parties, someone who has natural authority and commands widespread respect," he said.

"Who would that be?" I said.

"Linda McTavish."

"Do you mean Linda MacDonald, our librarian?"

"The very same. She can shush up the crowd if it gets out of control."

I think Jimmy was working from the book of old-fashioned female stereotypes, as I confess I had been. It included the nuns of yesteryear who wielded a nasty ruler, bench-pressed 500 pounds and had tattooed biceps under their habits. It also included female librarians who could launch death-ray stares at chatterers in the stacks and who possessed a terrible shush that would make people fall silent as far as a block away.

The Linda I knew was nothing like this but she did possess a quiet sense of authority. She ran a quiet library on the strength of her character and I am sure she could run a tight ship or a contentious meeting. Still, I would never have thought of her in this role but Jimmy had special insights when it came to people, even if he could never remember their names.

My surprise about Linda being called to the lion's den had no negative tinge. I did not know her well enough to have much of an opinion about her. She was friendly enough and had wanted to be on the newsletter staff – and that was good enough for me.

But I was a little disappointed that Jimmy was not going to be chairing the meeting. Watching him misstating the name of every resident who spoke would have been a hilarious diversion in a night that promised little joy.

Still, the generally eager anticipation of the meeting was undeniable. The month seemed to fly by and soon enough we were all filing into the main hall on a Thursday night – which was usually movie night and, of course, some grumbling went on about the usual show not happening. The Estate's distant Board of Trustees still hadn't decided on a new manager, as most of us had assumed would be the case. Pedro, the acting manager, decided to stay away to attend to his usual duties, confident that someone would tell him what decision had been made so he could approve it later.

The hall was full. Husbands sat on their hands, and their egos, and gave an impersonation of their best behavior, as instructed. The reporters for The Pine Nut – Gavin Halsey and Betty Bosworth – were seated close to the dais and poised to take notes. In Gavin's case, he had to sit nearby because he still had audio visual duties and he would have to leap up if the microphone malfunctioned.

Jimmy Devine did speak briefly at the start, calling for calm and good manners and respect for our chair for the meeting – here he looked at his notes – "Our very own librarian, Miss Linda MacDonald." A cheer went up. Whether the cheer was for Linda or Jimmy getting her name right was not completely clear but people seemed happy to see her.

She did have a reservoir of good feelings to draw upon. A librarian meets a lot of people in the course of her work, and readers moreover, are the smartest people in the world in my jaundiced view. In her other job for the last month, as commentary editor of The Pine Nut, she had scrupulously handled the editorial offerings of the pro-dressing-up faction and the casual-wear crowd. Beyond all that, she had an undeniable presence.

Sometimes firm, sometimes lenient, and always fair, she never let the crowd get away from her. They all addressed her as Miss MacDonald and Miss MacDonald heard them out. She was kind to the lady who asked about cookies being available – "There's some in the back, courtesy of our Pine Nut editor, Alistair Brown" – but laid the law down politely to Minnie Miller, who complained about the cancellation of movie night and the impropriety of taking a vote without the appointment of a new manager – "Thank you, Minnie, so noted, but both those points are a little beside the point. We are here on the only convenient night to take a vote, the legality of which can always be challenged later," she said.

She also proved adept at handling Microphone Mike, who was inevitably in attendance to ask his usual convoluted questions. In fact, if Microphone Mike hadn't been there, a lot of us might not have considered the meeting official. As it was, she managed to cut him off after two minutes and praised him extravagantly to make him shut up. It worked. Librarians have a way with words beyond shush.

After about two hours of discussion, when yawns had started to gape in the hall like a convention of elderly hippos, the vote was taken – and the casual party won with about two-thirds of the hands up – but this only after Miss MacDonald had managed to frame the question in a way that allowed freedom to everyone. From now on, smart casual wear would be acceptable attire in all parts of the dining hall but those who wished to dress up could go on doing so – which was actually the status quo. Still, everybody understood the vote to be a referendum on informality versus formality and informality had won.

Only Minnie objected. "In a month," she shouted to the crowd already leaving, "everybody will dress casual." In fact, she was to prove prophetic. In a month, after Pedro had signed off on the decision, most residents no longer went to the trouble of dressing up. In six months, few residents remembered that it had ever been an issue. Soon enough, another issue would be commanding our attention.

19 - AN OFFICE NEAR THE LOVE SHACK

Somewhere over the rainbow...
the dreams that you dare to dream
Really do come true
– Judy Garland, 1939

The morning after the residents made the historic decision that history would soon forget, I decided to pay Miss MacDonald a visit at the library. I had missed her after the meeting and I wanted to congratulate her on keeping the old cats in such good order without benefit of a lion tamer's chair and whip.

I hadn't gone far down the path when I ran into Romeo Rawlings, who I guessed was on his way to pay a social call to one of his lady friends. So was I, but a lady friend meant a different thing for him than me. I was dressed in the traditional Estate old-guy uniform of baggy sweatpants and untidy T-shirt, and, as always, he was looking pretty sharp. He had on a navy blue polo shirt with white slacks and sandals. His silver hair was slicked back and his mustache was trimmed and ready for action, because one never knows when the chance for romance might occur.

The biggest surprise was his buoyant manner. He was beaming and radiating good cheer. The blood had gotten back in his cheeks and, given his reputation, perhaps one other body part.

This picture of vitality was in sharp contrast to the last time I had seen him. Back then, he had the look of doom and he was warning everybody he met about the imminent collapse of civilization if the dress code rules were changed. Now that this allegedly ruinous step had been taken, he should have resembled a Roman bystander after the barbarians had sacked the city.

But far from it. He knew that for his purpose, as with all other types of salesmanship, a long face and downer manner were not the recipe for success. Optimism was the catnip he was depending on this bright morning, however dark he thought the previous night.

"Hey, guy, how goes it today? I didn't get to say hello to you last night but what a show our librarian put on, eh?"

"Actually, I was just going down to the library to tell her precisely that."

"I don't blame you for fancying her. Fine looking woman. I think the dust from the books must have preserved her complexion. I wouldn't mind walking out with her either, but she is not my type."

Not his type? Not her type, more likely. "You have it all wrong, Romeo. We are working together on The Pine Nut. I have no interest in Miss MacDonald as a woman, just as a nice, smart human being."

"Oh sure," he said. "Well, I hope it goes well with you and the nice, smart human being with the lovely hair, long legs and good skin."

My own skin crept up my arm a bit at this leering observation, but further argument was forestalled. Romeo had already turned off the path.

On the rest of the walk to the library I didn't think much more about what Romeo said. Of course he would say what he did. He viewed all women through the same prism; he could not imagine a platonic friendship with one of them based on respect.

My respect for Miss MacDonald had risen to new heights last night but it had been there from the beginning. I really looked forward to working with her.

But where? That was what now monopolized my thoughts.

Unfortunately, The Pine Nut had no office; in fact, it never had an office, if you don't count the manager's office where Mr. Higgins and Marge had done the minimum to keep the publication barely alive while attending to other matters.

Because of my bigger ambitions for The Pine Nut, we required a dedicated space where the staff of volunteers could meet and stories could be edited and laid out on a computer. This space would need to have a few writing terminals and one Mac computer for doing the layout.

Much to my relief, such a space existed and was currently underutilized. None other than Miss MacDonald was to find it. In truth, it wasn't very hard for her to find, being only about 20 feet from her desk in the library.

I had arrived at the library to discover that it was a slow day and we got talking, first about the previous night and then about the newsletter going forward. "So we need an office?" she said when I explained the problem. "How about this?" She swivelled in her chair and gestured.

I had walked right past it coming in. It was officially the library's computer room, separate from an adjoining bigger space that contained the stacks of books and the reception desk. This was perfect.

"Don't you still need this room?" I couldn't believe my luck.

"Not so much anymore. Early in the computer age, the librarian at the time was forward-thinking enough to have the Estate install computers for personal use and host classes to encourage residents to use them.

"But over the years, computer literacy became more general, even among the older seniors. As I have found, new residents coming to live at the Estate either keep personal computers in their cottages or they use iPads."

"Of course, there are some residents who never signed on for the computer age. They think they are too old to fuss with more technology. These folks aren't much interested in coming to the library to use something they have long done without. There are a few exceptions, but the computer room generally lacks computer users."

"We could do something about that," I said. "But what about the occasional person who still wants to use a computer here?"

"No problem. We can always accommodate one or two, except when we hold our weekly meeting – and that time can be reserved for us. After all, how many of us would generally be here? I figure no more than three or four of us here at any one time. How about you? Will you be here much?"

By now, I should explain, everybody on our volunteer staff had been given a job. I edited the stories and gave out assignments, although in time people came up with their own suggestions. Diane Gibson took the photographs but her artistic skills also extended to doing the layout. Miss MacDonald handled the commentary section of letters and columns but also helped with editing and reading proofs. Gavin, Martha, and Betty were our regular reporters and I filled in on occasion.

More and more, I regretted that I had ever thought of Betty as Betty Boop. My first impression of her as a mature Barbie Doll did not come close to doing justice to how capable she was. Having worked in the advertising industry, she knew how to make words count and now she deployed them to a new purpose with skill and verve. Although Martha and Gavin did a reasonable job, Betty was soon our star writer.

Sam Hudson became our sports reporter/editor, a role he embraced with all the fervor he mustered for politics. In doing so, he confirmed one of my long-standing suspicions – that party politics, in its unthinking allegiances and rivalries, was just sports by another name. It is the idea that our team is good, the other team is bad. If our team loses or does poorly, it must be the fault of someone else; likely the umpires in sports, the media in politics.

Sam was not one for being impartial and unbiased in his sports reporting, notwithstanding that bias was his chief complaint about the media in general. He was a "homer," as they say. When it came to teams at the Estate, he wrote everything from the perspective of a rabid fan. He used florid language and clichés galore and in another life I would have toned his copy down in the interests of professionalism.

But he was an amateur enthusiast not to be contained by a solemn lecture on the misuse of hyperbole, which, of course, the readers loved. Members of teams who barely had the results of their tennis and golf games reported before now were made to feel like champions even when they lost. They liked being compared to the Spartan heroes who held the pass at Thermopylae, even though the comparison was ridiculous.

Another Pine Nut staffer was Brenda Matthews. In every office of every type, a certain amount of routine material needs to be typed into the system, and that job was performed by Brenda, who was probably in her eighties but still a good typist. She had been a secretary when women office workers who typed and took dictation were still called secretaries and not administrative assistants. Brenda was a happy person whose good nature was not diminished by having to type up the dining hall menus for the coming week, a task that would have driven most of us nuts. She had no aspirations to be a writer – and had not attended my initial Sunday meeting – but just wanted to keep busy and useful.

Bill Gibson, who became our business manager, recommended Brenda. We didn't have much business for him to manage because we had no advertising or circulation sales. We just had a modest budget from the Estate for printing and other expenses and Bill kept an eye on that.

Miss MacDonald was right – not many of us would be using this room at the same time. With the exception of the weekly meeting at 10 am on Monday morning, most of the volunteers would type their stories on their personal computers in their homes and then email them in.

Miss MacDonald would work here because she was next door anyway. Diane would work here because she needed the Mac to do layout. Brenda would work here because she liked to be somewhere.

I liked to be somewhere, too, so I would definitely be working here. As a creature of habit, I was used to going to a central office for more than 40 years. The main reason I was doing this job was to get out of my little cottage and meet people. In time, I hoped I might look upon this small space as a little newsroom, a notion that was freighted with nostalgia for me.

However, when Miss MacDonald asked me whether I was going to be working in the office, I didn't answer immediately. I paused to ponder. I knew that I intended to work here but I didn't want to give the wrong impression.

Romeo, that sleazy rat, was to blame for this hesitancy. He had put a silly, illogical thought in my head. If he thought that I was coming on to Miss MacDonald romantically, maybe she herself had such a notion. Absurd, I said to myself, this is crazy. Miss MacDonald is not an idiot and I have never said or done anything inappropriate. As lonely as I often felt, I was determinedly not in the market for a girlfriend or partner. I was still at the stage where even contemplating such a thing pained me as a moral offense.

"Yes," I finally said, "I suppose it would be more convenient for me to work here. I have never done very well working at home."

"Good," she said. "I look forward to seeing you more often. But there's one thing I must ask if I may."

"Certainly. What do you need?"

"Please stop calling me Miss MacDonald. I am not that formal and this is California. You should call me Linda."

"I will, Linda, from now on."

"Thank you. I am sorry to be so particular but I feel I have been doomed by the Curse of the Librarian, which has cast me as a formidable Victorian lady in charge of manners. Perhaps if you call me Linda the 250 other residents here will do so too, now that informality is approved and they will soon be eating dinner in their pajamas."

I smiled at this and she smiled back and I felt that I was going to enjoy being in this nice sunny office. By the way, it happened to be located near Mr. Higgins' old office, now known by all as the Love Shack. I did not take that as any sort of warning of what can happen to a person.

<u>20 - MY INK-STAINED LIFE</u>

Those were the days my friend
We thought they'd never end
– Mary Hopkin, 1968

Miss MacDonald shared the next desk to me in the new Pine Nut office. (It was hard for my mind to adjust to the name Linda, which my mouth was now asked to say, but the name Pine Nut had been hard to get used to as well.) She still had her library duties to perform but her clients often came in clusters leaving her some free time. And after the library closed at 3 pm, she would turn her undivided attention to her newsletter job.

We chatted quite often, as happens when you work near someone. Brenda would sometimes chime in on these conversations but she wasn't there as much as we were. Diane Gibson would only be there full-time on Thursday to finish the layout before the newsletter was sent to the printer early the next day.

Familiarity breeds contempt, or so the old saying instructs. But that must have been devised by a cynic because some other feeling was at work with Linda and me. We found ourselves at ease with each other. When we talked, it was spontaneous, comfortable, never strained for a word or a thought. I now realize that slowly, without knowing it, we were building the foundation of a friendship. Best of all, I never felt guilty that we were straying into a relationship that, though strictly chaste, might have felt at least a mental betrayal of my beloved Susan. For me in my continuing grief, Susan had not completely gone away.

Of course, I was curious to know more about Linda, but I

suppressed my usual tendency to ask her all sorts of questions in case she was frightened off. Some people are very private and her manner suggested she was one of them.

Susan had always complained when she thought I was interrogating people about where they had been and what they done in their lives. "For goodness' sake!" she would say after I met someone new, maybe at a party, "You only just met that person and here you are asking all sorts of probing questions that they probably don't want to answer."

I always pleaded guilty to that charge and then would do another interrogation the next time a new acquaintance came along. I wasn't able to help myself. Maybe this tendency to unearth people's secrets was occupational hazard. My love of people's stories may explain why I liked journalism so much. That suggested a question. Did my love of stories lead me to journalism or did journalism teach me how wonderful stories were?

Whether the egg came first or whether it was the chicken was beside the point. I just wanted to know the chicken's story. My uncommon restraint on asking Linda questions led to something that was quite unprecedented in my life. She got my story before I got hers.

It took about two weeks working closely together. One Thursday afternoon, when she and I were sitting about after the proofs had been read, the subject came up in a wide ranging conversation, the one that for everyone I met at the Estate was the elephant in the room – Susan's untimely passing. Some never acknowledged the sad fact central to my life and they carried on blithely as if the elephant were not there. I could never decide whether that was an act of social cowardice on their part or a quiet attempt at kindness.

Others found graceful ways to bring the subject up, which is what I preferred. Linda, with her kind manner, did that now. So gently and naturally did she speak the delicate question, it was as if she gave the elephant a pat and a stick of sugar cane.

"Alistair," she said quietly, "I am curious about you. Can I ask you a personal question? Tell me not to continue if it is..." Here she paused as if feeling her way delicately among thorny emotions.) "...painful for you and too hard to talk about."

"Of course you can. You are a librarian and my life is an open book." I quickly wished I could have edited this cheesy declaration. Here she was asking me a somber question and here I was being flippant.

"Your wife...."

"Yes. Susan."

"I know that you are a widower and I heard that you lost Susan after you first arrived."

"Yes," I said. "It was the very first night. Not what we planned."

"How horrible. I am so sorry. I am not sure I could have coped. I would not have had the strength. What courage you must have. I know you must have loved her deeply."

I silently nodded.

"But you have carried on as she no doubt would have wanted you to do."

Sighing, I said: "I am afraid it is less courage than simply wanting to put on a brave face and not have our tragedy burden the spirits of anybody else."

"No question of that. Look at you – how long has it been, many months now? – and you are involved in a project that has given joy and purpose to those who work with you, me included, and the residents of this little community."

"Well, I am glad to hear that. This little adventure has partially filled a void for me. I have been busy and when you are busy you have less time to feel sorry for yourself. In a way, I have gone back to my first love as consolation for the loss of the love of my life."

Linda looked momentarily confused but quickly grasped that it was a figure of speech. "You mean, writing and editing?"

"Yes. That is it. I did it for years and years, from age 19 onwards, and then I didn't. What we do here is a tiny replica of what I used to do but that is OK. It has the same good feeling. It would be like an architect who has designed big buildings and then, in retirement, decides to build himself a garden shed. The scale is completely different but the same eye surveys the work and in that way a little happiness is rediscovered."

"I hope you do not think me a potted plant in your garden shed."

"No, not at all. I just got carried away with the simile. It happens to writers."

"How did you find this first true love of yours, this vocation?'

"My dad introduced me. He was a journalist and I loved him and what he did for a living. It seemed to me the best life that a person could have in the world. Other kids dreamed of riding a fire engine or flying a jet plane. I wanted to be the guy who told the stories of people who did those things." I paused briefly.

"You have to understand what newsrooms in the heyday of newspapers were like. They had a magic to them but it was a decidedly unromantic magic, like something cooked up in a witch's cauldron. They smelled. They smelled of paper, ink, and grease, and they had the stale air of old buildings with rudimentary plumbing and heating systems that circulated air fitfully and at temperatures defying the seasons outside. To top it all, sometimes the cafeteria would exude smells of dinner specials that had overstayed their welcome.

"Plenty of the people who worked there were as rumpled and soiled as their surroundings and alcohol was on the breath of more than a few of them. But everywhere there was bustle and excitement and life. What little kid could resist such a grubby and marvelous place?"

"When did you first see it?" she asked.

"I first saw it as a schoolboy of nine or so when I visited my dad's office with my mother. We were in town, probably on one of those dreadful childhood shopping expeditions for clothes, and my poor exasperated mother needed some relief. The newspaper office was on the main street in Brisbane near the stores, so a visit was convenient." I paused again for a moment to think back on those days.

"People used to talk about newspapermen – or women – who were so in character that it was said they had ink in their veins. That day I surely had my first transfusion. Dad showed me where he worked as a copy editor, or sub editor as they called them in Australia. You knew I was originally from there, right?" She nodded. "I met his pals and they were characters, I saw his office, and it was a place only characters could occupy.

"I remember meeting the paper's cartoonist. Dad told me that the cartoonist's work had offended the stevedores' union. Remember, this was still the Red Scare 1950s. and the wharfies, as they were called Down Under, were said to be led by communists and were notoriously militant. They had demanded huge wage increases and were threatening to strike if management didn't agree. The cartoonist depicted them as would-be millionaires wearing top hats, not surprisingly a comparison that annoyed them a lot.

"But the wharfies had the last word. At the Labor Day parade that year, they marched past the newspaper building like all the other unions. But they alone wore top hats, which they doffed with their steel bale-hauling hooks as they passed by. I have spent a whole career hoping to be saluted sarcastically by men in top hats."

She laughed but did not speak, sensing I wasn't finished with the story.

"You know, the sense of the power of words and images to influence events and move people never left me. With my father's help, I eventually landed a job as a cadet reporter at the same newspaper where my father worked. Ah, the power of nepotism, you might say. Actually, Dad wasn't in a senior enough position to hire me as so much as a copy boy. All he did was put in a good word for me with the bosses and because he was popular and had a reputation as a good hand, it worked. He felt very proud and I felt very lucky.

"During my cadetship, I came to see that a newspaper was really a word factory, with all the different occupations and classes working for the same purpose.

"I remember the grizzled veteran copy editors. They were once reporters themselves but were now permanently moored around the universal desk, the last berth of their careers. They would sit there hunched over the copy with their scissors and glue pots ready for when stories had to be patched together. They grumbled as they retooled sentences with their pencils, complaining that the new generation of reporters couldn't write and couldn't spell and didn't know the stylebook. I reckon they were right in my case. From time to time they would treat the insults to their craft with furtive nips from silver flasks. Those and the metal spikes on which they impaled rejected stories seemed their only source of joy.

"Elsewhere in the newsroom, this crazy symphony of creation had different notes of urgency: phones rang, sub-editors shouted Copy and pneumatic tubes sent the edited stories down to the composing room with a big whoosh of air.

"You should have seen the composing room. That's where the printers worked. To enter the composing room back then was to enter another realm where under bright lights operators would work alien machines with swinging arms and their own unique keyboards. The typesetters would boil molten lead to make single slivers of type. All the printers wore their blue collars on their sleeves and did not tolerate fools or young people gladly. I was both at the time, so it was a hard apprenticeship for me and a bit of amusement for them but I learned things that no college could teach." I took a deep breath of remembrance.

"Word factories. I miss them, Linda. Over the course of my career, I saw a way of life change. The hot type gave way to cold type which gave way to type digitally generated. Whole professions went away, including compositors, typesetters, photo engravers, proof readers, and many categories of journalists. Except at the largest papers, few editors remain, and those who do sit at terminals where cut and paste is not a physical act but a computer function for handling the stories of the last few reporters.

"And here I am, pretending in my old age that a little weekly newsletter at a retirement home can transport me back to an old-fashioned newsroom where, after the editions went to press, the hard core journos went to celebrate the effort with drinks into the night."

She had got me going, that librarian. I realized now that I had made a speech and she was the audience. But all throughout she had looked interested, even fascinated. I felt exhausted. I had not spoken so much in years. She remained quiet for a long time, which made me uneasy. Maybe I had made a fool of myself. At last she spoke.

"I think, Alistair, you have become a newspaper yourself. Full of information, full of turns of phrase, full of jokes and tragedy, full of life."

"I think that is the nicest thing anybody has ever said to me."

"Good," she said. "Now that you are in a good mood, would you like to go dancing with me?"

"What?"

<u>21 - LET'S DANCE</u>

I was dancin' with my darlin' to the Tennessee Waltz
– Patti Page, 1950

It turned out that Linda was inviting me to take part in a dance class. The Estate management was always scheduling educational classes or fitness sessions in order to keep the residents' minds off other things, with growing old and dying perhaps the most unstated but obvious.

Classes were convened for flower arranging, cooking, lawn bowls, gardening, yoga, low-impact stretching, bridge, and, in two weeks apparently, ballroom dancing. Notices were posted to encourage sign-ups. Six-week session. Learn the waltz, foxtrot and tango. Come by yourself or with a partner.

As the Estate was between management at this time, Mr. Higgins and Marge must have scheduled this activity before they themselves danced out the door. Some residents would have said that those two had done one tango too many already. If they didn't find another manager soon, all the classes would dry up and people would have to amuse themselves. Lord help us then.

Some confusion ensued when Linda asked me to take part.

"Wait! Are you asking me on a date?"

"No. It's a dance class. I need a partner. I don't want to dance with some lady."

"You need a partner?"

"Dance partner. Not the sort that hold hands when not on the dance floor."

"OK, but I have never been able to dance. I couldn't dance if my pants were on fire."

"That's why they have a class. I'm not an expert at cutting the rug either. An instructor will teach us the steps and I am sure fire extinguishers will be available in the unlikely event your pants start smoking."

"OK," I said very tentatively.

"OK. We have a deal," she said very positively. "I think it will be a lot of fun for both of us. More fun than any date."

As you can see, all of this came as a complete surprise, and even after I reluctantly sort-of agreed, because to say no seemed impolite, I was filled with a sense of foreboding. It was true that I was always a rotten dancer. Some people have rhythm, others have inertia.

Fortunately, dancing in my generation was easily faked. You didn't have to learn any steps for standard rock and roll; you could get by shuffling about, which is what I did at parties if dancing could not be avoided. I could shuffle about as well as the next hapless guy, leaving female partners unimpressed but only moderately disappointed. Disco dancing did require some expertise but most of us tried to avoid that even if we wore the fashion styles John Travolta popularized.

I have always believed that how a person danced – or shuffled in imitation – was set in stone early in life. The steps a guy does at 70 are the same steps he did at 20 or so. But ballroom dancing is another matter entirely. It requires actual steps.

When Susan and I were at our wedding reception 45 years ago, her mother looked at us shuffling around the dance floor during the bridal waltz like two puppies on their hind legs and said sadly: "I see that they will never be Fred Astaire and Ginger Rogers."

Susan had no excuse. She had attended ballroom dancing classes when she was a girl as many middle class girls of her generation did. Maybe she was a debutante at a coming-out ball. For my part, I was strictly a rugby player.

In fact, growing up, I always thought that ballroom dancing was distinctly weird. A boy and a girl, facing each other, held each other in public while they moved to the music. In that strict time, no other activity in polite society allowed an unmarried boy and a girl to hold each other in a crowd or anywhere else. Play the music, they can hold. Stop the music, they can't hold. Strange, the kid version of me thought, very strange.

Of course, as kids grew up, a good deal of holding surreptitiously went on at necking spots and drive-in theaters. But those were very private moments involving steps unapproved by society.

Ballroom dancing did not hold its monopoly on the culture as the 20th century advanced. By the time rock and roll captured the public taste, people were already happily dancing around each other without touching, perhaps a tacit confirmation that officially approved holding was no longer needed when illicit holding was occurring everywhere.

Yet ballroom dancing never died. Its devotees twirled on. I remember as a cub reporter being sent to cover the Pan-Pacific Ballroom Dancing Championship in Brisbane, Australia, in about 1967. My bosses at the newspaper could not have sent a less competent person to cover this event. It was the equivalent of sending a caveman to cover a seminar on brain surgery.

The competition was an eye-opener for me. The dance floor was full of dozens of couples dressed to the nines, the men in white tie and tails and the women in elaborate ball gowns, indeed looking uncannily like clones of Fred and Ginger. They twirled and smiled and dipped and did little leaps in step to some archaic tune.

Best of all, from my perspective, was that the men had numbers pinned to the back of their elegant black jackets so that the judges could identify the couples for scoring purposes. Those numbers were sort of like the numbers football players wore, except that these prancing men weren't covered in mud and blood, and they and their partners in the ruck did not have cauliflower ears or broken noses.

More surreal than this, the crowd in the bleachers yelled encouragement to their favorite teams. "Come on, Norm and Bobbi, you can do it!" "Go Jack and Debbie, show them how to waltz!" Strange, very strange, at least to my eyes at the time.

This is what Linda would have to work with, the un-dancing fool and his history of looking on astonished.

Our date with destiny did not affect our working relationship. (Well, it wasn't a date, I had been assured, and I hoped ballroom dancing wasn't my destiny.) We worked together but we did not dine together. I continued to go to breakfast alone and I had the staff at the dining hall make me a sandwich for lunch, which could be ordered in advance. I had always eaten lunch at my office desk while I worked and I kept up that routine. Linda did take time to go to the dining hall for lunch where I suppose she ate a salad or something else depressingly healthy. Sometimes I would see her at the dining hall in the evening but more often than not we ate with different people.

Our first dance class was scheduled at 4 pm, so we finished our work early that Wednesday afternoon. I would rather have stayed working, anything rather than trying to make my stumbles appear choreographed. But at 3:30 pm, Linda switched off her computer, then turned to me and said: "Are you ready to trip the light fantastic?"

I recognized the quote from a poem by John Milton. This is what you get when you go dancing with a librarian, I suppose. "Come! And trip it, as ye go, on the light fantastic toe," I said aloud, "and in thy right hand lead with thee, the mountain nymph, sweet liberty." I paused and added: "So, yes, my toes are ready but I can only guess whether they are up to mountain nymph standards."

"Very good," she said, obviously pleased that I had recognized something only English majors and people over 70 with old-fashioned educations would have a hope of understanding. Just as I was becoming pleased that she was pleased, she looked at me intently.

"Are you going dressed like that?" she said.

I looked down at my old guy uniform of sweatpants and sneakers. If it was one thing that 40 plus years of marriage had taught me, it was that if a woman looked at you and said, "Are you going dressed like that?" then it was time to change your clothes.

"Maybe I should put on pants and regular shoes."

"Maybe," she said.

I also knew what 'maybe' meant in womanspeak. Fifteen minutes later I came back dressed more appropriately for formal rug cutting. I even wore a shirt with a collar.

"Very nice," she said and then we strolled down to the fitness center for the class.

We were met at the door by the instructor, a flamboyant raven-haired woman with a big elaborate dress that, bolstered by petticoats, surrounded her legs as if she had stepped into a beach umbrella. "Welcome, welcome," she said. She was much younger than we were – meaning that she was middle aged – and very enthusiastic.

Other couples and stray singles had already begun to assemble. Most of them were in varying degrees of limber but one old gentleman and his lady had walkers. "Lordy," I said to myself, "how are they going to waltz? They will be like two withered elephants circling each other banging the ground." I wondered whether I should tell them what I knew about shuffling but immediately dismissed this thought as unnecessarily cruel. Besides, I would be in their condition soon enough. As it happened, their walkers did not bang the ground; they were tipped with tennis balls cut and re-purposed.

Ms. Zambona, our dancing mistress, took a roll call and then instructed us to take our places on the floor, "Not too close together please, ladies and gentlemen," she said.

"The waltz," she announced grandly. "Today we are going to master the waltz."

Good luck with that, I thought. She put on the music with a little portable disc player and then selected a random gentleman to be her partner for the purpose of demonstration. To be precise, he was random but not a gentleman. He was Romeo. It was not altogether a surprise to see him here. Holding ladies and leading them on a merry dance was his thing.

I had seen him out of the corner of my eye when I first came in and here he was, all spiffed up and cheesy-grinned, waltzing in his element. Ms. Zambona was an excellent dancer and Romeo was competent enough. "The gentleman leads, ladies. Look what we do. One-two-three, one-two-three...."

Having demonstrated the steps, Ms. Zambona now jettisoned Romeo so she could observe the rest of us. For his part, Romeo found another unattached lady to put in moral danger as his dancing partner.

I took hold of Linda's hand gently and put my arm on her back tentatively, as if I were in a bomb squad handling a sensitive device. Then we tried the one-two-three, one-two- three routine and I only stepped on her foot twice in the first minute.

However, this caused Ms. Zambona to split us for a short time so she could take me in hand to demonstrate how it was supposed to be done. Now mortified for having been singled out, I managed to trip over my own feet once but somehow managed not to step on hers, which were moving too fast for me to stand on anyway. Then I was returned to Linda and Ms. Zambona went to assist other hopeless cases.

I did marginally better. I was now able to adapt my lifetime shuffling to the one-two-three arrangement. Linda and I came to some sort of unstated understanding. She came to anticipate my moves, which she may have somehow signaled me to make. I only stood on her foot one more time in the rest of the hour and she stood on mine once too, although that was probably my fault. I was getting a little too relaxed and my concentration faltered.

By the end of the class, we had danced a number of different waltzes and I felt a little exhilarated for not causing too much mayhem. Linda appeared pleased as did most of the dancers, even the couple with the waltzing walkers. Ms. Zambona congratulated us all in her vaguely exotic accent and syntax. "Next time," she said, "because you do so well today, we tackle the tango."

The tango! Lordy, I'd have to check if Medicare covers it.

That evening Linda and I had dinner together, not alone but in the company of others. Still, we had this shared experience and we spoke mostly to each other. "Did you have a good time?" she asked.

"I did, much to my surprise. Sorry about your feet. I have to admit the tango has me worried."

"I had fun too and I am sure my feet will revive after a good soaking. And don't worry about the tango. I think you will surprise yourself again."

That night I thought about Susan but I did not feel guilty. Ballroom dancing was not something we would have done together, having learned our lesson early. For me, there were still some lessons left to learn and that struck me as good.

22 - THE NEW REGIME

Bye bye, love/ Bye bye, happiness
– The Everly Brothers, 1957

At last a new manager and an assistant were officially announced as coming to the Estate. When Mr. Higgins and his special office friend Marge left, the residents found this out at dinner time by reading an official notice posted on the bulletin board in the dining hall. The same happened when their replacements were announced. The Board of Trustees, it seemed, were not ones for new media or even revitalized old media in the form of The Pine Nut.

Now, at least, the board did The Pine Nut a favor, probably because its members didn't know the newsletter existed. Previously the news of the management changes had been posted on a Thursday evening, making us scramble to make the deadline for the newsletter; this time it was Tuesday evening, which gave us ample time to do a story on the impending arrival of the new manager and his assistant manager. And this time The Pine Nut was better organized and prepared.

Five months had passed since the old regime had left and the Estate seemed to be running quite well under the temporary leadership of the catering manager, Pedro Rodrigues, who kept the same low profile he always had.

His genial lack of attention to anything but serving meals and keeping lawns trimmed turned out to be a boon to the fortunes of The Pine Nut. Pedro didn't ask to be involved in the newsletter – he probably didn't realize that was one of his duties – and we were happy for the lack of management oversight. The newsletter found its feet in those early months, and by degrees we became more relevant and daring, although only someone who had lived a sheltered life could accuse us of tabloid behavior.

We ran one story about ducks landing in the main swimming pool and making it their personal pond. This might have concerned management previously. Had alert management been on the job, they might have feared that prospective residents would turn away due to the publicized presence of unhygienic water fowl doing laps. We even ran photographs of ladies in bathing suits at the pool trying to shoo the ducks away. They were waving their old-fashioned bathing caps at the ducks, which took no notice.

I remembered that Mr. Higgins, in my brief job interview with him, had expressed concern about pictures of "bathing beauties" appearing in The Pine Nut. But Mr. Higgins was gone, and whether the ladies qualified as beauties was open to argument. I am sure they would be flattered to be considered so.

By the way, only good came of this article. Apparently, someone on the maintenance staff read The Pine Nut because not long afterwards a worker was given the regular duty of rousing the ducks whenever they splashed in the pool. Ah, the power of the press!

I did feel sorry for the poor guy who became the duck irritator. But one day, when he has risen to become a captain of industry, he will be able to boast how far he has come from humble beginnings. Abraham Lincoln could say he was born in a log cabin but not many people rise to greatness after service as a duck irritator.

But what were we dealing with now? Would the new manager continue to take a hands-off approach to us?

The letter announcing the appointments was written in unhelpful officialese full of teasing clues but not much information. Residents gathered around the notice board wondering what it all meant and muttering to themselves, asking questions that nobody could answer. Well, The Pine Nut could answer them but it would take some work. The notice said:

"The Board of Trustees of the Whispering Pines Estate for Community Living is pleased to announce the appointment of Phillip D. Jones III, a graduate of Harvard College, as general manager of our Carmelito residences, effective on the first of next month. Until recently a member of the executive team at the management firm of Rylands Fenmore in Chicago, Mr. Jones later earned a diploma in Senior Life Care and Retirement Living Management. A native of Boston, he attended high school at the prestigious Frobisher School in Connecticut.

"The board is also pleased to announce the appointment of Marianne Crocker as assistant manager, as of the same date. Ms. Crocker, originally from Chicago, also attended Frobisher but returned to Chicago after high school to study at Northwestern University and later also earned a diploma in Senior Life Care and Retirement Living Management. She is particularly interested in promoting arts and crafts classes such as basket weaving as a way to individual personal understanding.

"After completing an extensive national search, the board is pleased that it has found two individuals who are not only knowledgeable about senior issues but dedicated to a holistic approach to senior life care. We believe that residents will greatly appreciate the fresh and dynamic approach that Mr. Jones and Ms. Crocker will bring to our beloved Carmelito facility." It was signed not by its chairman but simply The Board of Trustees.

I studied the notice as puzzled as anybody else. A familiar voice asked: "How can arts and crafts bring someone to personal understanding? Does this mean my knitting can bring me to a state of inner peace?" It was Linda speaking. As I was concentrating hard to make sense of the words, she had come up my side quietly without me noticing.

"I don't know," I said. "But it seemed to work for Madame Defarge. Didn't she knit contentedly as the guillotine lobbed off the heads of those aristocrats during the French revolution?"

She laughed. "OK, you got me there, but maybe Madame Defarge was just practicing a holistic approach to senior life care."

"Yeah, that's another gem of a phrase – more modern jargon signifying little or nothing. Unless they teach that in the diploma course for Senior Life Care and Retirement Living Management, I don't think it's meant to say anything. It is just meant to impress us and bamboozle us so we don't think too hard. It reminds me of an old saying we used back in Australia: BS baffles brains."

"Talking about brains," she said, "I suppose some school has a diploma for Senior Life Care and Retirement Living Management – they have courses in everything these days – but would Harvard or Northwestern? It seems unlikely."

"Yes, it does, Linda. Whatever college it is, maybe there's also a Department of Elvis Studies in the same building. The truth is that this notice raises more questions than it answers."

Linda and I ate dinner together that night, although it was not a dance night. We had much to discuss. We agreed that we needed to call The Pine Nut staff together the next morning to plan how we would answer the unanswered questions. I would send out emails and messages to everybody when I got back to my cottage.

The next day, the staff did gather dutifully at 9 am in our room at the library. By now they all had seen the announcement on the dining hall notice board and they had their opinions.

Gavin started it off. "I was struck that their education credentials were given more prominence than their experience. It said the Jones guy was on the executive team of some management company in Chicago that I never heard of. What does the company manage? What does he do in particular? How long has he worked there? As for the woman appointed assistant manager, they never said what she did, just where she went to school."

I spoke up. "Even then, it is not clear that she graduated from Northwestern. The announcement said after graduating from the private high school, Frobisher, coincidentally the same one that Jones was at, she returned to Chicago "to study" – those were the exact words – at Northwestern. Nowhere does it say she graduated from Northwestern. Maybe that's loose language by some PR person who wrote the announcement, but maybe it was done to cover up an embarrassing fact. And right after that, maybe to confuse us further, it very oddly said she wants to promote arts and crafts classes apparently for some goofy New Age-sounding purpose."

"Wait a second," said Sam, "This sounds like the old media carping. There's no crime in liking arts and crafts, although personally I prefer sports. And what does it matter if she graduated from college or not? I have known many fine people who never graduated from college.

"And what does it matter what college they went to for Senior Life Care and Retirement Living Management? Wherever it was, I say good for them for learning about the subject. Maybe they interviewed really well and are bright, go-getting individuals."

"Maybe, Sam," I said, "but we won't know until we answer these questions. The chairman of the Board of Trustees did say that they were looking for experienced candidates to be managers. Remember? We need to know how legitimate the credentials of these two are before we can tell if he has done that."

Sam took the point silently. It was hard to argue with that.

"It is really odd that they both attended an exclusive private high school across the country and they both are ending up here," Martha Evans said. "Do they know each other?"

"How old are they?" Diane Gibson asked. "If they are similar ages, that might suggest they were in the same classes if the school wasn't huge. What that might mean I don't know."

"They never put the ages in the announcement," Gavin said, "and that makes me suspicious. Maybe they are real young."

"To be fair," Betty Bosworth said, "the owners of Whispering Pines may not know their ages. These days that is not something you can usually ask someone straight out in a job interview. But there are ways to find out and I know how old Mr. Jones is."

"How old?" several of us said pretty much in unison.

"Twenty-three last month."

"How did you...?" I am not sure who squeaked this out but it was as much a joint thought as a stated question.

"While you were talking I was Googling. I don't know how old Ms. Crocker is but I will. Social media is the friend of those who stick their nose into other people's business. Oh, here it is on Facebook: She just turned 21."

"Alexander the Great was about their age when he first set off," Sam said. "Plenty of today's second lieutenants in Afghanistan are their age and nobody says they are too young."

"True, Sam," I said. "Warriors are young; the residents of the Estates are old. It might be an advantage for our officers in command to have lived more time in the century we were born in."

"Ageism," said Sam.

"Reality," said I.

"Here's another thing," Betty said. "There is only one college in the country that I can find that offers a diploma in Senior Life Care and Retirement Living Management, as stated exactly like that. It is Fuller College, in Evanston, Illinois."

"Never heard of it," said Martha, speaking for us all.

"It is an on-line school," Betty said. "You can do the course in six weeks. It costs $250."

"Who said the cost of higher education has gone through the roof?" Linda said. Everybody laughed.

Betty had found out more. "Someone asked about the management firm of Rylands Fenmore in Chicago. According to their website, they are industrial real estate developers, not retirement facility owners.

"Look, they have a profile of all their executives and here is Mr. Jones at the end of the list, all dressed up in his best dark suit. Wow, he is one sour-looking guy – talk about smile-challenged.

"I have seen this guy before. He was in a picture in Facebook taken at Ms. Crocker's 21st birthday party, so they know each other all right. And look at this – they recently announced their engagement!"

As we sat digesting these revelations, Betty found some more: "What projects did he work on, you ask? It says here he assisted on the building of a sewage treatment plant for some local municipality as a junior executive."

"I wouldn't smile for the camera either," Gavin said.

But we were all smiling broadly. We had a story. The rest of the meeting was spent deciding who was going to do what, and in the end everybody got a piece of the action, except Sam, who had his sports duties to attend to.

I reminded them, "Folks, let me remind you that The Pine Nut is still the official magazine of the Estate management, even if there is no management left to tell us what to do. What we will do is report the story scrupulously. We will not leave out pertinent facts but we will let them speak for themselves without editorializing.

"I am not worried about losing my job; I am only worried about not doing this in a professional manner. Go to it. Do the research and make the calls. We must get someone from the Board of Trustees to comment on the facts we assemble."

"I'll do it," Betty volunteered. "I'll call the chairman of the board. Martha has his number from when Mr. Higgins left."

"Good," I said. "Remind me what his name is?" I worried in advance what his reaction might be. I am not sure he and the rest of the trustees understood what The Pine Nut was – being, as they were, mostly from out of town and unfamiliar with the workings of the Estate. They might think it was some independent local paper calling. But there was always the chance that the chairman might know and forbid us to publish anything.

"Wait," said Betty, as she looked up the board chairman's name. "Here it is...Phillip D. Jones II of Boston, Massachusetts."

Wait a second....I had benefitted from a little nepotism in my life too but this was of a different order. I shared my thought: "No wonder that the announcement of the appointment of Phillip D. Jones III, aged 23 and formerly of Boston, as general manager of the Estate was made in the name of the Board of Trustees, not the Board Chairman Phillip D. Jones II of Boston. They appear to be father and son."

23 - PROGRESS REPORT

We passed the time away
Writing love letters in the sand
– Pat Boone, 1957

Dear Susan,

It has been a year since that night when we smiled and lifted a glass to the future and the next morning when I saw what that future would be and I cried. In one sense, it doesn't seem so long ago but in another way it is like a memory from a lost land. My new life confounds the idea that time only flies when you are having fun.

My old life had its fun. Now I just have...activity. In this, I have faithfully honored your words: Stay active, stay busy, even if this frantic effort to stay upright and in motion is often ridiculous.

The other day I went to a dance class. Can you imagine that? Me. Two-Left-Feet Alistair. True to the old form that you knew and loved, I was a danger to passing toes and my sense of rhythm remained hidden from view. A lady I work with in my new job asked me because she needed a partner. I went because I didn't want to give offense and I was assured that it wasn't a date. Good thing that it wasn't a date because I would have failed the test and would have been propelled back to my socially inept teen-age years in everything but the acne.

By the way, that job I mentioned is an exercise in going back to the future. After looking for something to do, I landed the position as editor of the Estate's little newsletter, which in my vanity I think of as my little New York Times, only with the amended slogan All the News That's Fit to Print and Read If You

Can Find Your Glasses.

By the way, the newsletter is called The Pine Nut, a name that seems especially designed to be humbling. How the mighty have fallen, eh? Of course, the editorship is a volunteer position. The one thing you can say about a non-paying job is that you can do it well or badly and your bosses are still getting their money's worth. Nevertheless, I do put in long hours and that does help me forget that my life has come to this.

The Estate has its share of odd characters that might bring a smile if my mood allowed more smiles. There is a guy called Microphone Mike, who loses no public opportunity to broadcast his voice to captive audiences. There is a guy named Romeo who thinks he can charm every single lady on the Estate by bringing smarminess to a high art.

And remember Mr. Higgins, the manager who met with us? He disappeared without a trace one day, as did the woman who was his assistant manager. Popular scuttlebutt insists that the two of them ran away together for a new life of romance. This may or may not be true but in a place where there is generally little to talk about the gift of rumor was gratefully received.

A new manager and his assistant are about to take over. They are apparently young people who know nothing come to rule the realm of elderly people who think they know everything, which ought to be another boon to conversation. The writers of The Pine Nut stand ready to shake the tree.

Much has changed and yet nothing has essentially changed for me, despite my frantic activity. Susan, I was the one who was supposed to die first.

As farce has dogged all the serious events of my life, I always thought my time would end with some stupid misadventure that would make my pall-bearers giggle as they hauled away my pall. A fissure would open up on the golf course and swallow up my cart. A speeding drone would come out of the blue and nail me. Or I'd go somewhere like Fiji, only to be hit fatally on the head by a falling coconut.

Instead, alone in my room, with my heart overruling my head, I am reduced to writing to you an occasional report of what is happening. I am not sure dead people can receive mail. The Post Office is slow enough for the living. If you were still alive and here with me, I am sure you would be the first to say that this letter-writing habit of mine has become weird.

But if my writing is mainly for the purpose of sorting out my own feelings for the benefit of myself, I pray that you will sense the essential truth: You are not forgotten.

Love always,

Alistair xxxx

24 - THE UNQUIET LIBRARIAN

Good golly, Miss Molly
– Little Richard, 1958

A few days after the new management team was announced, Linda and I had dinner again together. It was not planned. We just happened to go to dinner about the same time, which would be about 6:15 pm – positively late-night dining by Estate standards. Most of the other residents were in the final stages of their meals. As we sat down together, I asked her only half-jokingly: "This is not a date, is it?"

"No, you can rest easy, having dinner together in the dining hall is not a date. I'll tell you if ever it's a date." Thank goodness for that. If I were on a date, I'd have to make mental peace with the ghost of Susan sitting in the bleachers of eternity with nothing better to do than to keep an eye on me.

We talked again about the management changes at the Estate and how The Pine Nut was responding but that conversation was soon exhausted, as we had been discussing that most of the day. To my surprise, the conversation turned to what we did in our earlier lives. She knew some of the details of my past life but I knew next to nothing about her. I had made some assumptions about her but, the more she revealed, the more I realized almost every assumption I had made was wrong. That was becoming a pattern of mine.

The biggest surprise was when she told me she had a tattoo of a leopard on her inner thigh. I remember being so taken by surprise that all I could say was an old word from my old life. "Crikey!" I said. "Crikey!" The cry of a man confounded, at least where I came from.

But that revelation came later in the evening.

I had ordered a bottle of wine, one of the pleasant amenities that made the Estate's dining room seem more like a quality restaurant than a chow house for the elderly. Fortunately, this was not a place where bland meals went to die of excessive steaming before the diners did.

Linda, I knew, liked the occasional glass of wine and I liked several glasses on many occasions and a bottle seemed a better deal with two sharing. The wine drinker's rationale was ever thus. The wine, a local Pinot Noir, worked its familiar magic in lowering our social defenses.

I wasn't planning to do my usual social interrogation that night. I always understood that she would probably tell me what she wanted to tell me about herself in her own good time. This was her good time. For one thing, we were by ourselves. Because this was not a ballroom dancing night, we were not joined by other dancers happy to regale each other with tales of collegial ineptitude and the colorful instructions of Ms. Zambona to remedy the curse of two left feet.

"I want to thank you, Alistair, for introducing me to the world of letters again," she said, after we had pretty much talked out the management situation. "I am a librarian. I am a custodian of words but you have given me a place in the word factory, as you call it, although it is a modest word factory, as we both know, serving a very small and select readership, but a word factory nonetheless."

"You had aspirations to be a writer once upon a time?" I asked, afraid that I might be blushing from her flattering testimonial.

"Yes, I was an English major at Bardhurst College in Ohio, which has a reputation for literary pursuits. I loved books and I pretty much lived in the library when I wasn't training for the cross country team. I soon joined the college paper, which is part of the appeal of working at The Pine Nut with you and the others. It takes me back, it really does. All we need is to order pizza to turn back the years."

"Not a bad idea. I have been bringing cookies, as you know, because I found out the hard way that this place is cookie crazy. But, before the thought escapes, did writing for the college paper put you off creative writing?"

"It sort of did. That was the downside. I found that creative writing is not the same as newspaper writing. It's not just the style of newspapers, the short sentences written in the active voice. It was also about being tethered to the facts. A car crashes and you proceed to answer the how, when, where and why questions. In creative writing, you make your own facts in a leap of the imagination. I hope you don't take offense at this description."

"Not at all. You have described it accurately. These days many people – the people with a political grievance usually – assume journalists make up facts but that is not the journalism I knew."

"My problem," she said, "was that my imagination was not informed enough by life experience that I could write fiction that seemed plausible. I could write a fair story for the college paper about a student fund-raising drive but in creative writing class I didn't know where to start. I was just a girl from suburban Cleveland who had been nowhere and done nothing."

"So you wanted to write a book but life hadn't given you enough material?" I asked. She nodded.

"I am sure you are selling yourself short," I said. "I look at you and you strike me as a wise woman, someone who understands people very well. People are not usually born with innate wisdom, they usually acquire it the hard way. I always say that I went to the University of Hard Knocks and graduated with a degree of concussion."

"Well, I have read a lot of books. And books are not just engaging little stories. The best of them are primers on life. They teach wisdom. The Brontë sisters sat there in rural England in something like genteel obscurity, their lives limited by their female social standing, and yet their imaginations leaped beyond all the boundaries invented to contain them. And their education from the books they read surely did let them grow in wisdom."

"I take your point. But, still, you seem worldly, experienced – in a quiet and dignified way, of course. I have to think that there is more there than was found between the covers of a book."

"Hmm, I am not sure that is the image I want to project."

"Forgive me, I don't mean to offend you," I said.

"No," she said, looking unoffended and now quoting one of my favorite poets, Robert Burns, "O wad some power the giftie gie us, to see oursels as ithers see us."

"My dad used to say that line," I said quietly, savoring the memory. "Dad would lay on the Scottish burr, as if he were a real Scotsman and not an Englishman by descent. And then he would translate it for me in his usual voice: 'Oh would some power the gift he give us, to see ourselves as others see us.' "

Looking up at me now, hesitant, almost in the manner of a confession, she said: "You have it right. I did have a wordly, experienced life before I entered this geriatric cloister. Before I became everybody's idea of the spinster librarian, Miss MacDonald treading the racks in comfortable shoes, I danced a wild dance."

I did not say a thing, although it was hard to stay quiet. I knew her story would be told without my usual prompting.

"It started in college. The Vietnam War was going on, I was 19 years old and our little campus, while not Kent State or Berkeley, had its own little version of campus unrest. There was a young man...."

"There is often a young man in a young woman's story of personal disaster," I offered.

"A cliché it was, certainly. His name was Bernie. He thought of himself as a big student leader on campus, the Che Guevara of Bardhurst, complete with blue jeans, ripped T-shirt bearing some lame slogan of the time, and a motley beard that looked like it might have been defoliated by a topical application of Agent Orange. Of course, I thought he was the most exciting man I had ever seen. It was love, as only love can be for someone who knew nothing and had been nowhere.

"Did he have the iconic Che Guevara beret?"

"No, that was the one thing he didn't have. What he had instead was a motorcycle. Bernie turned out not to be much of a student. The only book I ever saw him read was Zen and the Art of Motorcycle Maintenance. He really was a biker and maybe he rolled into college by mistake. And he rolled out of college as soon as the road got rocky, which happened when exams came. Unfortunately, I rolled out with him on the back of the motorcycle."

"You quit school? Weren't your parents mad?"

"Yes, and furious is too mild a word for how Mom and Dad felt. But I never mentioned Bernie to them, not wishing to set off strokes in chain reaction. I told them that I was just taking a break, for a year, so that I could travel and, of course, find myself. I suppose it was a scene playing out across America that year. Kids were searching for something and not knowing what. In the interim, they settled for more dope.

"We were very young and stupid. I remember Thanksgiving 1970 as the worst. I was grilled more than any turkey, and dried out by my parents' anger and sorrow. And yet, I still stayed with

Bernie. I was gone not one year but close to two and I never went back to Bardhurst."

"Where did you go? What did you do?"

"Odd jobs in odd places all over the country but ending up in California. Some of the jobs were disreputable. Pretty much all of them were trivial and stupid when they were not actually morally destructive. Eventually, I tired of the life and Bernie both. He was still trying to read his one book. He tired of me, too. He took up with a woman with tattoos on her chest." Linda shook her head. "It was after that that I got a tattoo of a leopard on my inner thigh. It was sort of tit for tat, or maybe tat for tit, except he liked her tits more than my tat."

I must have raised an eyebrow at this remark. She seemed to rush now to reach some more positive conclusion to her story.

"The turning point came one day after a boozy, drug-hazed party. I woke up in what I took at first to be a garbage dump but was actually someone's trashed apartment. I was lying next to some wasted hairy guy and it wasn't clear what had happened. Bernie was nowhere to be seen. The thought that something might have gone down between me and Sasquatch in the corner added a special touch of nausea to my hangover."

"I had always kept in touch with Mom. Dad was too far in his rage and grief then. I called her sometimes and we had a temporary pad in Bakersfield and she had sent a letter there about a week before. I was carrying it around, unopened, afraid of what it might say. When I did finally open it later that day, it said that Dad was very sick and might not last and could I come home. I took a Greyhound bus back to Ohio that same night."

"Did you make up with your Dad?"

"It was hard at first. He found it difficult to welcome the prodigal daughter back home but, yes, he did come around, even as he grew sicker. Just before the cancer took him, we made our peace. He said: 'Do one thing for me, Linda. Take care of your mother.' And I, who had never done one thing for him, promised to do that one thing. And I did. It turned out that Mom was sick herself and for the next two years I nursed her. I did not work, I devoted myself to her, but I went to college at night to finish my degree. They accepted my credits from Bardhurst and it took me two years but I graduated. It pleased Mom very much but then she died."

"What did you do then?"

"I first got a job at an insurance office and then I decided to become a librarian. I had gained all the experience in the world, but I had lost a bit of my creative soul. I didn't want to depress myself and other people by writing novels based on sordid memories. So I went back to school again and got my degree in library science. After that, I decided to make a fresh start. I once visited this area in my vagabond days and it struck me as very beautiful. I got a job out here, helped sell my parents' home and moved. After my late start, I ended up having a happy 25-year career."

"Ever see Bernie again?"

"No, never, thank goodness. I am sure he is fat and bald and is still trying to finish his book."

"A little more respect for the bald, please."

"Sorry. Believe me, you are no Bernie."

"Did you ever meet anyone else?"

"No, well...I dated some, but no one ever seemed so exciting again, which is probably a good thing after what happened the last time. I'm lucky in library cards, unlucky in love."

"Can I see your tattoo?" I was shocked at myself for saying this but after such a sad tale some friskiness seemed the only path to a lighter mood.

"No. Remember this is not a date. Even if it were, I am no longer the sort of girl who shows her tattoo on the first date."

"Good to know," I said, because I couldn't think of anything else to say in the circumstances.

25 - GOLDEN OLDIE

One, two, three o'clock, four o'clock rock
– Bill Haley and His Comets, 1954

When my mother was old and sick back in Australia, and she and Dad were still surviving on a meager fixed income, she had to go to a nursing home of a much more modest variety than the Estate and one with a different mission. She wasn't in an independent living situation. Because she needed round-the-clock attention, she was in a medical care facility where nurses' aides mostly cared for her. They were cheerful enough and treated the patients' inevitable bouts of depression by making numerous cups of tea...the Aussie remedy in those days for almost everything that troubled body and soul.

The place had an institutional aroma, as such places often do, which made me wonder whether this was where all life's once pleasant aromas finally retired to ripen into unpleasantness and decay.

As soundtrack accompaniment to the rattling teacups, the staff piped in sentimental songs from the '40s and '50s during the daylight hours and into the evening. These were the songs the patients once danced to. And the thought also occurred to me that when I was old and sick, and laid up in a way station like this, they would play the songs of my generation. The playlist would probably include Mick Jagger, then no doubt about 80 years old himself, singing "I can't get no satisfaction" – as if I needed any reminder of that fact in my senior years.

This morbid thought came back to me a few days after my dinner with Linda, seemingly in the form of a ghost from good times past. While we were still processing the news about the management changes, a newcomer to the Estate sought me out in The Pine Nut's office.

His name was Billy Franks and he looked like an old hippie or rocker that a taxi-driver, not knowing what else to do with him, had dropped off at the front gate. He was certainly an apparition.

Billy's sparse hair was dyed blond and hung scraggly down from his balding crown like a mullet gone to seed. He wore beat-up blue jeans held up by a big leather belt with a brass buckle, cowboy boots, and a ripped and soiled T-shirt that said: 'Rock 'n' Roll Rocks' – a statement remarkable only for its stunning redundancy. He wore sunglasses in a vain attempt to make himself look cool. I am not sure if he was around for the recent dress code debate but I think he would have voted with the informality faction. Just a stab in the dark there.

"Hey, man," he said, not surprisingly, because dressed like that what else could he possibly say, and introduced himself as a newcomer to our little community. He said he had formed a rock and roll band at the Estate with a few other guys and his wife, Babe, and they wanted to play a gig. "Man, like we need some publicity to get this show on the road." Actually, that was just a figure of speech. As much as Billy might long for the road, he would settle for a gig in the dining hall.

It turned out that Billy had been a professional musician, not a character from central casting or stereotype heaven as might be supposed. He had played in rock bands all his life with little success and in retirement couldn't put it aside. The Estate wasn't cheap and a lifetime of playing in dives could not have been that lucrative, so Babe must have inherited some dough. As much as Billy and I were different people, I knew the feeling of wanting my career back. Here I was pretending to be practicing journalism after a lifetime of not much (pecuniary) success and still not smart enough to give it a rest. So I was naturally sympathetic.

"Sure, Billy. What is your band called and what do they play?"

"Well, we haven't got a name yet but we rock. We do heavy metal, vintage rock, classic rock, Van Halen, Zeppelin, Stones... you name it." The mention of the Stones confirmed my worst fears but the news did explain something: The infernal noises that had been heard about the Estate lately were Billy's doing, not unidentified rowdy characters living up the canyon as had been suggested.

"Who is in your band?"

"Well, I play lead guitar and sing. Babe does backup vocals. Let me see...there's a guy named Charlie on bass guitar, Freddie does rhythm guitar, Bobby plays sax and Donnie plays the drums." He couldn't remember any of their last names and I recognized nobody from his description.

Apparently everybody in his band had a boy's name ending in "y" or "ie" – except Babe. Whether that was her real name, or the legacy of Billy calling her Babe as a habit of rock and roll speak, was never explained.

"Oh yeah, almost forgot, we have a sound man. His name is Havin something."

"You mean, Gavin?"

"Yeah, man, I swear by that dude."

"I am sure he swears by you. When is your gig planned?" I asked.

"We booked the dining hall not this Saturday night but a week later."

"That gives us time to do a story." It was my idea that the Band With No Name would make an entertaining diversion from the coverage of the new manager and his assistant.

"Tell you what, Billy. Let's run a competition for the readers of

The Pine Nut to give your band a name. That should create some interest."

"Yeah, man, I really dig that idea." Then, thinking a little longer than usual, he added: "But what if the name, like, really sucks?"

"You get to choose the name you are comfortable with."

"Oh yeah, that really rocks, man."

So it was settled. Betty would normally have done the assignment but she already had her hands full. As it turned out, Linda volunteered to write the story, her first, which previously I would have thought a bad idea. But as a result of our recent dinner, I now knew that Linda was another book that couldn't be judged by its cover.

Linda did a fine interview with Billy and Babe and the rest. Babe was something of a character in her own right and was no doubt the source of the blond dye bottle for Billy's hair. As Linda discovered when she interviewed her – and as I confirmed when I later got to know her personally – Babe was not the hard-boiled rock and roll chick that her brassy blond appearance and her very name might suggest at first encounter. She was kindly and thoughtful and well-spoken.

Where Billy would speak in hipster sentence fragments informed by clichés, Babe spoke standard middle-class American in complete, sensible sentences. If you closed your eyes, or you heard her over the phone for the first time, you might think she was a kindergarten teacher reporting on a generally lovable kid with slight problems.

While I don't believe they had children of their own, Billy was a man/child who obviously needed her supervision. She was devoted to him and their life together had to have been hard at times. Even if he had been a true rock star, it wouldn't have been easy – and perhaps harder, given the temptations of the trade.

As it was, their life on the road – as Billy played for bigger names in back-up bands – required exceptional effort on her part. But there she was, cleaning and pressing his clothes, telling him kindly not to drink too much or smoke, making him sandwiches for all-night studio sessions, paying the bills, putting gas in their van and driving it when he slept between gigs, and translating his grunts into intelligible conversation. She even got up on the stage and sang, which seemed more a duty than a calling. And now she had got him here, into the safe harbor of the Whispering Pines Estate at the end of their long adventure. All this for love apparently. I have to say I was quite jealous.

The rest of the band members also had some musical experience, so their concert would be loud and bust a few hearing aids but otherwise might be passably entertaining.

Linda asked me if I wanted to go with her. "And, no, this won't constitute a date," she quickly added.

"OK," I said, "seems fair." I actually looked forward to it as something completely different.

Linda's story on the aging rockers in The Pine Nut turned out to cause as big a stir as the report about the youthful managers. Amazingly, the little sidebar inviting readers to come up with a name for the band drew an amazing number of responses. In my long career in newspapers, I was always amazed at what caught the public fancy and once again I was not prepared for the reaction. Only institutional boredom could explain the fact that a sizable segment of the Estate's residents weighed in.

The proposed names for Billy's band pretty much covered the landscape of geriatric concerns and conditions. Linda now had the job of collating the various responses to her own story.

I'll never forget her reading out the suggested names at our weekly editorial conference. Her dignified librarian air of formality made for a risible recitation. She could hardly keep a straight face herself.

"OK," she said, "here is what The Pine Nut readers have come up with, at least so far. Everything related to the prostate, forgetfulness, bowel movements, flatulence, general physical ruin, and failing libido is here. Don't blame me – I didn't come up with this stuff – and forgive me if I blush."

She cleared her throat slightly and began to read aloud as solemnly as she could: "Billy's Boys, Franks and the Frankfarters, Big Billy and the Small Willies, Twice a Night, Midnight Wanderers, Where Are We? Up and Down and Up Again, Tell the Kids to Come Get Us, On the Throne Troubadours, Wind in the Pillows, In Our Dreams, Pill Rattlers, Walker on By, Last Call, Rock-Roll-and-Nap, The Hot-Water Bottles, Billy the Geezer and the Rock Gang, The Geriatrics, the Rolling Bones, Silly Billies, Prostate Patrol, Wild Bill Hiccup, The Bandy-Legged Boys, and Sunset Serenaders.

She came up for air, then continued. "Three Times a Night, Stood on a Frog, One Tooth for the Steak, The Medicine Men, Rheumatoid Rendezvous, The Prime Ribs, Give Me a Big Pour, Senior Songsters, Too Old to Care, Five Times a Night" – here Linda stopped to say, "I think someone is boasting now."

She took another breath and pressed bravely on: "Blue Pill Bluesmen, We're With Babe, Forgot the Music, Forgot the Lyrics, Guitar Gasbags, Nothing in the Pants, All Our Yesterdays, the Wrinklies, Mummy and the Papas, the Golden Oldies, Last Resort, Deaf to Complaints, Nothing for the Kids, The Knee Replacements, Artificially Hip, Old Duck Whisperers, The Flaccid Five, Not Dead Yet, Pining for Love, Estate Eagles and Alcohol by Mouth."

"Wow," Martha Evans said seriously when Linda had finished reading and blushing. "That's a lot to choose from."

A ludicrous debate proceeded among us to weigh the relative merits of the suggestions. When it was done, all the women in the group voted for "We're with Babe" and the guys were split between "Nothing in the Pants" and "Midnight Wanderers."

"Well, no consensus there," I said, "but at least we didn't pick Franks and the Frankfarters. Anyway, it's ultimately up to Billy because it's his band."

Billy's choice ended up being – and go figure – The Hot-Water Bottles. The name would not be revealed until the night of the concert.

When we printed all the name suggestions in the next edition, the bland and risqué together, the concert generated interest in an unlikely quarter – our small local daily picked up the story.

How an outside reporter came to read The Pine Nut I don't know but the story was a natural. The headline in the local paper said it all: "Old Rockers Never Die – They Give Concerts at Rest Homes." This in turn caught the eye of the local bureau of the Associated Press, which sent it out around the country. Soon TV stations were calling to ask if they could come to cover the concert, now eight days away.

Billy Franks had suddenly become more famous than at any time during his career. Babe was handling his calls.

26 - THE ICE MAN COMETH

Hit the road, Jack
– Ray Charles, 1961

As we sat in our editorial conference in the week before the concert, we noticed lights on in the manager's office across the way. Figures were moving about inside and members of the Estate's maintenance staff were outside maneuvering trolleys to move furniture. The new manager and his fiancée were not expected for a week but it appeared they were arriving early.

Then we caught a glimpse of a little man wearing a dark suit of old-fashioned style complete with bow tie and suspenders. Accompanying him was a woman who looked like she might be interviewing for president of the Junior League. Her woolen coat and dress also seemed to be of another age and she wore long gloves and high heels to complete her ensemble. Eskimos arriving clad in seal skins would be less incongruous in our little community where nobody appeared in the daytime wearing formal suits, not even a visiting undertaker come to sign up prospective clients.

Phillip D. Jones III, the new manager, and Marianne Crocker, his assistant manager and apprentice life companion, had arrived – not that we got to meet them immediately. They only stayed long enough that first Monday morning to give directions to the workers. First, the old furniture was moved out, then the painters arrived with their brushes and drapes, and after they were done a day or two later, new furniture was moved in.

The somberly dressed Mr. Jones and Ms. Crocker were not seen again until Friday of that week. Even then, they did not exactly get out among the residents and introduce themselves. I went over to their office next door to welcome them but I was told by a flustered Ms. Crocker that they were far too busy to see anyone today and that I should come back Monday. The Pine Nut goes to press on Fridays so there was no chance to get a statement from them on their arrival.

But they had been busy and they had made their own statement of sorts. When I went over to the dining hall that evening, I was told by everybody I met that Pedro Rodriguez, the catering manager who had done an excellent job filling in as Estate manager in the interim, had been fired late in the afternoon.

I immediately went back into the kitchen, normally out of bounds to residents, and found Pedro sitting disconsolately at a table wondering whether he should leave immediately or else get up and help with the evening meal this one last time.

"Pedro," I said. "What the heck happened?"

He looked up sadly and said, "I don't know, Mr. Brown. I was just doing my job like always when Ms. Crocker calls the dining room phone and says, 'The new manager, Mr. Jones, must see you immediately.' "

" 'OK,' I say, 'Is there a problem?' "

" 'Just come now and be quick,' she says and hangs up. So I am anxious and so I go over to the office and I find Mr. Jones, the new manager, but he does not introduce or shake my hand or even smile, he just says: 'You are Rodriguez?' "

" 'Yes, sir,' I say."

" 'This is your last day. Pack your things and leave right away.' "

"I am shocked. I stumble to make a reply. I say, 'Please, sir, did I do anything wrong?' "

"He says, 'Don't make a scene, Rodriguez. There's a new sheriff in town now and you are gone. That's all you need to know.'

"That was it. Our meeting was over. He turns around and starts to look at papers. Ms. Crocker is embarrassed – she does not even look me in the eye.

"Mr. Brown, I have worked here for 15 years without any trouble. I do so well they ask me to be temporary manager as well as run the kitchen. There's no trouble then either. And then the new manager comes and I am terminated immediately. I don't know what I did or what I will do. I forgot to ask about severance pay."

"That's awful, Pedro," I said. "That makes no sense at all. But I know one thing: You never did anything wrong. And I have no doubt that you will find a new job without any problem. I bet there are 200 residents here who would be glad to write you a personal reference to get you started. Thanks for all your good work."

Half an hour later, after finally resisting the false call of duty to complete his shift, Pedro walked out of the hall carrying his folded apron and a few other meager possessions in a cardboard box. He was given a standing ovation by all the diners and people came up to shake his hand and wish him well for all the kindnesses he had done for them. He looked defeated but allowed himself a little smile.

"Not a good start for young Mr. Jones," I said to Gavin, who let out an epithet as if Mr. Jones were just a robot gone rogue.

But they say it's an ill wind that doesn't blow somebody some good. With the sense of grievance shared by all, rock and roll now had its chance to provide some emotional release. Billy Franks and his senior rockers were primed for their Saturday gig in the dining hall and so was their audience. The residents were of a mind to shout and let their hair down, such hair as they had.

What can I say about the concert when Saturday night rolled in like thunder at the dining hall? It was fun. It was loud, which took away from the fun somewhat. Seniors do not do well with loud. But those in the audience with hearings aids – which is to say, most of the audience – turned them off. Gavin also had the good sense to turn down the amplifiers from earthquake shattering to merely throbbing. The band didn't notice because they were deaf too.

Another senior moment was notable. After all the attention The Pine Nut had given to letting residents vote to name the band, Billy never once mentioned it. He forgot. When he introduced his fellow rockers, he just mentioned the old boys and their kid names. They were not told by their leader that they were The Hot-Water Bottles, and perhaps they still don't know to this day.

Distracted as they were by the spectacle of 70-ish men in tight jeans, frilly lace shirts, and platform shoes, the people in the audience who voted for a band name also forgot that they had done so. And The Pine Nut staff, including me, forgot too. The canny Babe probably didn't forget but decided to keep humoring Billy and not make a fuss. She sang on, ever the loyal backup.

The beat went on. The residents, Linda and I among them, danced in the aisles or at least they swayed from side to side in an impression of dancing. We didn't do any moves learned in Ms. Zambona's class, but we impersonated the kids we once were and laughed, especially when Billy played the Chicken Dance, an unusual part of his rocking repertoire. A crowd of oldies pretending to be chickens is a sight to behold. If real chickens had seen it, they would have ceased laying for a month. The local TV station that covered the event couldn't believe their luck. "Tonight, senior band rocks the roost, film at 10!" said the promo.

By Sunday, life had returned to what passed as normal these days, although residents continued to wonder what new surprises the Jones administration would bring to the management of the Estate. They did not have long to wait. But on Monday morning, Mr. Jones and Ms. Crocker did not do the customary bright-and-early arrival for people having their first day on the job. They arrived dim and late in their formal suits – no earlier than 11 am. Again, they made no effort to get out and meet people.

Visitors came to them, and when they came they encountered one new change immediately. As well as the cosmetic changes to the office, Mr. Jones had hired himself an administrative assistant, a Mrs. Fothergill, who was just as stiff and starched as her younger employers.

Mrs. Fothergill was both sentry and keeper of the dragon's lair. With a supercilious air, she performed all functions deemed to be beneath Mr. Jones' dignity, which turned out to be pretty much everything, from brewing coffee to handling the paperwork. In Mr. Higgins' time, Marge handled all these duties but now Ms. Crocker would be assisting in some other way, perhaps by inspiring her fiancé to Great Thoughts in his inner sanctum.

Mrs. Fothergill sat in the front part of the office by the door with Ms. Crocker across the way from her. To see Mr. Jones in the inside office, visitors needed to have an appointment made by Mrs. Fothergill. In practice, this meant you needed to visit the office twice to see Mr. Jones once. Mrs. Fothergill made it clear that she did not accept appointments made over the phone. You had to state your case for seeing the Estate's manager in person, who, she always reminded people, was a very busy man, and she would then decide if you were worthy of an audience.

Emails could not be sent directly to Mr. Jones, only to Mrs. Fothergill. She did allow grumpily that she could not stop you sending emails to Ms. Crocker but made it clear that she was not in favor of this. In fact, Mrs. Fothergill's general attitude was that it was a shame emails were ever invented.

As for the appointments, they could only be made between 1 pm and 3 pm on weekdays (Mr. Jones and Ms. Crocker did not work weekends). As best as we came to understand his schedule, the very busy man arrived at 11 am, drank his coffee, made calls and read his paperwork, then went to lunch off campus precisely at noon. He then returned at 1 pm, maybe. A person with a 1 pm appointment often had to wait at least half an hour. He went home precisely at 4 pm However, Ms. Crocker was more hard-working. Sometimes she left as late as 5 pm but otherwise observed the same timetable as he did.

As Bill Gibson accurately observed later, "These two work fewer hours than most of the retired people we have here."

It was Wednesday before I finally got to meet our new manager. I was preceded by Jimmy Devine, the chairman of the residents' board of directors, who had the 1 pm appointment but finally got in at 1:45. I was booked for 2:30 but wasn't seen until 3 pm. I brought Betty in with me, because she would be the one who would do the story of the new manager arriving at last. We hoped he would tell us what his plans for the future were.

We had been lucky to get an appointment at all. Mrs. Fothergill let it be known that she "didn't approve of members of the press" – which was flattering in a way, even if she was clearly under the false impression that we represented the local town paper and not the internal newsletter of the Estate. But I made a veiled threat that it might not look good for Mr. Jones not to receive us and so she did book us, although with considerable ill grace.

And now we were kept waiting, which she must have enjoyed. When Jimmy came out, he stopped briefly where I was sitting in what passed as the waiting area. Both Mrs. Fothergill and Ms. Crocker went in to the other office for a moment at Mr. Jones' summons, so we had time for a quick word.

"How was he, Jimmy? " I inquired.

"What a sour little twit," he said. "My charms did not work on that nut case." Coming from Jimmy, whose gregarious charms worked on just about everybody, it was not a good report.

27 - THE YOUNG AND THE FECKLESS

*It was a one-eyed, one-horned,
flyin' purple people eater.
– Sheb Wooley, 1958*

At first glance, it seemed Phillip D. Jones III was dressed in the same somber clothing that he wore when we first caught sight of him the previous week. But now, standing before us in his office, he was attired more formally still, appearing more like a Victorian banker going about his business. He wore not only a dark suit, but also a waistcoat with golden fob watch chain, a white shirt, red bow-tie, red socks and black highly polished shoes. He may have been wearing suspenders too but the waistcoat made confirmation difficult.

He was reading a note he held in his right hand when and Betty and I were ushered into the room. Without looking up, he yelled to his retreating administrative assistant, "Mrs. Fothergill, can you get me Simpson on the phone?"

Then he looked up to reveal a young face serving as a mask to an old man's severe manner. Not quite looking me in the eye, he said: "Mr. Alistair, is it? You are the editor of that rag, The Fine Mutt." He did not acknowledge Betty at all.

"The Pine Nut," I corrected him, suppressing a smile. "And I am Mr. Brown, Alistair Brown, and I am editor of the newsletter, which we don't think is a rag." I now put out my hand to greet him, which he reluctantly took as if he were being offered a fish to squeeze. "This is Betty Bosworth, a reporter for the newsletter." He took her proffered hand with even less enthusiasm.

"Let me tell you this," he said, when he was done with the

inconvenience of shaking hands, "That story you had in your little rag was highly offensive to me and my assistant manager, Miss Crocker."

"Oh," I said. Betty and I glanced at each other for half a second.

Before he could explain, Mrs. Fothergill buzzed him to say that Simpson was on line one. He picked the phone up and immediately launched into a long and boring conversation – more a monologue really – with the mysterious but certainly hapless Simpson. We moved to get up and give him his privacy but he gestured with his hand to stay where we were.

And so we sat and we sat and we sat – for 15 to 20 minutes – as he carried on this inconsequential phone call. And as we sat, I went over in my mind what possible offense our story could have given to the junior power couple now in residence.

Was it the reference to the online college from which they got their senior management credential? Was it the explanation of Mr. Jones' former job, where he had nothing to do with retirement homes and really not much responsibility for anything else? Was it mention of her scant work record? Were they sensitive about their ages?"

Finally, Simpson made his excuses to get off the line, perhaps because he had developed a bad migraine or a case of cauliflower ears from the assault of nonsense on the phone at his head. Without pausing, Mr. Jones immediately buzzed Mrs. Fothergill to make coffee.

"Where was I?" he said.

"You were telling me why you and your fiancée were horrified."

"That's it," he said at once, angrily.

"That's what?" I said.

"You called her my fiancée. How dare you?"

"I am sorry," I said, completely baffled, "but you had an engagement notice in The New York Times. You announced it on Facebook. Has all that changed?"

"No," he said. "But you should not have put that in your little newspaper without my permission."

Mrs. Fothergill now brought him in his espresso and a cookie. Nothing was offered to us. As he slurped his coffee and dropped cookie crumbs down his front, I pointed out the obvious. "With respect, Mr. Jones, we shouldn't need anybody's permission to publish facts already in the public domain. By definition, an engagement notice is a public declaration that someone is to be wed."

Even as I said this, I realized that the conversation had gone through some strange portal and come out on the other side in a topsy-turvy world. I was being logical in a place where reason was suddenly unknown. Thank goodness for Betty. She rescued me by taking an entirely different tack.

"But, oh Mr. Jones, our residents loved to read that you and this delightful young lady of yours are engaged. What a wonderful love story. That detail in the story won you more goodwill than you can imagine."

"You think so?" suddenly perking up into some mood resembling agreeable.

"I do, Mr. Jones. But what I can't understand is why you would want to keep your engagement a secret?" Betty said this in a most sympathetic way, as if she were a confused aunt striving for clarity from her nephew.

"Well, it would be OK with me but Marianne, my fiancée, is very worried that the people here will, you know, think we are living in sin by coming out here together."

Even Betty had a problem trying to digest this astounding thought.

Before she could remind him that this was the year 2018, and living in sin was a concept that had largely gone the way of whalebone corsets, Mr. Jones seemed to sense the silliness lurking in his statement. "Marianne says seniors stand for traditional values," he added. "They are not like young people. They are grandmas and grandpas, and the rest of us must stand up for what they hold sacred. So, out of respect, she does not want to cause a scandal as First Lady of Whispering Pines."

"Mr. Jones, what a wonderful thought," Betty said, recovering quickly. "But you can tell Ms. Crocker that my generation still loves a love story with a happy ending – and to be engaged like you two are is the guarantee of that happy ending. Nobody is going to think badly of her for coming out here with you. Why, it is just lovely. We are too old to be sitting around harboring nasty thoughts concerning upstanding young people with the best intentions."

She laid this on so thick it was almost humorous and I now feared she had gone too far. But Mr. Jones sat there and beamed, an attitude I would have thought against the order of nature in his case. Thus, the matter of mentioning the engagement in public was now officially cleansed of all bad, if imaginary, associations.

I picked up where Betty had left off. "Mr. Jones, if you don't have any more complaints about The Pine Nut, we would like to interview you on the record about your first impressions here and what plans you have for the future."

"Very well, let me tell you this. I think the Whispering Pines Estate needs to return to good business practices. We need to cut costs. The Estate is a business and when the business is losing money, the residents are losing money."

"The Estate is losing money?" I was surprised to hear this as residents paid large sums to live here and fairly hefty annual home owners' fees. Never before had anyone suggested that the facility was losing money.

"I mean that money is being lost through the waste and misman-agement of previous executives. Do you know how many pickleball balls we have to replace every month? Maybe two dozen! Residents just lose them and expect management to buy new ones. I have decided that henceforth residents cannot be reimbursed for more than two pickleballs every three months."

"That would seem a little expense in the overall scheme of things," I offered.

"That's just the attitude I am here to change," he said, becoming more heated again. "Every penny counts. My father has the expression that if you watch the pennies, you will save the dollars. My father is a great businessman. He knows what he is talking about."

"No doubt," I said. "But I wanted to return to something you previously said. You said that 'when the business is losing money, then the residents are losing money.' How does that work? If you are going to make economies in things like pickle-balls, then how does that save money for the residents? They will be paying for more pickleballs."

"They can just save the ones they already have. Problem solved. But the bigger point is that every economy I make will help us keep down increases in the monthly owners' fees."

"You are going to raise the monthly owners' fees? They haven't been raised in five years."

"Everything is fair game," he said.

"How much are you thinking of raising them?"

"Nothing has been decided. I will decide that when I decide it."

Betty sensed that the questioning was irritating him so she tried another ploy.

"How would you describe your administration? What are its hallmarks going forward?

He was happy to answer this. "We will be business positive and pro-active. I will put an end to all policies that hamper our effectiveness and do not make good business sense. I will have an open door policy and practice transparency."

"So anybody can walk in the door and see you?" I asked.

"All they have to do is walk in and see Mrs. Fothergill to make an appointment."

"Will you see everybody?"

"Mrs. Fothergill will decide if they need to be seen."

His understanding of an open door was obviously too silly for further questioning – obvious to me and the rest of humanity at least but probably not to him.

"Why did you fire Mr. Rodriguez?"

"He was not fired. He was let go. But that is a personnel matter I cannot discuss," he said. "I can only say that he was the temporary manager and no business can have two chiefs."

"But he didn't want to be manager for even five minutes. He took on that role as a favor to the Board of Trustees. What he wanted to be was the catering manager."

"I don't know about that," he said. And then he said his foolish aphorism again as if saying it twice would make it true: "No business can have two chiefs."

"Will you be filling the position of catering manager?"

"I don't know if it is necessary. I am here to save some money. I can't afford any luxuries."

I thought how this would read in The Pine Nut; probably as a heartless parody of good sense. So in an attempt for some semblance of balance, I now asked the greater question: "Mr.

Jones, you have not spoken much about the residents, other than people who will bear the brunt of small economies like fewer pickleballs that will somehow benefit them in the long run. What about your commitment to the residents?"

He was peeved at this question. "My fiancée and I love old people. We wouldn't have come here if we didn't want to help them lead better lives. And they will, make no mistake" In his resentment, I noted, he had again used the "f word" – fiancée.

"But why do you go on about pickleballs? Lots of changes have to be made around here. The entertainment program needs serious attention. I read in your rag that some goof was putting on a rock and roll concert in the dining hall Saturday night. We were made out to be a laughingstock on local television. That sort of thing won't be tolerated in the future."

"That goof was a resident and many other residents came and enjoyed the concert."

He ignored this. "And do you know what Marianne found out? That some foreign woman has been putting on dance lessons – including the tango. Can you imagine that? Old people doing the tango with its lewd and suggestive steps under the guise of dancing. Disgusting! I have canceled this. I am so glad that Marianne alerted me." He tilted his head back and said, "Well, that's enough for one day. The interview is over. Don't screw up what I said."

Well, I thought, how could we improve on the original?

On the way out, I whispered to Betty, "Let's try and get a cell phone photo of him." Normally, Diane Gibson would take the shot but he looked like he might be hard to pin down in the future.

In the event, Betty, with her superior social skills, persuaded both Mr. Jones and Ms. Crocker to pose for her together and he even deigned to smile, although it looked like his face was rebelling from the effort. And she also did something else brilliant. She said to Ms. Crocker, "We have been hearing about some of your interesting views. Could you sit down and have an interview with me?"

"Oh no," she said, "I couldn't possibly" – and she was all demure and self-effacing and glad to be asked as she said this.

"I understand," Betty said, "that could be a little awkward for you. How about I arrange a little tea party with the ladies so you can feel relaxed in a social setting? I will just sit in the back and take notes."

"That sounds wonderful," she said. "I love old ladies." And so it was arranged for next month.

Once we were outside, I said to Betty. "Very well handled."

"First Lady of Whispering Pines? Can you believe that?" she said.

28 - THE CANDIDATES

Every way you look at this, you lose
– Simon & Garfunkel, 1968

Jimmy Devine, chairman of the residents committee, was up for re-election in October but to the surprise of everyone he announced that he was standing down after four years in the job. Friendly and capable, Jimmy was expected to be unopposed and the election for the chairman and half the resident committee board members was widely considered to be a formality. Jimmy now told the board that he felt new leadership was needed for what he called the "challenging times ahead."

This was as close as he ever got to saying that the arrival of Phillip D. Jones III as manager of the Estate spelled trouble for everyone. According to a popular saying, when the going gets tough, the tough get going. As it happened, Jimmy did not lack the tougher sinews of character. If he had been a real public official in a real leadership position, he might have got going to meet the challenge. But when the going gets tough for a retired tough person, there is no dishonor in asking whether the trouble is worth it and then deciding to take a figurative nap.

None of the residents blamed Jimmy for leaving the gavel for someone else to bang furiously, even as they came to realize that trouble was indeed brewing. I am proud to say that The Pine Nut, simply by stating the facts in an impartial manner, had sounded the alarm.

The initial reporting had raised the question of whether Mr. Jones was a boy sent on a man's errand. Then came the story of his peculiar views brought to light in the interview conducted by

Betty and me. The idea that he thought of the Estate first and foremost as a business and was threatening to raise the homeowner dues went over with the residents like a concrete balloon.

The cancellation of Ms. Zambona's dancing class, to save the residents from the moral danger of the tango, and the new policy for conserving pickle tennis balls, were further irritants, as was his intention not to allow Billy Franks and his band to give any more concerts in the dining hall.

After meeting with the manager, I told Linda that we were not going to be dancing the tango together after all. "Something I said or did I just scare you off?" she responded.

"Neither. It was something our new manager said." Part of me was glad that she and I weren't going to attempt the tango, which sounded like an opportunity for major embarrassment, but no way was I going to admit this to her.

Of course, the tango ban and the rest of the manager's trivial dictates paled in comparison to the prospect of higher homeowner dues, which threatened everybody. Nevertheless, all the ingredients added to the bitter stew of bubbling unrest. As Bill Gibson said, "I get the impression that young Mr. Jones thinks he is the boss and the residents are his employees."

Our new leader apparently didn't understand that if you hit a hornets' nest with a stick, you were likely to meet buzzing, angry hornets. If only he had seen the Great Dining Room Dress Code Controversy, he might have known that it didn't take much to get the residents of the Estate riled up. Now they were fast headed for full riled up mode. Even those who didn't read The Pine Nut could see the writing on the wall – or rather the writing on the dining hall menu.

As I have mentioned, the food served to residents at the Estate was generally excellent, with lots of choices offered. But in the absence of a catering manager after the departure of Pedro

Rodriguez, quality began to suffer and attention to detail began to fray. One evening the residents came in to find six desserts to choose from and the next night they discovered none at all. Some residents whose sweet tooth had been outraged thought to take advantage of the manager's open door policy to make their complaints. Instead, they found that Mrs. Fothergill, the keeper of the door, did not think desserts qualified for Mr. Jones' attention. As dampers on resentment go, this reverse variation of "let them eat cake" worked about as well for her as it did for Marie Antoinette.

So here we were in September, a month away from a residents committee board election that had appeared a forgone conclusion, and suddenly we contemplated an election that was certain to be a vehicle for carrying forward all the people's grievances and fears – in other words, like many elections in the real world.

Of course, the residents committee had no real power. As Martha Evans had remarked in one of her wittier moments, the difference between the residents committee and a bunch of old guys shooting the breeze over coffee was the board members were officially elected and drank only water at their meetings. Still, as a sounding board for the community, the residents committee might be able to bring some influence to bear on the young master – i.e., Mr. Jones.

The duty of the board on hearing that Jimmy Devine was stepping down as chairman was to recruit possible replacements, as it had been doing for the other vacancies on the board. The system at the Estate was somewhat unusual and mimicked towns where the mayor and council members were voted upon separately.

However, residents at the Estate did not usually put their own names forward as possible candidates. They had to be invited by members of the board and then voted upon at the annual membership meeting. As the board had no power and not much prestige as a result, finding likely candidates was usually hard. Not this time.

In one of his last acts as chairman, Jimmy opened up the process to make it more democratic. He moved that residents could suggest themselves for the positions on the board, including chairman, and he would nominate them himself no matter how absurd their candidacies. As he told me, "Anybody stupid enough to want one of these thankless jobs should be able to nominate themselves." The board agreed and The Pine Nut ran a little story informing residents that if they made their candidacies known, they would be on the ballot.

However, some board members still recruited their own candidates. Of the six openings on the board, four positions were currently filled by incumbents who expressed a willingness to serve another term.

Linda was approached by Jimmy Devine himself, who was among many residents who were impressed with how she had handled the meeting on the dress code. He wanted her to be on the board.

In fact, Jimmy proposed that she be the new chairman, although she had never served as a regular board member. Although flattered, she declined the offer and I was secretly happy. She would be great in any capacity but Martha Evans was already on the board and I wanted Linda to stay on the newsletter without the burden of further possible conflicts of interest. Besides, I had grown accustomed to having her around.

Between the board members themselves and the residents who came forward independently, every vacancy had residents who wanted to fill it. One of the incumbents up for re-election, Peter Hamilton, now decided that he would prefer seeking the chairmanship. An engineer in his past career, he was a solid character but decidedly low-key. His only hope of besting the new manager in any future dispute was possibly boring him into submission. Sam Hudson, purple prose sports writer on The Pine Nut and conservative partisan in other arenas, also put his hat in the ring, being of the belief that no board experience was necessary.

The third candidate for chairman, Robert Norman, was in some ways the most interesting. He was a retired history professor who had served one term on the board four years ago but had stepped down because of illness. Now recovered, he brought a reputation for good manners and good sense and generally looked the part of a distinguished senior academic. With his silver hair and penetrating gaze, he projected a gravity and wisdom that even the likes of young Mr. Jones would find formidable.

Professor Norman was remarkable in another way too. In our little community, he was one of the few African Americans living at the Estate. Apart from a few residents of Asian descent, the Estate was seriously lacking in diversity. But as an individual with a familiar face, he was accepted by almost everybody. No doubt he sometimes suffered thoughtless slights but he kept his dignified and friendly demeanor. I think he was too wise to have anything but pity for the ignorant.

We now all found ourselves in a committee election that nobody could remember the likes of, not even those residents at the Estate who were as old as Galapagos tortoises.

For the six positions open for members of the board, the nominees included some residents every bit as unlikely as those who were standing for chairman. Three incumbents stayed in the running – all of them women, as it happened.

Among the other nominees were Billy Franks, who had taken the manager's insult to rock and roll personally, Minnie Miller, the Estate's professional complainer, and Brian Cooper, my old tennis buddy who could never remember the score but off the tennis courts still successfully practiced part-time as an attorney in the law courts.

The fourth new nominee was another old friend, Gavin Halsey, who played a small role as a writer for The Pine Nut but was still mostly involved in handling uncooperative audio- visual equipment.

Surprisingly, Microphone Mike was not a candidate. His questions were always sappily sentimental and perhaps he figured that the nuts-and-bolts subject matter of committee life would not suit his talents.

With six positions open on the board and seven nominees, the pain of losing would be felt by only one candidate. This was just as well. Those of us who remember the sting of rejection from a prospective prom date at age 17 wouldn't wish the same humiliation to return for many others seeking a different sort of song and dance at age 77.

Because of the sudden interest in the election, the committee took the unprecedented step of booking the dining hall for two candidate forums on consecutive nights two weeks before the election. My fear was that Mrs. Fothergill might object but in fact the duty of hall booking was part of the duties of Ms. Crocker. She had little interest on what might be going on. As long as it wasn't a rock concert or a tango gala, she was fine with it.

The first and liveliest meeting, given the cast of eccentric characters running, was for the six board member vacancies. At the invitation of Jimmy Devine again, Linda MacDonald chaired the event. The format consisted of each of the seven candidates giving a three-minute presentation on why they were running. Then Linda asked them each questions suggested in advance by members of the audience, which saved everybody from Microphone Mike holding forth at great length. At the end, the candidates made closing remarks of no more than a minute.

The event was over by 9 pm, which was quite late by Estate

standards. Most of the crowd stayed to the end, despite the yawners and snoozers finally setting the tone.

The meeting had some memorable moments: When it came his turn, Billy Franks said, "I love rock and roll, man, and I just think we got to tell the Man that rock and roll is never going to die at the Estate."

Somebody asked from the back of the hall: "When you say Man, do you mean Mr. Jones, the new manager?"

Billy was confused by the question: "If Jones is the Man, man, then he is the Man."

His wife, Babe, then turned around to the questioner and said good-naturedly, "The point is that Billy just wants to help everyone get along and have a good time." This sparked applause among the confused listeners and Linda had to call the meeting to order.

Gavin spoke and took the new manager strongly to task, as did almost all the speakers, including the incumbents. They were not going to stand idly by as their rights and prerogatives were trampled upon. They would fight to the last pickleball.

In the general spirit of over-reaction, they spoke as if they were council members or state legislators. They spoke as if they could pass laws. They spoke as if the residents committee was really the seat of power, not a seat of ineffectual grievance airing.

The meeting was both ridiculous and heart-warming. If Mr. Jones had any social sense, which of course he didn't, his ears would have been ringing. It fell to Brian Cooper to take the discussion back to sanity.

The old lawyer stressed that the board would have to make representations to the manager and try to negotiate with him. "We can't be promising to do more than that. If all else fails, we may have to consider legal action."

One speaker took exception to the manager-bashing. Minnie Miller, ever the carping contrarian, could probably take no other stand but to support Mr. Jones and all he stood for. My guess is that if everybody had approved of the new management, she would have been against it. As it was, her defenses of the new policies brought mild boos. Linda again had to insist on fair play for all speakers, no matter how annoying. She did not say this directly, of course, but to me it seemed implied.

The chairman's forum the next night was shorter for having fewer participants but it wasn't as entertaining. Peter Hamilton, the incumbent board member seeking a promotion, made his low-energy case for strong action and set off some premature yawning in the process. Robert Norman was as sensible as ever and kept his promises in the realm of the reasonable. In my opinion, he was the most impressive speaker of the night.

For his part, Sam Hudson made all sorts of wild promises. He accused his opponents of appeasement, even before they had done anything. Knowing little of the job and thus unencumbered by facts, he spoke with certainty. His turns of phrase echoed his sports writing, full of hyperbole and fractured metaphors.

He was a puzzle, though. A person might think that his anti-government political leanings would make him a natural ally of the new manager and his pro-business model of operation of the Estate. But it was clear that to Sam, the Estate's management was the government in our small world. And when Mr. Jones threatened to raise home owners' dues, he was as good as promising to raise our taxes. And Sam, the champion of the people, was against it.

The thought passed through my mind that if Sam somehow won, it would be my fault. I had made him the sports writing celebrity of Whispering Pines Estate. But he wouldn't win. His pitch was a small and absurd echo of what we had seen in Washington, D.C., and just look at the division and absurdity that had resulted there from misplaced populism. Our voters were a council of tribal elders, cloaked in wisdom; they would know better than to discount experience.

Those two nights were good for community democracy and good for The Pine Nut, which faithfully recorded the events. And Linda again demonstrated her ability in a public setting. In the days ahead, the candidates took to writing commentary pieces, which Linda handled with the same impartiality.

Mr. Jones was still in his office but the people were speaking out and even Mrs. Fothergill could not bar the door to their voices. And Ms. Crocker had yet to take tea with the ladies, which carried with it the potential for further rattling the crockery.

29 - THE MAD HATTER'S TEA PARTY

Go ask Alice when she's 10 feet tall
– Grace Slick/Jefferson Airplane, 1967

A tea party with the ladies was duly held as Marianne Crocker's introduction to polite society at the Estate. Of course, gentlemen were not invited, even if I qualified as one, so my account of this event comes from Linda and Betty, with Betty later writing a report for The Pine Nut and both of them giving a more personal account to me.

Thank goodness that men were deemed unsuitable to attend. In my jaundiced view, a man would have needed to be on his very best behavior not to have burst out laughing. As it was, Linda confessed to a suppressed case of the giggles.

The tea was held at 10:30 am in Betty's cottage. Half a dozen ladies were there to meet the young newcomer, a fair cross-section of the Estate in terms of age and their involvement in the life of the community. All of them dressed up smartly for the occasion but they weren't prepared for the arrival of the assistant manager regaled as if she really were the First Lady.

She wore a little hat with a veil, which no doubt protected her from the bees in the garden as she tip-toed down the path on her high heels, and her sky blue outfit was from some other age, with the hem of her skirt flouncing somewhere between knees and ankles. As the piece de resistance, she wore long white gloves that extended almost to her armpits. Many of the ladies were quite elderly but none of them was ancient enough to recall a time when this outfit was fashionable.

To say she was dressed to the nines would not do her justice according to all who attended. Marianne was dressed to the tens, elevens or even twelves. She was seated by design in the grandest chair in the horseshoe arrangement of chairs, some of which Betty had borrowed from friends for the occasion. Amid nervous giggles, unnatural politeness, and forced small talk, Marianne was offered refreshment. She would like some tea, please, one lump of sugar, with milk. Betty, a social being, was an accomplished hostess and the tea came out on fine china. She brought cookies too, placed on elegant little plates.

It was all very jolly, except that it wasn't, with everybody at first trying to be on their best behavior. At the appropriate time, Betty formally welcomed Marianne, thanked her for coming and reminded her that she would be taking notes and using a little tape recorder to help her in this, as she wanted to be absolutely sure she was quoting her correctly. She hoped this would be all right. Marianne nodded – her mouth being full of cookie at that moment – and the conversation started in earnest.

As my knowledge of polite society at the Estate or elsewhere was never extensive, being a long-time ink-stained wretch, I did not know some of the ladies in attendance. I was told they included a Miss Curtis, who had apparently misplaced her first name permanently years ago; an Emily Parsons; a Ginger Hawkins, so named for her hair, which once may have been red naturally but now was red unnaturally; and a Gertrude Connor, who might have been better served if she had lost her first name in transit.

As well as this formidable crew, Betty was of course the hostess and discreet reporter, and Linda was a guest, but her presence owed more to her friendship with Betty and her librarian status than her work with The Pine Nut. Linda was there to convey respectability according to the traditional librarian reputation.

As an icebreaker, Betty asked about Marianne's interest in basket weaving, which in the original announcement of the management changes was singled out as a pastime she hoped to introduce in a class at the Estate. "I see you have a fondness for basket weaving, Marianne. That is unusual for a young lady. Where did you get this interest and what is it about basket weaving that you think would be entertaining and helpful to the residents here at the Estate?"

"Well," Marianne said, "I remember my grandmother on my father's side, Nana Beatrice, who was in a retirement home much like this one back in Ohio. After her husband, my grandfather, died, she became very sad, so sad that she wouldn't even watch television anymore. Then my mother said, 'Nana Beatrice, what you need is a hobby. How about basket weaving?'

"So my mother set her up with the basket-making materials, found a corner of the recreation room, and Nana Beatrice got to work. One of the nurses' aides knew how to weave baskets and she showed Nana Beatrice how. A few other ladies joined in, not many because some still liked to watch television.

"It was so cute. There she would be weaving baskets from morning until night. When we came to visit, we would say, 'Nana Beatrice, what a beautiful basket.' She didn't smile exactly, but you can see she was pleased inwardly. The only problem was that after a while we had dozens of baskets and we didn't know what to do with them. So we kept some to sell at the Christmas bazaar and put the rest in the recycling bin."

Betty, still trying to be helpful, asked: "And did Nana Beatrice's spirits improve? Did she regain her zest for life?"

"Well...." Marianne paused here, not knowing how exactly to reply. "She was never the most zestful person in the world but the basket weaving gave her something to do and she was keeping busy, which is the main thing."

As the guests considered how to react in a polite and encouraging way, Ginger Hawkins piped up: "I tried basket weaving once. It was as boring as all crap."

As Marianne formed a horrified look, Betty said: "I think the point Ginger is making is that something like basket weaving is not going to appeal to all tastes. The activities here at the Estate have traditionally been meant to stimulate the mind and senses."

"Yeah," said Ginger, "we don't do things just to keep busy so our minds can be anesthetized by mindless repetition as a substitute for TV."

Marianne was visibly trying to square her conception of a traditional morning tea party with the blunt and coarse language of this woman with the dreadful red hair. It was perhaps her first inkling that the image of kindly old people in rocking chairs did not account for another part of the picture: that some were old and cranky, and cranky precisely because they were old, a state of being not always conducive to contentment.

Ginger was one of that dyspeptic clan; she had evidently reached the to-heck-with-everything stage of life where false pretensions of courtesy had been outgrown. Feisty old ladies are figuratively the sisters of curmudgeons.

Miss Curtis, with old-fashioned manners and deportment suggestive of her name, now entered the discussion with soothing words for the unnerved Marianne. "My dear Miss Crocker," she said. "Perhaps it would be helpful if we told you about some of the many clubs and activities we have here at the Estate."

Looking like the private girls school principal she once was, she proceeded to give a list as if she were reading an announcement at a school assembly. "Let me see, we have the gardening club; the knitting society; the speakers group – they arrange interesting people to give lectures; the welcoming group – they give tours to prospective residents; the yoga club; the tennis players and golfers; the Bible study fellowship; the amateur artists and photographers; the bridge players, we can't forget the bridge players; the wine tasting society; the dog and cat lovers groups;

book of the month club; the hikers; and the happy dreamers club."

"Which is your favorite, Miss Curtis?" Marianne asked.

"My partner and I like the gardening club very much but we have become quite fond of the happy dreamers."

"Wait! I mean, excuse me," said Marianne, "you have a partner? Who is this gentleman?"

"Actually, it is not a gentleman but a lady. We have been partners for 45 years. We did not marry after it became legal – we both think that would have been a little bit silly at our age – but we do share our cottage together."

"Is it common to have partners here?" Marianne managed to ask as curiosity battled bewilderment in her mind.

"Not uncommon, my dear," Miss Curtis said calmly. "More seniors than you might suppose live together in loving relationships at the Estate – either they came here together or else their original partner passed away and they had a sunset romance with someone else. Of course, most couples are men and women but I never cared for men – such dirty, hairy beasts – although I am sure your fiancé is different, my dear."

(When Linda was telling me this later, she added: "In Mr. Jones' case, I am not so sure.")

On hearing these revelations, Marianne sat in her throne-like chair in what I think is technically called stunned silence. In the interim, Miss Curtis took the opportunity to return to the original question.

"Miss Crocker, I did not explain what the happy dreamers group does. We are a bit like the wine fanciers but we do cannabis tastings. The happy dreamers formed when only medical marijuana was permitted. Most of us had various ailments but our primary condition was that we were old. Since recreational marijuana became legal, we have dropped all excuses. We just like to get high. Of course, somebody brings munchies."

In Marianne's continuing silence, she added, "The name happy dreamers is a bit of poetic license; it is not like we are smoking opium. In fact, we don't smoke anything, it's all edibles with us, just the cannabis and the potato chips. You are most welcome to attend."

She then asked Marianne whether Mr. Jones might allow the gardening club to grow some marijuana in some of the glass houses on the Estate property. As she put it, "Some of the people who go to cannabis dispensaries and stores are not the sort of people we would normally associate with. It would make us much more comfortable if we could just grow our own supplies in accordance with the limits prescribed by the law."

At this suggestion, Marianne let out a muffled sound that was not quite a word and not quite a squeak.

The question of the tango ban came up. Marianne revived enough to defend her position if only meekly: "I think that dancing the tango does not qualify as stimulating the mind," she said.

"You are right, Marianne," Emily Parsons said. "That activity is entirely about stimulating the senses."

"Quite right," said Gertrude Connor. Marianne was aghast anew, shuddering to contemplate old people stimulating their senses with dirty dancing.

Ginger noted her surprise and added helpfully, "Yeah, when I first came to the Estate, I never guessed how many people still had a healthy sex drive. I thought it was a place where the un-hard flirted with the unlubricated. Boy, was I wrong."

At this, Marianne's ruin was complete. To be fair to her, most people arriving at the Estate would be shocked to find traditional looking older people behaving untraditionally, say as couples living unmarried with a partner and/or partaking of cannabis. I know this was my reaction when I first arrived.

The easiest explanation would be to put this situation down as a case of vintage liberal California. But the state also has its conservatives and older people who live in expensive retirement homes would seem more naturally inclined to be conservative at heart – as indeed I found many were. Sam Hudson was not that unusual at the Estate, only louder than most.

Perhaps there's another explanation: Some people grow stronger in their convictions later in life, others find their social and moral moorings fraying a little as tides of cynicism or fatigue pull them to different shores. Some just become more open as they no longer have an image of themselves to uphold. However they choose to live and why, the elderly as individuals cannot be easily categorized in a group.

No one knew this better now than Marianne Crocker. At the end of the tea with the ladies, she walked out into the sunlight again with the tentativeness of someone for whom stereotypes had become like fallen roof tiles shattered on the path before her. What would Nana Beatrice have thought of this? Why, she probably would think it was like something out of a TV show she watched when she watched TV.

30 - THE DAY OF WINE AND ROSES

I like the gin / It makes me feel thin
But give me the good old vino
– Rugby song, circa 1971

There are many things to dread about growing old. You can forget, you can be flatulent, you can forget that you are flatulent, you can sleep too much or too little, you can easily break your bones in a fall, you can bruise just by thinking about a fall, you can lose your libido, you can lose your reading glasses (though they are probably on the end of your nose), you can lose your sense of smell, making your nose only good for resting your glasses, you can be hard of hearing, you can see double or dimly or not at all, you can have multiple pains in multiple places, you can be incontinent, you can be constipated and discontented; and you can find yourself playing bingo. In my book, playing bingo is among the greatest of the dreads haunting the elderly.

I say this knowing that bingo gives pleasure to some people. Then again, eating turnips gives pleasure to some people. Each to his own, says one proverb, but there is no accounting for taste, says another. If I ever find myself playing bingo, I will quote the Immortal Bard to myself, assuming I can remember the quotation: "What a piece of work is man! How noble in reason, how infinite in faculty!..." And then I will say, "How not like a paragon of animals is it to sit in a hall" – not that I have anything against halls – "trying to match numbers on a sheet to those announced by a caller, thus imitating a chimpanzee counting bananas at the urging of a fellow ape. Bingo indeed!"

This fear and loathing of bingo has from the beginning made me wary of special activities put on at the Estate for the alleged benefit of its senior residents. I didn't want to be at any event where bingo could break out unexpectedly. My general view is that if young people don't do it, then older people probably shouldn't either. That takes care of basket weaving and bingo.

That said, if young people are doing it, older people don't necessarily need to do it too. Seniors should not be enrolling in skateboard classes, as the elder posterior is not as cushion-like as it once was, generally speaking. Tango lessons probably are a bad idea too, but that possibility is moot now thanks to the new management's embrace of old Puritanism.

However, the Estate also sponsors field trips for interested residents. Sometimes these trips involve a trip to a museum or an art gallery in the city. One day a few months earlier, I had noticed a flyer for a day trip posted on the community notice board. It offered wine tastings at select local vineyards. I doubted any outbreak of bingo would occur at this event as everyone would be too wine-sodden to remember their numbers.

As one who likes a glass of wine, I signed up at once. I really didn't know many people at the Estate back then. I was not yet the editor of The Pine Nut. I just thought that it might be easier to meet people when their wine glasses were up and their social defenses were down, a tried-and-true strategy for curing loneliness.

The cost of the trip was reasonable and covered the bus, a lunch at one of the wineries, and the tastings at the various venues to be visited. But what once seemed a chance to get out and meet people now seemed an inconvenient burden on my time when I really needed to be meeting the people covering the election.

But the outing was on a Saturday and I could afford a day off. I did not have a clue who had signed up but when I went down at 10:45 am to the front gate to catch the bus I did see some familiar faces. Martha was there, which was puzzling as I knew she wasn't much of a drinker. "Martha," I said. "Have you developed a late taste for the vino?"

"Oh no," she said, "I just like bus trips."

More promisingly, Gavin boarded the bus, as did Sam Hudson, whose heartiness and ruddy complexion marked him as one who needed a little more than a bus to make him cheerful. Then Bill Gibson climbed aboard too. Both of them had left their wives behind to play in a lawn bowling tournament.

"Aren't you supposed to be covering that for The Pine Nut?" I asked Sam. "That's too exciting for me, Alistair, I'd get palpitations. I'll get the results from the ladies when their pulse rates have returned to normal."

Just before the bus left, Linda MacDonald came up the stairs too. I knew she liked her wine but she didn't look like she was going to match the boys taste for taste on this trip. She sat down with a bunch of seriously sober-looking ladies, including Martha, at the front of the bus, though she smiled and gave me a cheerful wave when she saw me. I was sort of relieved. I was with the guys and I wouldn't have to be so much on my best behavior.

Gavin sat next to me and we started to chat as the bus made its way to the first of several wineries. What I never before realized about Gavin was how much he liked food and drink. Our conversation turned to the places we had visited in our lives. Most of the places I had visited were planted in memory by some great vista upon land or sea. Gavin's memories were all about the scenery of his dinner plates as viewed over knife and fork.

He did not much recall ancient ruins or the mountains' purple majesty but he did remember the little restaurant just down the road. "Speaking of Athens," he recalled, "I remember the octopus in ouzo and the retsina we drank in a little place at the foot of the Acropolis." That was all Gavin had to say about the Acropolis. The octopus' succulent tentacles had wrapped themselves around all memory of his visit.

Most people have a storehouse of memories. Gavin had a pantry. Not only could he remember exactly what he ate and drank to the last detail, he could remember dates and times. "That lunch in Stockholm was the first time I really got an appreciation for herrings. We didn't get to the restaurant until late, about 2:30 on that first Wednesday of our trip, but it was not a problem at all. We had a few drinks, country club pours they were, too, and everybody seemed very convivial. I think the Swedes get a bad rap about having no sense of humor. The more we drank, the funnier they were."

"Funny that," I said. "When was this trip?"

"It'll be 12 years next April the 5th," he said.

I had heard Gavin use that expression "country club pour" before – at the Estate at the dinner hour. It was almost his favorite expression, although of course he had some choice ones for misbehaving audio visual equipment.

As the waiters at the Estate were either Filipino or Mexican, "country club pour" was probably not something they learned in English class. To tell the truth, I was a bit baffled at first too. But everybody soon came to understand that Gavin liked a big pour of any drink he ordered, his glass full to the rim, and anything less he considered to be a source of disappointment and complaint. And, as often as not, the waiters would give him a bigger pour than everybody else, on the sound theory it is best to placate the elderly, not irritate them.

I never found out what country club had spoiled Gavin into expecting very large drinks in his later life. The few country clubs I have visited served more or less conventional-sized drinks. But I can only believe that somewhere in Pennsylvania, where Gavin was originally from, there is a club where members stagger under the weight of large vodka and tonics while their wives struggle to hold up giant Chardonnays as big as fish bowls. Maybe Gavin could give a lecture one night: The Country

Club Pour – Fact or Fantasy?

You would think that Gavin would show the signs of his food and drink loving ways. Not so. He was trim and apparently fit. Unlike some, he did not have a stomach resembling a cask full of big pours and assorted pastries and sauces.

After stopping at various locations for tastings, the bus eventually reached the last winery where we would have lunch. As soon as the ladies had taken their ponderous time to disembark, the guys proceeded to walk to the tasting room with Gavin nimbly leading the way, making up for lost time. "Gavin," I said, "have you ever been here before?"

"Yes," he said, "June 14, 2016. They had a pretty fair 2013 Pinot Noir." Unfortunately, Gavin's appreciation of the winery was spoiled a bit this time. He was rebuffed on the big pour by a no-nonsense, patronizing young woman. "At wine tastings we pour only a little taste so your taste buds are not overwhelmed. Then we have a little cracker to clear our palate."

Her little lecture did not go over well with Gavin, who had been to many tasting rooms in his lifetime, knew the drill, and hoped that the drill might be relaxed for once. If our server had been a piece of audio-visual equipment, he would have said something harsh. As it was, he just made a low grumble of displeasure in her direction.

It was probably just as well that the pours were small because small adds up to big after you have quite a lot of them at successive wineries. By the time lunch was served, we were probably not fit for the company of the ladies. That did not stop them joining us.

All the obvious teetotalers seemed to flock to our table, perhaps to be a good moral example but more likely to enjoy the pleasure of looking down their noses at us. They ordered tea – tea! In a winery no less! – which seemed to me an offense against Bacchus.

But I resisted the temptation to say anything. For one thing, I saw Linda across the room eyeing me with what I took as suspicion, although maybe it was the ghost of Susan hinting that I needed to watch myself.

In fact, all the guys remained restrained and cheerfully polite, so much so that we were relieved to be called to get back on the bus, so that we could be our unbuttoned selves.

As we walked back, I turned to Sam, who was even more hearty than usual, and told him a story: "This reminds me of when I was about 21 growing up in Australia. A mate of mine had a flat and he was talked into hosting a wine appreciation night. The members of the wine society brought 24 bottles of different choice wines, which an expert was going to lead us in sipping. He also put two really crappy bottles in the mix to enliven his commentary and make a point.

"Well, the expert made the mistake of coming late. He was supposed to come at 7 but he didn't arrive until 9 pm, by which time everyone was lying about as paralytic as possums after drinking all the bottles, including the two crappy ones, which by then nobody noticed were crappy."

Sam enjoyed the story immensely, not surprisingly, as all of us men were now in an elevated state of cheerfulness. I am not sure when the drinking songs started on the bus ride home. We certainly did not lack for a ribald repertoire of tunes. I knew a few from my rugby playing days and others had obviously been sung long ago by bunches of guys around rowdy campfires. Our singing voices were probably too slurred and off-key for the delicate ears of the ladies to fully comprehend but they may have guessed we had been over-served.

All I know is that we were in the middle of one song "Dinah, Dinah, show us your legs, show us your legs, show us your legs, a yard above your knee" when the tour coordinator came on the intercom and shushed us up. "Gentlemen, a little quiet please, it's time to play bus bingo!"

Oh no! My greatest fear had been realized. What luck: A man has a drink and a headache of another sort sneaks up on him when his guard is down. Needless to say, my friends and I did not join in the alleged bingo fun. Back at the Estate, I slept for the rest of the afternoon and on Monday, when I arrived for our editorial meeting, Linda said pointedly, 'Well, you had a good time on Saturday.' "

31 - ELECTION NIGHT

Oh, I won't be afraid
Just as long as you stand
Stand by me
– Ben E. King, 1961

In my old newspaper career, Election Day was always a special event to be savored. With most government offices closed, the beat reporters who covered council meetings and courts in daylight hours were now rostered on the evening shift, and they came back to the newsroom like birds returning to their old roosts, adjusting their eyes to the unaccustomed light. The result was that the newsroom was more than twice as full as usual.

Even for the dullest election, the building was an accelerating engine of energy and excitement. The results would dribble in most of the evening and then came in a big rush as midnight approached. All the while phones rang and frantic editors yelled for copy in the time-honored way. When the home edition was finally put to bed, the newsroom managers – in an uncharacteristic fit of generosity – arranged for boxes of pizza to be delivered for the workers for a late dinner.

Whether it was because of the rare largesse that provided it or the frenetic work done to earn it, no pizza ever tasted better. Later, in the early hours, some of the traditionalists went down to a bar a block away that had promised to stay open late to tell the backstory tales over frosty mugs. No beer ever tasted better either.

Of course, the election for a new chairman of the Estate residents committee and six board members was in no way comparable to a real election. Until the arrival of the obnoxious Mr. Jones to the manager's office, resident committee meetings hardly registered in the community's consciousness. Now, off course, everybody was riled up and the election was suddenly a big deal.

And now the day of the vote had arrived. With the candidate forums behind them, most residents prepared to cast ballots for the very first time or else thought they were voting for the first time as previous elections were so boring they could not remember participating in them.

That still did not make this a real election in the way that I formerly experienced them. But, then again, The Pine Nut wasn't a real newspaper, so my nostalgia for the old days had its limits. Nevertheless, I succumbed to the temptation of inviting the staff of The Pine Nut and a few other friends over to my cottage for pizza and beer after the vote.

One slight awkwardness was that at least two of the candidates for office were members of the newsletter's staff – my friend Gavin Halsey and Sam Hudson. This would never have happened in real journalism. I hoped, in particular, that Sam would take his certain defeat gracefully, as graceful was not a word often associated with Sam.

The polls closed at 7 pm, so it would not be a long night. The volunteer vote counters had only about 250 paper ballots to count and that was if everybody on the Estate voted, which was highly unlikely. After dinner, people stayed on in the dining hall and milled about in conversation. The vote counters set up a table to work on and a blackboard next to them to record the running tallies. Every few minutes, one of them would post new results. Being elderly, and much given to fussing, the vote counters were not as quick as they might have been but trends slowly started to emerge.

In the race for chairman, it was a struggle between the accomplished Professor Norman and the man-of-the-people Sam

Hudson, who was doing better than I imagined, although by the time 150 votes had been counted he trailed the professor by 34 votes. It was a great relief to see that the good professor had the race in the bag. Peter Hamilton, who had quit his seat on the committee to run for chairman, trailed far behind.

Only one group had not been heard from. Residents could vote at four locations – the dining hall, the library, the gym and across the street at the permanent care center, whose votes had not yet been counted. I said to Linda, who was in the group watching the results with me, "Sam would have to win almost all the votes of the sick and infirm folks across the street to pull this one out." She nodded in agreement.

Just about then the box arrived with the last 50 or so votes from across the street and 10 minutes later the final tally was posted. Sam had won almost all the votes from across the street and with that he had won the chairmanship too by about a dozen votes. Oh no! He would be unbearable.

That was the only prediction of the night that I got right. He was unbearable. For his part, Professor Norman was the soul of sportsmanship and civility, shaking Sam's hand, congratulating him and wishing him well. As soon as that was done, Sam was exulting and fist-bumping and behaving as if he had just won the Super Bowl.

More surprises were in store. In the race for committee seats, seven candidates were vying for six spots. Minnie the Moaner was the leading vote getter across the board; she did better than even the three women incumbents who kept their seats. Gavin was behind them and Billy Franks, the rock and roller, just squeaked by to win the last seat. This meant that probably the most accomplished candidate of them all, Brian Cooper, the still practicing attorney and sometime forgetful tennis player, was not going to be on the board. At least Brian took it quite well.

But the results made no sense. I was reminded of the quotation that a candidate for the California state senate had famously declared after his electoral defeat: "The people have spoken. The bastards."

With our hopes and expectations for the night shattered by 8 in the evening, we trudged over to my cottage for what was supposed to have been post-election festivities, but seemed now about as festive as an invitation to an autopsy. Jimmy Devine, the outgoing chairman, had been invited too and he walked with me and shared my hovering cloud of depression.

"Jimmy, can you explain how it is that Sam Hudson, the most vociferous and loud opponent of Mr. Jones, is elected as chairman by the same people who then turn around and give Minnie, the one person who perversely likes that little twit, the most votes to be a board member."

"I don't know," Jimmy said, "the election turned out to be a strange little parody of the national mood, don't you think? The candidates with the biggest mouths are elected by the people with the lowest attention spans, and rhyme and reason fly out the door. And I think I am partly to blame because I allowed people other than board members to nominate these guys. It would have been far better had we stuck to the old way with the existing board members nominating a slate of candidates who were then voted on more or less as a formality."

"Don't blame yourself, Jimmy. Who was the dope who turned Sam Hudson into the darling sportswriter of the Estate, and elevated Billy Franks to our own rock and roll hall of fame, senior division? That dope was me. I wanted The Pine Nut to become a force in the community but a force for good, not absurdity."

"Actually, I think there's more to it than that," Jimmy said. "Part of the national mood is the desire to give the establishment, or the prevailing thinking, or accepted norms, or whatever you like to call it, the elevated finger. This was just one big general 'screw you' from folks who are not only a microcosm of the larger world but also have a more personal reason to be generally irritated, being as they are old."

That may have been part of it but when we reached my cottage for the post-election party further enlightenment soon followed from the man of the hour himself. Sam and a few others were waiting for us outside and Sam was still congratulating himself and enjoying the moment.

"OK, Sam, my congratulations to you," I said, "but how come all the residents across the street voted for you en masse?"

"Simple, Alistair," he said. "I just used an old political trick."

"What was that?"

"In a word, cookies."

"Cookies?"

"Yes, cookies. I went across the street and visited the sick folks and gave cookies to everyone and told them to vote for me. I figured that was the one place my opponents would forget about. If the patients were napping, I left them cookies wrapped in a note. They were really glad to have a visitor but they especially liked the cookies."

Of course they did. What was it with this place and cookies? I should have known. In my mind's eye, I saw empires crumbling like so many cookies, the old fortresses of fact and reason collapsing under a barbarian bombardment of chocolate chips.

Surely nothing good was going to come of this night. My taste buds seemed to confirm this. I thought the pizza was mediocre and the beer seemed strangely flat. Still, some of the guests enjoyed the party. Gavin, who for once had not been stymied by technology, was enjoying the fruits of victory delivered by the paper ballots. "Excellent pizza, Alistair," he beamed. I didn't doubt that a year from now he would remember exactly what time he ate it.

In the corner, Linda was surveying my apartment with a careful eye. This was her first visit and I had cleaned up a bit for her and the other visitors. When I say a bit, I mean that I spent almost the whole of the previous day making the place presentable. The Estate has maid service and I avail myself of that but a man suddenly thrust into living by himself tends to become cluttered. Maids can put newspapers and books in neat piles but someone has to come along as if on a mission to throw stuff away.

I had lately gotten out of the habit of imagining what Susan might have thought about the details of my life and what I should do to keep up standards. But I could clearly hear her voice again when it came to tidying up; it sounded like a direct order resurfacing from the depths of memory. "For goodness sake, Alistair, you can't have people seeing this mess!" And I did not quit until her voice – to me, the voice of conscience – receded once more into the background noise of my new situation.

It was impossible to read Linda's thoughts to know if she thought the apartment looked smart enough for company. With my luck, she would view the state of the cottage as another disappointment on a night of them. But I soon had bigger things to worry about.

32 - FIRED

Oh, the shark, babe, has such teeth, dear
And it shows them pearly white
– Bobby Darin, 1959

The next day the staff of The Pine Nut met in the library to plan and produce the election edition. Everybody already had their assignments and we had talked about the results at the pizza party, so our meeting wasn't planned to be long. Before it began, though, Linda asked me a question in a confidential whisper.

"What are you going to do about Sam Hudson?"

"What do you mean?" I replied, but I think I knew already what she meant. His success had raised a concern that I didn't really want to address.

"Well, I know you care about conflicts of interest. I know you really didn't want Sam and Gavin to run in this election and now they have won. Granted, Gavin is not a problem; he only says bad things to computers but Sam was brutally vocal in his opposition to Mr. Jones and now he is at it again."

"How so?"

"Here's the statement he gave Betty after his victory."

I picked up the paper that Linda had printed out from an early draft of Betty's story.

"Mr. Jones better be awake tonight because we had an earthquake at the Estate. The residents have spoken with a loud voice. They want this pipsqueak out of the manager's office and as chairman I will make it happen. He better not mess with me. There will be no more talk of raising our annual dues. And we demand the full range of desserts we love at the dining hall. This boy and his fiancée need to wake up and smell the coffee. I am going to make the Estate great again!"

"Enough clichés for you, Alistair?" Linda said, as I stood there shaking my head in sorrow and disbelief.

"Pipsqueak boy, eh? Yes, that will make Mr. Jones more amenable to reason."

"And Sam?" she asked.

"He's only the sports editor, so he will have no influence on our coverage of the election. In fact, as the committee has no power, which Sam doesn't seem to have grasped, he will have no influence on anything, except to make the pipsqueak harder to deal with." But I still hadn't properly answered Linda's question.

"As the first step, I will ask Sam to tone down the pipsqueak boy language a bit, then I will think about what we will do going forward. The dual sports editor/strongman dictator role may be too much for us to bear going forward. If he were a real journalist at a real paper, I would fire his ass. Instead, he is a volunteer hack on a phony paper who won a faux election and I, a pretend editor with nostalgia-induced illusions, have been given an unreal ethical issue to deal with." Here I stopped and sighed and Linda sighed in sympathy.

In any event, Sam did consent to change the wording of his statement. He complained long and loud about political correctness and his First Amendment rights being violated – both irrelevant to the matter at hand – and I made the case for courtesy and sounding professional, even if we weren't. I also hinted darkly that maybe he couldn't write sports for us if he couldn't stop sounding like a jerk who hurt our reputation. In the end, after much haggling, he consented to the following amended version to be printed in The Pine Nut:

"Mr. Jones better be awake tonight because we had an earthquake at the Estate. The residents have spoken with a loud voice. We won't tolerate such behavior in the manager's office. There will be no more talk of raising our annual dues. And we demand the full range of desserts we love at the dining hall. Mr. Jones and his fiancée need to wake up and smell the coffee. I am going to make the Estate great again!"

The statement was still ridiculous but marginally less so. For the time being, Sam would stay on as sports editor but I wasn't sure whether this arrangement would work in the days ahead. The compromise was certainly imperfect but then I don't think King Solomon, if he had edited the Temple Times, could have done better in the circumstances.

What a dilemma. In a 40-year career I had never encountered a problem quite so stupid. On one hand, I wanted the full flavor of Sam's pronouncements to be presented unabridged to the readers; on the other, The Pine Nut was the officially funded organ of the Estate management. A certain ingrate factor was involved in having one of its staff writers, in his separate capacity as residents' committee chairman, calling Mr. Jones a pipsqueak, even though he was one.

That was on Wednesday and The Pine Nut came out on Friday morning as usual with all the news that would fit, as always not quite The New York Times. On Friday just before noon, Mrs. Fothergill made an unusual call to me on my cell phone number. She was not one for polite preliminaries. "Mr. Brown, this is Mrs. Fothergill from the manager's office. Mr. Jones has summoned you to appear in his office at 2 pm."

"Summoned me?"

"Yes, at 2 pm, come by yourself and be prompt. Mr. Jones is a busy man." Click.

And I am not a busy man? I thought. Well, I suppose not on a Friday afternoon, although I resented the assumption, as anybody would. But I am a curious man at any hour so at 2 pm on the dot I showed up at the manager's office to answer the summons. Of course, I was kept waiting until 2.45 pm until the great man had done whatever passed as work for him.

For a man so formal in his appearance, Mr. Jones was not one for the formalities of social interaction, much like his private assistant, Mrs. Fothergill. The two were perfect for each other.

Barely looking at me, he proceeded straight in on what soon became a tirade. "I am very disappointed, Mr. Brown, I am disgusted and disappointed. Once again, that little rag of yours has printed rabble-rousing stories about the ridiculous little residents' election you have stooged up to make me look bad." He paused here for theatrical effect.

"You should know that this committee has no power, no power at all, Mr. Brown, to do anything. I am manager here, I am in charge, not this Sam Houston fellow who thinks he is such a big shot with his insulting remarks."

He was now pacing around the room using his arms alternately to make his points – one arm up, one arm down, arm up, arm down, back and forth, so a passerby looking through the window might think a demented marionette was putting on a show.

"Hudson," I said. "Not Houston."

"Whatever."

"And The Pine Nut didn't stooge this election up, as you put it, to make you look bad. The interest in the election was stirred by recent events that residents did not like. We just reported the facts."

"So you think that there's been an earthquake at the Estate because of this election? You call that a fact?"

"It is a fact that Sam Hudson thinks it is so and his opinion deserves to be known. It is fair comment."

I regretted to myself now that I hadn't let Sam call the pipsqueak a pipsqueak. If I was going to be condemned for the milder version of his statement, I should have gone with the original.

"I refuse to meet with that lying man. How dare he call Miss Crocker my fiancée."

Oh no, I thought we had gotten beyond that. But this was the start of the second part of his tirade, which lasted at least 20 minutes more. The subject matter reprised the best of the looney tunes hit parade and was punctuated by more pacing and hand waving. I didn't know what was more remarkable: His talent for spouting nonsense or the resilience of the carpet in not wearing out. I gave the winning medal to the carpet.

As he spoke in a torrent of angry words, and my mind took temporary refuge in pleasanter thoughts, I thought of two positives to possibly take away. First, he didn't seem to realize that Sam worked for The Pine Nut – he knew him only as the recently elected "lying" committee chairman. Second, he was probably just letting off steam and this too would pass.

But like everything else I had recently been wrong about, the ending was not happy. His lip finally curled, "Well, Mr. Editor, who thinks he is so great, consider yourself unemployed. You know what I found out from the accountant? The Pine Nut is completely funded by the Estate."

"Yes, I know," I said, "I thought you knew too."

He looked a bit sheepish but he was having too much fun for his inadvertent admission of ignorance to spoil the fun. "You are fired. The Pine Nut is no more. It has fallen off the tree. Finis. Good riddance. It has done nothing but spread dissent. My only regret is that I didn't close it down immediately to save more money."

He paused here for my response, hoping I think that it would be pleading, remorseful or pathetic.

"OK," I said.

"What?" he said. "You are not going to plead your precious First Amendment rights?"

"No, the First Amendment is about government power being used to censor free speech. You are not the government, despite what you may imagine. And you are entirely within your rights to close down a publication you fund if you don't like it. Good day," I said, and got up and left his office.

I left him with a puzzled look on his face that I hoped was shock tinged with disappointment.

The staff of the now decommissioned Pine Nut met at the library in a hastily convened emergency session at 5 pm. I did not tell them in advance what was going on – just that it was urgent. Just before people arrived, I had a disturbing thought.

"Linda," I said. "Are you paid for your library work?"

"Sort of. The money I earn goes towards reducing my monthly dues. I still pay something but the little I make is how I afford to live here, as I didn't grow rich as a librarian."

"Oh, sorry, I didn't mean to pry into your financial situation. But tell me, if you were to fall into disfavor somehow, and you were fired as a librarian, you could end up having to pay more to live here?"

"Yes, I suppose so. I have never thought of it before."

They came in shortly afterward but when they took their places around the table one chair was empty. "Where's Gavin?" I asked.

"Oh, his wife called," Linda said. "He's not feeling well and he's taking a rest."

I would have to tell him later. So I told the story to the rest of them – the summons, the tirade, the bringing down of the curtain on our little paper. They were suitably disgusted and angry and even despairing.

Then Betty said, "Alistair, I know you are furious, as we all are, but something tells me you don't think this is the end."

"You are right, Betty. I have a plan. On Monday morning, I am going down to the printer's office to see if they can still print us a newsletter for the same price that the Estate was paying. I have some savings. I don't mind chipping in."

"I will come with you," Bill Gibson said. "Maybe I can finally do some business as business manager."

"Yes, I think we should have advertising as well."

"Can we do this, run a magazine and distribute it here privately?" Betty asked.

"I really think we can. The pipsqueak has his rights but we have ours. He thinks he has won and solved his problem. What he doesn't realize is that he no longer controls us. Instead, he has given us freedom and his problem just got a whole lot worse."

There were smiles and cheers in the room now. Despair had been routed by hope.

"One last thing," I said. "We have to find another place to meet and work. Mr. Jones doesn't have a clue who works for The Pine Nut but we can't risk him getting mad and firing Linda as librarian because she is aiding and abetting the rebels."

And so we all went to dinner, hungry for the plan.

33 - GOODBYE, OLD FRIEND

The greatest thing you'll ever learn,
is just to love and be loved in return
– Nat King Cole, 1948

At 7 the next morning, when it was not yet fully light, I was awakened by someone knocking urgently on my front door. Curious and anxious, I felt compelled to get out of bed faster than my usual lazy creep, throwing on a pair of sweatpants and a sweater over my pajamas in order to answer the door with some semblance of decency.

To my further great surprise, I found Linda at my doorstep, looking anguished and shaken.

"Linda, what is…" My sentence trailed off at the sad spectacle of her, the last person I expected to see at that hour, in that place and in that condition.

"It's Gavin," she said, "He's dead."

"Gavin? He can't be dead, we just saw him. What happened?"

"I don't really know the details but apparently it was a heart attack. Trish texted me a few minutes ago that he died late last night."

Then suddenly she was hugging me and crying inconsolably on my shoulder. Amid her sobs, she managed to say: "I didn't want you to find out from some random person over breakfast."

I thanked her for that and led her inside and sat her down at my little kitchen nook and made her a cup of coffee. When she had recovered a little bit, she said: "Will you come over to their cottage with me?"

"Of course," I said, not relishing the prospect, as much as I wanted to help. As she drank her coffee and composed herself, I took the opportunity to put on something a little classier than sweat pants. As for Linda, she did not have to go back to her place. Even in her shock and distress, she had managed to dress appropriately.

It was almost fully light by now and I felt a bit better about paying our respects at this hour, even though Trish had probably been awake for a long time, if she had ever been asleep at all. As we walked over to Gavin and Trish's cottage, I wanted to cry, too, and envied Linda her freedom to express her emotions more visibly. The convention that big boys don't cry seemed at that moment less like a masculine virtue than an emotional defect. Gavin was my first friend here. I knew I would miss him terribly. Despite my outwardly stoic shell, I was shattered inside, lost and confused, and even a little angry at the cruelness of fate.

Death, even sudden death, as I well knew from my experience with Susan, was no stranger to the Estate. Everybody who takes a breath is under a death sentence, but the older we get, the closer we get to the day of reckoning, the day we go down that long one-way road stretching to God only knows where. It doesn't get any easier knowing that Death is so well acquainted with our address at the Estate. For every resident, he's just out of view, hiding around the corner, sensed but not seen, polishing his scythe, biding his time, his presence near, his call anticipated. Yet until Death comes, we who live at the Estate are mostly in denial. So when the time comes, we are as shocked as anyone.

When Linda and I arrived at the cottage, heavy with sorrow, we found other friends had gathered there, too. I knew some of them but I didn't know them all. Trish was in a terrible state and to look at her was to break your heart. Somehow between all the well-intentioned words that were useless to dispel her loss, the story came out.

Gavin had complained of not feeling well. At first, he thought he had indigestion, the result of liking his lunch a little too well, but later he began to sweat and complain about a pain in his arm and Trish didn't like the sound of it. Over his continuing objections that it was nothing, Trish made him come over with her to the medical center, just a short walk from where they lived.

The nurse on duty took one look at him and called an ambulance. He was made to lie on a bed but his condition quickly deteriorated and the staff began working on him with increasing urgency. By the time the ambulance arrived, he was gone. Heart attack? Probably, but it wasn't quite clear yet. Only the result was.

We stayed at least an hour, promising to help with any grim formalities that might come up. With inexperienced management in control at the Estate, there was no assurance that the usual procedures would be followed.

Other friends came in as the word spread. As I was saying goodbye, Trish leaned over to me and whispered, "Gavin thought of you as his best friend here and I know you felt the same. Would you say the eulogy for him at the funeral?"

"He was my best friend, Trish, and I will." And I kissed her lightly on her cheek.

In the several days before the funeral, visitations at a local funeral home were held. I went to all of them; Linda went as much as her library duties would allow. If Gavin had died back in Pittsburgh, where I spent many years in my newspaper career, the coffin would have been open and Gavin would have been lying there in his best suit, looking like he wanted to be somewhere else, somewhere less formal. He also wouldn't look like Gavin. His features would be immobile and waxy and his friends and relations would think that a mannequin had been placed in his coffin.

Fortunately, funereal practices in this part of California do not so much reflect old country ways and a lid was mercifully placed over Gavin for the visitation. While there was no viewing, as such, Gavin being safely out of view, some of the features of more traditional viewings were obvious.

Trish was now supported by their two sons, both grown up to be middle-aged men. As visitors came and paid respects to the family, some would share cheerful meetings with folks they had not seen in a while and were glad to see again. Funerals do bring people together and sometimes people, with no disrespect meant, laugh so they won't cry. Ironically, visitations, wakes, and receptions can be events that the deceased might have taken some joy in if only he hadn't died.

Laughter was a stranger to my mood those several days that seemed to pass so slowly. I mostly recited in my head what I might say to honor Gavin at the funeral service. He was a lively, happy person and how to convey that on such a somber occasion was my challenge. I finally decided to take a cue from the hearty exchanges I had witnessed in the reception line at the funeral home. I would faithfully honor Gavin the man and let the traditional service for the burial of the dead speak to the sadness of the hour.

A fog to match our spirits blanketed the countryside the day we gathered to see Gavin off and it stayed foggy for much of the morning. By noon, the scheduled hour of the service, the sun was at last piercing the gloom. The service was held in Trish's church, a little Episcopal church in a forest a few miles away from the Estate. Shuttle buses ran from the Estate and by the time relatives and friends were summoned to rise for the opening hymn, the pews were packed.

For the next half hour, as the prayers were recited and hymns sung, and Gavin's sons appeared at the lectern to make their readings, I waited my turn with a case of severe failing nerves.

Not since I was asked to speak at my son Sean's graduation from a traditional private high school had a speech held so much terror for me. On that occasion, a Hindu priest in flowing robes had given the first benediction, an unlikely choice that was meant as an inclusive gesture to acknowledge that some students were of Indian descent. As incongruous as this was in such a preppy habitat, the Hindu priest managed to put me at my ease by chanting, even though he startled much of the audience. But Hindus were in short supply on this day. All I could see were Episcopalians in every direction, or at least people who looked like they might have the makings of being Episcopalians if they had sufficiently good table manners, not that the lack of them had disqualified me.

I was called up to speak at last and, staring out at my friends in the gathered assembly, a sort of calm came over me. As I have learned over many years, often the hard way, the secret to making a good speech is about the confidence of the delivery. A speaker can read a shopping list and be successful if it is done with verve. People in an audience don't want to feel embarrassed for the speaker. At the very outset, when they are prepared to cringe, the speaker must reassure them that they can rest easy. A speaker may be shaking in his boots but his words must be full of authority. For whatever reason, my confidence had returned not a second too soon.

"Thank you. I have the sad honor today to be called to say a few words about Gavin Halsey, whose untimely passing has gathered us all here. I have no more standing to do this other than the fact that I was his friend. Of course, all of us here are his friends and some of you are his relatives too, with his beloved Trish and his sons John and James being the first among us all.

"I note that the audio equipment is working perfectly on this occasion. Of course it is. It doesn't have Gavin to yell at it, so there is no sport to be had in breaking down. I sort of wish that static would crackle from this microphone or the speakers would emit a piercing shriek so that the lack of cuss words coming from Gavin's casket would confirm for us who can't believe it, that he has truly gone.

"We all remember those outbursts, so profane as to be comic. But I would have you consider: Can you ever remember Gavin ever yelling at a person? Or even a dog? He had nothing but understanding for creations of flesh and blood. With his wise and gentle spirit, he knew the imperfections of living things and generously allowed for them.

"But as an engineer, and a scientist who traded in empirical facts and the perfection of numbers and the soundness of theorems, he expected the machines that serve us to be flawless and was angered when they weren't. He argued with entities that he thought had no excuse, at least this side of highly advanced artificial intelligence.

"Gavin was a distinguished scientist and engineer, but a career alone does not make a person good or great. Gavin's real virtue was in the human vocations – husband, father, and friend. He was one of those rare people that you felt better for meeting. His goodness animated him while inspiring everybody else. He was simply good. There is goodness and evil in this world but goodness is so much stronger and Gavin was its emissary.

"As a scientist, it is true, Gavin liked his theories of life to be amenable to proof; so in matters of faith his head was inclined to be skeptical but his heart believed in what was right as if it were a fixed star in the sky. If he did not always attend church, he nevertheless was away somewhere doing something for somebody and living the essential love preached by the church.

"Because he was good, and heaven is the place where good souls are meant to go, I pray that Gavin's skepticism melted at last in the presence of the almighty engineer whom he then praised and thanked and then was blessed in return, and was admitted to heaven with the understanding he cannot use cuss words in the presence of the divine computers or the celestial organ.

"I suppose I should now read the words of Psalm 23, the eternal and traditional comfort of the fearful or bereaved on occasions like this. You know King David's wonderful words, of course: 'The Lord is my shepherd, I shall not want....' But I have spoken long enough so let me repeat that part which I believe is now Gavin's reward, the part that says "You prepare a table before me in the presence of my enemies."

"Gavin had no enemies so he can enjoy his dinner unmolested – and we remember how he liked a good dinner and a nice glass of wine, in fact, he enjoyed his life until the very last slice of pizza. So I pray now that we his friends or loved ones can perhaps one day join him at that table and he can make us smile again. In the meantime, our memories of him sustain us.

"God bless you, Gavin, and God bless the Halsey family."

The audience had seemed to be with me during the eulogy, projecting warmth, at turns smiling, laughing, perhaps daubing away tears, but it is so hard to gauge a reaction from a single vantage point. Insecurity was setting in as I walked back to my pew as swiftly as dignity would allow. My colleagues from the newsletter were seated in a row there and I sat back down next to Linda. I was surprised to acknowledge to myself that I wanted her reaction more than any of the others. She turned to me, smiled and gently squeezed my arm.

Soon, we came out with the crowd into what was now bright sunshine and she said, "I am emotionally drained and we still have to go to the reception in the church hall. Can we go out to dinner tonight in Carmelito?"

34 - BONSOIR

I keep a close watch on this heart of mine,
I keep my eyes wide open all the time
– Johnny Cash, 1957

The reception in the church hall after the service was again one of those times when sadness rubbed shoulders with cheerfulness. To the extent that people were uplifted in spirit, it was because they were buoyed by memories of Gavin and life was now calling them back to pick up the daily routine where he had left off. There was relief, too, that for them the time of deep mourning was coming to an end and smiling would again seem natural, at least until the next funeral. Of course, Trish and their sons would be burdened with sadness for a long age more.

The emotional release did not entirely raise my morale. I ate little cucumber sandwiches sadly and made small talk. People came up to me and said that they enjoyed my tribute to Gavin – and that was nice of them – but I had no way of knowing whether they were just being polite. It's not like they felt free to say, "Alistair, your eulogy was awful!" So I wasn't completely insulated from the thought that indeed it might have been awful.

Feeling drained by the day's events, both Linda and I retired to our respective cottages when we returned to the Estate, with the agreement that we would meet outside the library at 6 pm to go to dinner. I had made a reservation for a French restaurant called Bonsoir in Carmelito at 6:30 pm.

In the meantime, I lay down on my bed for an afternoon nap. Grief can be exhausting, perhaps because we have an instinct to use sleep to escape the emotional burdens of reality. As it was, my nap almost extended past the time agreed for our rendez-vous. I woke in a panic and hurriedly threw on some passably spiffy clothes, resisting the strong temptation to put on an ascot in order not to look too ridiculous in Linda's eyes.

As I walked as briskly as I could toward the library, a shrill woman's voice yelled out: "Coming through!" Then a grumpy man's voice added: "Watch your back!" and a moment later "Get out of the way." I turned around to see two electric-powered sit-down scooters bearing down on me at a great rate of knots. I stepped quickly off the walking trail and in an instant they breezed past me without so much as a sideways glance. I heard the old man say: "Stupid old people hogging the trail."

Well, he should talk. But by the time I had recovered my senses enough to yell, "Slow down!" they were gone around the corner. Around that corner Linda was waiting for me, looking down the trail to where the elderly daredevils had disappeared in a cloud of grass clippings.

"Did you see those old coot maniacs?" I asked Linda.

"See them? They almost knocked me down without a word of apology."

"Me too. And the replica Mario Andretti said I was a stupid old person."

"That's only half true," Linda said, leaving me to guess which the true part was.

"You know," I said, "we have this vision of the elderly as being wonderfully sweet and polite, contentedly sitting by the fire with a shawl over their feet, bathed in a shaft of sunlight, but some old folks go crotchety and decide they have no time left for manners. Their attitude is: To heck with everybody."

"Maybe they were just late for dinner," Linda said, more charitably.

We kept discussing the topic of elderly people behaving badly as I drove her in my little mini car into the nearby village of Carmelito, where we found parking easily. "Ah, the governor's spot," I said. I remembered ruefully that was what Gavin used to say whenever he was parking-spot blessed.

By the time we were seated in the restaurant, my mood had improved markedly. And why not? Linda was the embodiment of vitality after a day dominated by death. I could not tell you exactly what Linda was wearing that evening but she was as stylish and as fresh as ever. I swear she could emerge from a train wreck looking as if she were on a fashion shoot.

"This was a good idea, Linda, having dinner here tonight. I feel an old joke coming on. Do you think it's time for a joke?"

She was sipping her white wine, a Muscadet, so she simply smiled and nodded.

"So, a guy walks into a French restaurant and asks the maître d': "Do you have frogs legs?"

"The maître d', a stuffy sort of fellow, as you might expect, looks at him disdainfully and says: "Oui, monsieur.""

"And the guy said, "Great. Hop over the bar and fetch me a cheese sandwich.""

"Do the jokes get any better?" Linda asked.

"What's the matter with it?"

"I think it's what kids call a 'dad joke.' In your case, perhaps a 'granddad joke.'"

"Well, yes, I suppose, but it is the prerogative of old guys to tell old jokes, so that they are not lost to posterity. We believe jokes are like fine wine, they get better with age."

"I wonder when that process of improvement starts," Linda said. But she seemed amused by the conversation if not by the joke.

As it turned out, I ordered the frogs legs, in the absence of cheese sandwiches on the menu, followed by coq au vin. Linda had the onion soup and some salmon. I could not help wondering what Gavin would have advised. And soon enough the conversation turned to my eulogy.

"Do you want to know what I thought of your remarks?" she asked.

"Well, not particularly, well, maybe, yes," I said, unsuccessfully trying to be indifferent but eager at the same time. I did not say – although she could read it in my face – that I wanted to know her reaction at that moment more than any secret in the universe.

"I thought your eulogy was very fine. Well-delivered, well-spoken, funny and sad and therefore a bit daring – and above all heartfelt."

"Thank you."

"But.."– uh-oh, I said to myself, there's the inevitable but – "… I was surprised how religious you seemed to be. I didn't know that about you."

"I think deeply religious people would take issue with that. For them, my eulogy might have struck them as theologically suspect, this idea that good people might be admitted to heaven on a special pass. My problem was that Trish is a very religious person and Gavin wasn't. He was basically an atheist. I think he had an unhappy experience with religion early on as a kid and after that scientific explanations were his creed."

"That was my take, too," Linda said.

"But, you see, my duty was to praise Gavin while comforting Trish, and how could I comfort her? I thought that the best way to comfort her was to suggest the possibility she might see him again. You know, in the afterlife, in heaven.

"I suppose I was expressing my own feelings there. I want to see my wife Susan again. I want to see my parents again – they were very dear to me. So the idea of eternal life has terrific personal appeal to me. I don't want to believe that a great black curtain finally descends on us and that is the end.

"My Susan was religious like Trish and so were my parents for that matter. But the thought has always haunted me that I might not be able to join them because I did not believe like them. I am a journalist, after all, and I might be damned by professional definition." I meant this as a little joke to relieve the seriousness of the discussion and Linda obliged by giving a little smile.

"It seems terribly cruel that a loving heavenly father would separate those who loved each other on Earth because one had the faith and the other didn't. Yet that is what conventional Christian belief seems to say. Like all religions, it says that people must do what the Bible says – its way or the highway – and we all know what wretched place that highway leads to. But I take comfort in what St. Paul said, we understand as through a glass darkly. I also note that there are hundreds of different religions, all reading the same Bible, and all disagreeing on the meaning of some of the particulars.

"So I reckon I might be right yet. I hope there's a get-into-heaven pass for all good people – not only church-goers but good Hindus, Muslims, atheists, agnostics, anybody who is pregnant with celestial fire, anybody who lives a loving life and thus honors the Almighty without realizing it. Anyway, we won't know until we die. What do you think of my theory?"

"I think you are naïve, confused, possibly illogical but motivated by a kind and well-meaning heart that is itself pregnant with celestial fire – and thank you for the literary nod to Gray's Elegy Written in a Country Churchyard."

Well, that allusion was something only someone like Linda would know. As for the rest of it, I would take the criticism with the praise as the best a wacky theory could hope for.

"If it's any consolation," Linda added, "I don't think a soul in the church thought so deeply about it, not Trish, not the pastor. They would have just heard you saying good things about Gavin."

"So, my eulogy was awful in one way and good in another?"

Linda ignored that. "So, Alistair, you are confused but are you religious? Do you believe? Do you go to church?"

"I didn't go to church much when Susan was alive – she went every Sunday and I went on special occasions. You know, Christmas and Easter. But now I find myself wanting to go regularly and I do most Sundays. I find it is a comfort for me. Maybe it was Susan's death that left me adrift and in need of a mooring. Maybe it is just growing old and the realization that I am closer to the great divide now than most people are, and I had better think about what lies beyond and behave accordingly.

"Do I believe? It is not an easy question for me. My head doesn't believe, there's just too much about the church's narrative that I find illogical or unlikely. But my heart does believe, whole heartedly and no pun intended. For example, when I receive communion, I find my mind erased of all extraneous thoughts. A stillness comes over me, I leave the world behind. There's no words to describe it, but it seems to me like a foretaste of the everlasting. Search, it is written, and thou shalt find. I am still searching."

"Do you pray?"

"Yes, briefly, before I go to bed, as I learned as a child. I pray for Susan, my mother and father, my children and their children. More things are wrought by prayer than this world dreams of."

"Tennyson," she said. "Morte d'Arthur."

"Oh you are good, Linda. That is one of my favorite poems. But enough about me. How about you, now that you think that I am a weirdo?"

"I am searching too in my own way. I did not grow up in a religious family and religion is a curiosity to me, not a source of resentment or criticism. If all weirdos were like you, the world would be a better place."

We also talked of lighter subjects that night but that is the exchange I remember. She had peeked into my soul in ways that almost nobody had before. I felt embarrassed but I remember the evening as a happy one overall. This had only happened because I was so at ease with her.

The one thing we did not discuss was The Pine Nut, although that was a topic very much at the back of my mind. Linda did seem to hint at it when we were driving in the car going back to the Estate.

"Alistair, do you remember another quote from Morte d'Arthur that seems to speak to everything that has happened to us? 'The old order changeth, yielding place to new, and God fulfills himself in many ways, lest one good custom should corrupt the world.' "

I walked her back to her cottage. Just before we reached there, the crazed scooter riders from the senior division of the bat-out-of-hell brigade came roaring down the trail, as they had done earlier in the evening. "Out of the way," the man shouted.

This time I managed to shout back: "Late for your own funeral, I see."

Linda smiled and kissed me lightly on the cheek. "Good night," we said both at once. "Bonsoir," I added and immediately felt corny.

35 - EVERY DOG HAS ITS DAY

Somewhere over the rainbow, skies are blue
– Judy Garland, 1939

The Pine Nut was no more but Gavin's death postponed the effort to resurrect it in a new form. As Gavin was part of our team, it seemed unseemly to have his friends at the newsletter concentrate on something besides paying our respects to him.

To delay its return even for a week was nevertheless contrary to my every instinct. I believed that the paper must be published, the show must go on, lest the fine machinery that keeps the world on its axis be disturbed. I remember when I was a real editor and the 1989 earthquake left my old newspaper without power – yet we managed to type out stories on vintage typewriters by candlelight and take the copy to a printing plant in an adjoining county that still had power. And in this way the paper came out, very late but in the same day, and God was in his heaven and the readers were in their parlors and everybody was happy and equilibrium was restored to our little part of the planet.

But this was an old-man's nostalgic conceit. I recognized that in our circumstances it was too hard to get out another newsletter right away.

Besides, bitter recent history has proved time and again that presses fall silent and the world continues to turn. People may be left in a wobbling state with no firm information to hang on to but they don't seem to know it. I had every expectation that residents of the Estate would not even notice that The Pine Nut had gone missing. Only the puffed up pipsqueak in his office would note its absence and he would be glad, thinking that he had won.

Yet to my great surprise, the residents did notice. Boy, how they noticed! By Friday, they had not received their usual copy and by dinner time it was the talk of the Estate. When I came to the dining hall that night, I was bombarded with questions, the first of which was: "Where is The Pine Nut?"

"Mr. Jones has pulled the plug on it," I would answer.

"Why?"

"Because he didn't like the stories about the reaction to his management decisions as demonstrated by the recent board election."

"That's not good."

"Not good at all."

"Can't we do something about it?"

"Yes, we can and will. A new version of The Pine Nut will come out next week with a different name and different management."

"Who will own it?"

"We the residents will own it."

"That will be good."

"Yes, very good."

As I had seen before, it didn't take much to get people at the Estate riled up. They were old, they were used to certain things, they were relatively wealthy and they had time on their hands – all the ingredients of social dynamite ready to blow up the calm at any supposedly sleepy place like this.

The number of agitated residents who came up to me that night amazed me. People who had never read The Pine Nut were suddenly outraged by its disappearance. And, of course, Mr.

Jones had made no attempt to explain his side of the story, so his decision was added to his snub of the newly elected board president, our own Sam Hudson, whom he still refused to acknowledge.

But the most amazing person to be outraged by The Pine Nut's demise was Minnie the Moaner, who in my tenure as editor was The Pine Nut's first and most consistent critic. Almost every issue carried a letter from Mildred Miller, her formal complaining name, about some story or other that she didn't like. So after she had personally expressed to me her displeasure about The Pine Nut's official extinction, I had to ask her: "But Minnie, I thought you couldn't stand The Pine Nut."

"Yes, but that doesn't mean I want it to disappear. It is something I have come to love to hate."

"Don't worry," I said, guessing at her real motive. "We will still keep printing your negative letters in the replacement newsletter." At this she visibly brightened. "Now that you are on the residents committee," I added, "maybe you can help us make that happen."

I hoped this suggestion wasn't pressing my luck. During her baffling, ultimately successful campaign for a seat on the residents' committee, she had expressed support for Mr. Jones. But I figured that was then and now she had something new to be contrary about.

Buoyed by the residents' reaction, I went down with Bill Gibson the following Monday to the printing plant that handled the production of The Pine Nut and met with the account executive that we had been dealing with, a very attractive middle-aged woman named Sharon Price.

I mention that she was attractive not because I am degenerating at this late stage to a leering old man, although I suppose I have my moments as I am not yet immune to the charms of beauty, being as I am not yet dead, but because Sharon bore a striking resemblance to my Susan when she was younger. I looked at her – probably to the point of staring – and had to remind myself where I was and what I was.

Bill, our business manager hitherto with little business to do, helped me explain to Sharon our predicament and our offer. We wanted to print a newsletter about the Estate but financially independent of it. How much would that cost? She seemed sympathetic. We said we hoped she could give us a break, at least initially. She could and it was quite generous, half the price of what the Estate had been paying, at least in the first three months.

From Sharon's perspective, her company was losing the Estate's business but we would be an immediate replacement and she wanted us to succeed. Bill told her that he would be seeking advertising so in three months' time we would be self-sustaining and would be able to afford the full freight.

It was a deal. We shook on it and I looked at Sharon and thought longingly of Susan. "Alistair," she said, as an afterthought just as we were about to leave to return to the Estate. "What are you going to call your new newsletter? You can't call it The Pine Nut."

"No, we can't, "I said, "but I have an idea."

After lunch, we journalistic conspirators met at the back of the dining hall, as the library was no longer a venue that could be safely associated with our rebel enterprise.

"So what do you think?" I asked them. "The Pine Nut has died, long live the...whatever. What shall we call our new publication?"

The Piney News, the Estate Bugler and the Retiring Times were suggested and received with not much enthusiasm so I put in my two cents. "Do you remember what Mr. Jones mistakenly called

The Pine Nut in our first interview with him?"

"Was it The Fine Mutt?" Betty offered tentatively.

"Yes, Betty. Well done. The Fine Mutt, a name for a publication which hopes to have some bite."

"Oh, I like it," said Betty.

"The man who banned it is the man who renamed it," Linda observed.

"And Fine Mutt rhymes with Pine Nut so everybody will recognize what it is," said Sam.

"Yes, Sam, that is sort of the point."

"Oh," he said.

So by popular acclaim, The Fine Mutt came into growling being. Everybody was dispatched to their own quarters to start writing the first issue. And we had a new recruit to replace Gavin. As an engineer, writing was never really Gavin's forte, and I think he did it as a favor to me. Any kind deed for a good friend, any bad word for a malfunctioning machine – that was Gavin's philosophy.

Our new recruit was Deidre Williams, who long ago I thought might be a dreaded casserole lady with designs on me. She wasn't. She was just a nice woman who was outgoing and knowledgeable, especially on the importance of keeping cookies handy in any public meeting. She was the one who taught me that lesson when I first sought people to write for The Pine Nut. As she had attended that meeting, I half expected her to join the staff but she had other duties, including the welcoming committee which gave tours of the grounds to prospective residents. Perhaps she thought herself too busy back then for any extra duties but now she had come forward to volunteer her services.

By chance, the day we started our new adventure – a Monday – was the very day that Mr. Jones decided to raise the residents' monthly dues by 10 percent. A note appeared on the notice board at dinner time, causing even more consternation among the residents. If Mr. Jones had known that a new independent newsletter was in the offing, he might have postponed the announcement to Friday when it was too late for us to make the edition.

The timing was nearly perfect: I had looked forward to The Fine Mutt arriving unannounced at his desk. I could imagine the look on his face even if the first edition was not explosive. But now our lead story was going to be about the most incendiary story of all – the 10 percent rise in residents' dues.

That would require some comment from the manager's office – even if it was going to be a no comment. Betty volunteered to write the story and she didn't have much to work with. The announcement was bare bones. The increase would start next month. That was it.

This begged several questions. While most of the residents were well off, some had come to the Estate long ago and their assets had dwindled over the years. What provision would be made for anyone who was suddenly struggling? Could the management give a discount if residents paid annually? Would Mr. Jones meet with members of the financial committee to discuss other possible means of reducing the Estate's costs if that was the problem? (We knew the answer to that but the question had to be asked). Most of all, what was management's justification for this steep rise?

"Don't worry," Betty said. "I'll email Ms. Crocker and appeal to her. I'll tell her that it is in her fiancé's best interest to try and justify what he is doing." In the event, despite all of Betty's logic and charm, nothing worked. Mr. Jones wasn't going to have anything to do with the residents' committee or its new champion, The Fine Mutt.

So her story was all about the arrogant little notice, the unanimous condemnation of it by the residents and a report on an emergency meeting of the residents' committee called to discuss the matter the same night. This led to more incendiary language – including the term pipsqueak, which was left in this time – that Mr. Jones would not have been happy to read. By his silence, he had again guaranteed that all the criticism of him would go un-contradicted.

The residents' committee meeting was mostly all talk and no action, although it did pass a motion condemning the fee rise – if that symbolic move could be called action. I realized that Gavin was supposed to be at that meeting; it would have been his first. His place was taken by Brian Cooper, the old lawyer who was the one candidate who did not win a seat but was the natural choice to be Gavin's replacement by virtue of being on the ballot. The last shall be first, I guess. Brian did promise to look into the residents' legal rights, which might be a help in the coming weeks.

But Gavin was still on the front page – only as the subject of a remarkably good obituary done as Deidre's first assignment. When The Fine Mutt finally appeared on Friday, he was grinning at me from the page. And all I could do was grin back.

Part of The Fine Mutt's masthead was a mongrel bulldog showing his teeth, standing on a scroll that said: "Nobody Can Keep Estate Residents in the Dog House." The main headline said: "Residents Furious Over Big Dues Rise." And so they were and in their fury they were grabbing copies of The Fine Mutt as fast as they could.

<u>36 - THE MUTT FINDS A BONE</u>

You ain't nothing but a hound dog
– Elvis Presley, 1969

Over the next 10 months, The Fine Mutt continued to bring comfort or consternation to its readers, depending whether you lived in a cottage or worked in the manager's office. The new normal for residents at the Estate was sustained grumbling, although to some extent that was the natural state of things anyway. People always had their aches and pains but now a layer of institutional irritation had been added.

The cost-saving and fee-raising policy did not change. After the arrival of the first edition of The Fine Mutt, a decree was posted in the dining hall that reading the "unauthorized publication of certain disgruntled residents" was hereby forbidden and staff were instructed to pick up and remove any copies on the premises.

Brian Cooper then wrote a threatening legal letter on behalf of the residents' committee reminding management that the Estate was still in America and residents could read whatever the heck they wanted. Further, a lawsuit would be filed if any attempt were made to interfere with The Fine Mutt. The decree was removed the same day it was posted and this particular silliness was no longer mentioned.

The committee came to my personal rescue too. I had planned to pick up the cost of publication out of my own pocket until advertising started to kick in. Indeed, Bill Gibson's efforts were starting to pay off, with several funeral homes being the first to buy ad space. But the residents' committee decided that money raised by our thrift shop Secondhand Rose, formerly used to help fund programs to benefit residents, would also be used to subsidize The Fine Mutt. The thinking was that the residents needed a voice more than they needed basket weaving classes.

This was a relief to me. I had some savings in my bank account but I wasn't one of the Estate's resident millionaires; I didn't have the funds to sustain The Fine Mutt for long. Better yet, the committee left me with a free hand to get on with the job. There was no suggestion that he who pays the piper calls the tune.

The tune I called was not so different from what we had done previously. Sam Hudson, in perpetual personal eruption as board chairman, vented his frustration in the sports columns with no forays into anything that could be thought political. Deidre continued to shine as a fledgling reporter and all the others continued their good work. In everything that we did, whatever our personal feelings, I am proud to say we strived to be fair, never failing to seek out Mr. Jones for comment on stories although he never failed to ignore us.

Freed from our previous constraints, we now had a proper editorial page with editorials that I wrote and columns from any quarter. Linda took care of all the editing for the revamped page, as she had done before. While we took the precaution of no longer holding staff meetings in the library, Linda and I did continue to see each other there every day. After all, a man going into a library is more naturally suspected of wanting to read a book.

Often we would go to lunch together. One day we were walking over to the dining hall and the two scooter demons were back on the track, again yelling "Out of the way!" "Out of the way!" But this time they were closely pursued by two residents on Segways, those ridiculous stand-up scooters that are technology's hope of replacing human leg exercise. The four of them were apparently in a race.

Round the corner and out of sight they flashed and a few seconds later came the sounds of a terrible crash. We rushed to the scene of the accident and found the two Segways on the ground and one scooter overturned. Their riders lay sprawled. In addition, a deaf pedestrian, foolish enough to think she was safe from traffic on a walking trail and who had not heard the cries of "Out of the way," was bowled over.

The various victims lay moaning on the ground, bruised and slightly bloodied and blaming each other. Ambulances were called - not unusual at the Estate, where they are on speed dial – and their approaching sirens added to the drama. As it happened, the neck-breaking speed of the racers did not end up breaking any necks.

After offering such assistance as we could before the paramedics arrived, and in seeing that the injuries appeared minor, Linda and I resumed walking to the dining hall without having to be worried about being run down by a scooter.

"See, Linda," I said, "here is another proof that there is a God. Vengeance hath been wrought."

This accident, by the way, was duly recorded in The Fine Mutt. I took a picture with my cell phone as a warning to all.

As we went on chronicling life of the Estate, unbeknown to us The Fine Mutt was approaching its finest hour. The tip for the big scoop that was to change everything was delivered by none other than Deidre Williams, the newest member of our team.

She rushed into the dining hall at lunchtime one apparently ordinary day and sought Linda and me out. She had just come from leading a group of prospective future residents on a tour of the Estate, the volunteer job that she had been doing for years and never given up. She said she had "very big news." Well, I thought, that would make a change from dessert shortages and scooter wrecks.

Deidre always had an enthusiastic personality, perhaps due to cookie-induced sugar highs, but now she had been loosened of all constraints. Her words spilling out, she said: "I was leading a tour of three couples. The men were serious but the women looked like they were on vacation; they were there to have fun. I figured the guys were on some business convention and their spouses had come along too.

"They were a little younger than our usual attendees on these tours; guys in their fifties, maybe the gals in their late forties. Well, I really hit it off with the gals. The guys were busy taking notes and mumbling to themselves while the gals and I were cracking jokes and having a gay old time. I reached into my handbag and shared a little treat with them and they loved that."

"Cookies, by any chance?" I asked.

"No, candies. The cookies came later when I took them to my cottage."

"You took them to your cottage?"

"Yes, I wanted them to see how an average resident lived here. We shared a bottle of white wine and that's when the cookies came out. They loved it."

"Isn't that unusual?" I asked, now completely baffled. "How did that come about?"

"Well, see, the guys announced that they had an appointment with Mr. Jones and could I direct them to his office. Well, my eyebrows raised a bit at that one, because that was highly unusual. Nobody on these tours has ever asked to see the manager. And certainly not at 10:30 in the morning even if they did, because that is the crack of dawn to young Mr. Jones and he doesn't see anyone until the afternoon anyway."

"OK, so the men went to see the manager and you stayed with the women and showed them around a bit more?"

"Yes, they asked me to. The men were going to call on their cell phones when they were done, but it took an hour and a half. So I first showed the gals some other stuff – pickleball courts and such – and then we went to my cottage."

"So what happened then? What exactly is the very big news?"

"The manager is trying to sell the Estate. Those people weren't prospective residents, they were potential buyers."

"How do you know that?"

"One of the ladies told me. She obviously is not great at keeping secrets but the wine might have had something to do with it. I had said to them that they appeared more youthful than most of us and that it was worth remembering that you couldn't move in here until you are 65, except if you are married to someone older. So at this, they looked awkward, which also made me suspicious. When someone tells you that you look young, the average person will look flattered and happy.

"After a slight pause, one said, 'Oh well, it doesn't hurt to be prepared,' but it came off lame. Later, when the other gals were helping clean up the dishes, the most talkative one, her name was Sally, sidles up to me and whispers, 'I shouldn't be telling you this but you are so nice. We aren't actually interested in living here. Our husbands are partners in a retirement community company that is interested in buying this place.'"

"Oh," I said, "That is interesting."

"Yes, we have retirement communities all around the country," she said.

"But then her pals came back and she winked at me. Nothing else was said."

"That's great, Deidre, but we don't know who these people are, do we?"

"Actually, I do. At the end of the tour, Sally gave me a card with her cell phone number written on it. She said: 'You are so friendly. If you ever come to Cincinnati, you give me a call and I'll give you a tour of the city.' It turned out to be her husband Larry's business card; he works for an outfit called Retirement Solutions."

"Wow!" said Linda. "I'll bet that's the reason for all the belt tightening. Mr. Jones is trying to make the books look good to make the Estate seem more of a bargain. He's not thinking about the long-term, it's all about a sale in the short term. No wonder he doesn't care what the residents think. He's not planning to live with them much longer."

By dinner time, we and the other members of the staff had assembled in a remote corner of the hall for yet another emergency meeting. How to proceed? That was the question. I quickly told everybody the state of play. "Thanks to Deidre, we have learned that Mr. Jones is trying to sell the Estate. We know this because Deidre was told this confidentially in her volunteer capacity as a hospitality tour guide. It turns out the group she was leading were not interested in living here; they were here to check out the place for a possible sale. The men in the group had a meeting at 10:30 this morning with Mr. Jones.

"This is a terrific scoop Deidre has uncovered but it presents difficulties. It's going to be hard to confirm. I almost think the information doesn't need confirmation – appearing as it does as coming from the horse's mouth – but just to be safe we should make every effort to confirm it. We don't want to be sued for some cause.

"The woman who told this to Deidre just thought she was a tour guide; she didn't realize she was a reporter for us. Deidre made no promises, of course. She was not seeking this information and it's not her fault that this woman is a blabbermouth. At the same time, we don't want to burn this gabby lady and perhaps ruin her marriage by outing her as the informant. If we do get confirmation from another source, we could just state the facts unattributed if it comes to that."

Deidre now added: "I don't feel comfortable being a tattletale after this lady trusted me with her secret, but I realize that this is something everybody who lives here should know. I just don't want that lady to get into trouble."

"Agreed, Deidre. Perhaps there's somebody else who knows and can help us confirm it."

"I think Ms. Crocker might be able to help us," Betty said. "She might be able to tell us whether this group was the first to visit or were there others."

"Really, Betty, she could help? The last time you tried she could do nothing."

"I think things have changed a bit with her. But if she can, she too has to be protected. The king in his castle can't suspect in any way that she is talking to us."

"Fair enough," I said. "And someone needs to check something else. The retirement home industry probably has a trade paper – most industries do – or maybe a broker that checks out properties for clients. That may be a way to shake something loose."

So everybody got their assignments. Although Deidre was the hero of the hour, it was agreed that she should stay in the shadows and let Betty write the story. I reminded them, "Folks, what happens in the dining room stays in the dining room. Mum is the word. Goodnight and be careful of flying scooters on the trails, although I have reason to believe that tonight you will be safe."

37 - THE END IS NIGH

Heavenly shades of night are falling,
it's twilight time
– The Platters, 1958

Amid this excitement, my daughter Roberta called me that night and said she was unexpectedly going to meet with a client in our area the next day and could she come see me for lunch before her meeting.

It was my habit to call my children at least once a week, usually on Sundays. Both are married and have families of their own, Roberta in Palo Alto, and Sean in New York City, and I hadn't seen either of them for a few months. As busy as I was, I could spare a couple of hours at lunch time and return to my newsletter work in the afternoon. After all, my first and last job was being a dad, and from that job a man should never retire.

"The Estate is hopping at the moment and not necessarily in a good way," I said. "Let's meet at Hernando's Tavern and I'll explain everything. Let's say noon?"

Next morning I sent Linda a text message that I couldn't have lunch with her today. She replied: "OK, you are forgiven (smiley face). I have other plans too."

I went to Hernando's a little early and grabbed us a place in the courtyard, which is in the back.

Hernando's is popular with Estate residents who want to get off the reservation for a burger and a salad and I didn't want to run into anyone. It's not that I am unsociable – well, maybe a bit – but my time with my children is precious and I wanted Roberta to myself.

On the way over, something occurred to me. I had been so busy with the newsletter that I had forgotten what day it was. How time had flown by! This was the second anniversary of Susan's passing and I immediately felt guilty for not remembering.

Then I wondered whether this sad and morbid date was one I should remember. Wasn't it better to remember our wedding anniversary? Just as a new husband sometimes forgets to celebrate his wedding date, and of course I had done that in the past, then maybe a new widower can be forgiven for forgetting the day he was left alone. Then I sadly concluded that I should probably remember both. I wondered whether Roberta had remembered the date.

She arrived just two minutes after noon, looking happy and relaxed and apparently dragging no cloud of sadness. "Hi, Dad," she said, leaning over the table to kiss me, "you look good."

"You always look good, darling, so I have to keep up." As always, I cheered up at the sight of her and I wasn't going to spoil the moment by immediately reminding her what day it was if she didn't already know. Besides, while she had some of me in her, a long nose for one thing, her beauty was all from Susan and to see her was proof that in a way Susan still lived.

One of the challenges of the modern parent can be that you don't understand exactly what your children do for a living. Roberta worked for a computer company; software was involved somehow, and she was some sort of salesperson. And she had clients whose parents in turn were no doubt baffled by what they did. All I knew was that she was well paid and the hours were flexible so she could care for our grandchildren and keep them well-housed and fed. Her amiable husband, Dave, was an eye doctor and that I understood, as did his parents.

"My clients are sometimes irritating but this meeting is great because it gives me a chance to catch up with you beforehand. How is it going?"

"Oh busy, busy. If I was any busier, I'd have a real job." Then I told her about The Pine Nut/ The Fine Mutt. She laughed at the farce of all our adventures and scowled at the folly of the Estate's manager who was keeping us so busy.

We then talked about her kids – Kyle and Erica – and how they were doing well in middle school. We talked about their father, Dave, and how helpful he was as a dad when she was away on business trips. It was all the stuff a grandparent wanted to hear.

"And have you made any friends, Dad?" she asked.

"Well, you know me, Roberta. I have many acquaintances but not so many friends. This is the curse of the curmudgeon, I suppose. I had one really good friend but he recently died."

"That's sad. What about lady friends?"

I paused for a moment to think about that. "No," I said.

"None?"

"Well, there's one lady I work with at The Fine Mutt and have lunch with quite often."

"Really, and she doesn't qualify as a friend because she is a woman?"

"No, I mean, well, maybe she is a friend, but I don't think of her like that. Men and women…" My thought trailed off and then I added: "Friendships between men and women can become complicated."

"That's a very old-fashioned thought, Dad."

"Maybe," I said. "But the only woman I ever thought of as a friend was your mother." Then my emotions, roiling under the thin veneer of pleasant chat, suddenly burst through and tears rolled down my cheeks and a half-swallowed sob escaped from my mouth.

"Oh my goodness," said Roberta, surprised and afraid. "What is wrong, Dad?" And as she said this she leaned over and took my hand to comfort me and looked at me with a deep concern I had not seen since she was a little girl.

"Your mother died two years ago today. I wasn't going to tell you." There, I had said it, against my will and better judgment. I daubed my tears with a napkin and prayed nobody had witnessed this.

The moment only lasted a half minute and I was soon myself again, embarrassed enough to resume my normal composure.

"Well," Roberta said then, "I hope you encourage that lady friend of yours. It sounds like you need someone – and Mom would certainly have approved. You are coming up for Thanksgiving, aren't you? You can bring your friend if you like."

"Really, Roberta, it is nothing like that, but thank you for the offer. I'll be there myself to see you."

The talk of my lady friend struck me as being too silly for further discussion. I felt I was getting my daughter's blessing for a relationship that wasn't that sort of a relationship. But I appreciated her kind sentiments.

With happiness restored, I am sure we both walked out of the restaurant feeling like the time had been well spent, despite my uncharacteristic squall of emotion. On the way to the front, I spied Bill Gibson and another man seated at a table across from where we had been sitting. Bill was not so close that I felt the need to introduce Roberta, so I just waved and smiled.

Back at the Estate, I bumped into an excited Betty as I made my way to the dining hall to see if anybody else was around. "Bingo," she said. Bingo was not a word I usually associated with good news but I put that thought aside.

"Bingo?"

"Yes," she said, beaming. "I found a broker in Los Angeles that specializes in these places and has the listing. A picture is posted on the Web. It doesn't identify where we are – it just says Northern California – but it clearly is us. In the photo, you can see the pines and the little turret on the dining hall. Even the flagpole. Also the details match our situation exactly."

"Do you know how much they want for the Estate?" Betty asked, pausing for dramatic effect and then answering her own question: "Thirty million dollars."

"Was that in the ad?"

"No, it said call for particulars. So I did. I said that I was resident of the Estate, I worked for a residents' newsletter, we knew the Estate was for sale and thought that some of the residents here might be willing to buy it, as there were quite a lot of wealthy residents here. He was pleased with this suggestion – I don't think it was an angle he had thought of – and we got talking about the potential of the place and the many amenities and I told him that I had dabbled in real estate back in Chicago. He asked me if I really thought a residents' group might be interested. How much are we talking about? I said. "Thirty million," he said. By this time, I think he had forgotten the mention of the newsletter and he obviously didn't think talking to an old lady was dangerous, anyhow."

"It's another lesson in never underestimating an old lady," I said, hastily adding for gallantry's sake, "although you are hardly an old lady."

"Thank you, Alistair."

"Thank you, Betty, for your good work, although that stuff about residents buying the Estate was a bit of a stretch."

"It might be true," she said. "Who knows? All is fair in love and war and real estate."

"Not so much in journalism," I said.

"I am not so much a journalist," she said.

Seeing a slight touch of concern on my face, she said: "Don't worry. Ms. Crocker confidentially confirmed all this. She also confirmed those buyers the other day were not the first interested group to visit. Two others did too."

"What is it with Ms. Crocker suddenly becoming so cooperative?"

"I'll tell you when we have more time."

That evening we had another emergency editorial meeting in the back of the dining hall, which is all we seemed to do lately. The story would be stated as fact with no attribution – this to protect our sources – that the Estate was for sale for $30 million, the broker was in Los Angeles, the ad was in the public domain on the Web, and that several interested parties had already visited. Deidre would interview Sam for the official residents' committee reaction, a touch too incestuous for my taste but that problem had not gone away, and Betty would write the bulk of the main story. Martha Evans would help by contacting the board chairman for his comment.

As it turned out, Mr. Phillip D. Jones II, father of our nemesis, Mr. Phillip D. Jones III, was no longer the board chairman. Martha was directed to one Eric Curtis, the new chairman, who lived in Sewickley Heights, Pennsylvania, not far from where I used to live, although I did not know him. He knew nothing at all about a possible sale. He didn't deny it; he just expressed shock and promised to look into it. We thought for a short time to hold off on the story, but as we were confident that we knew more than the board chairman did, we saw no point in delay.

At the last moment, as agreed, Betty went to the manager's office to get the last quote for the story. She was met by Mrs. Fothergill and asked if Mr. Jones was in, as she needed to speak to him urgently. "Mr. Jones is in but not for you," she said.

"It is really important. It is about the Estate being.... "

"Don't tell me what it's about," she interrupted angrily. "I don't care if it's about the Second Coming. When are you people going to get it that Mr. Jones won't speak to anyone from your nasty little rag. Now get out of here right now or I'll call security." She closed the door on all further discussion, hard enough to send a message, not slammed enough to bother his lordship in the inner sanctum.

At my urging, and despite this rude behavior, Betty later sent an email to Mrs. Fothergill to be forwarded to young Mr. Jones. It was clearly marked Sale of Estate. We heard nothing more. Mrs. Fothergill either didn't check her email or deleted it immediately on seeing Betty's name. So when the deadline came around, we sent the edition to the press.

"You know, Alistair," Betty said, "This really will seem like the Second Coming to Mr. Jones when the newsletter comes out."

One odd detail must be reported about this dramatic day. Linda did not come to our editorial meeting. Everyone else was there but not her. When I got back to my cottage and checked my email, I saw to my relief an email from her. But what it said was a cause for anxiety.

"I am resigning my job at the newsletter effective immediately. Thanks for the opportunity."

That was it. What was this all about? Was she sick? Had I offended her? All I knew was that I would not be sharing The Fine Mutt's finest hour with the person who was only just revealed to me as my friend.

38 - POWER TO THE PEOPLE

And I think to myself
What a wonderful world
– Louis Armstrong, 1967

Judgment Day for Mr. Jones broke about mid-morning Friday with the arrival of The Fine Mutt in all the glory of print. The front-page story on the prospective sale of the Estate could not have summoned the living and the near dead any faster if Archangel Gabriel were blowing the last trumpet.

Alerted by word of mouth, the residents came to the library where the papers were stacked in bundles outside. They came in yoga and sweat pants, in dressing gowns and in white sports-wear and muddy gardening clothes, the attire of whatever they happened to be doing. Like a slow-moving stream, they came from across the community, from their cottages, the gym, the gardens, the pool, and the tennis and pickleball courts, and they lined up none too patiently for their newsletters. In all my career I had never seen anything quite like it.

And as they put on their glasses and started to read, they said things like "Oh my word, Harold, look at this!" "I can't believe it" and "This is the worst news ever." Some cried and others hugged each other. And quite quickly the mood of the crowd rose from curiosity to anger. They now drifted over to the manager's office nearby and they started chanting in high-pitched voices. "No sale, no sale, no way!" and waving bony fists.

Mrs. Fothergill now came out briefly, clutching a newsletter in one hand, in fact, the very first copy to be distributed, because I had earlier made a point of dropping it off in person. At first she was in her no-nonsense sergeant major persona, but she quickly beat a frightened retreat behind the door again as an elderly gentleman crept toward her waving a cane in a distinctly ungentlemanly manner amid a chorus of "No sale, no sale, no way!"

Then young Mr. Jones appeared but only half way out of the door, which he used as a sort of shield. He needed it. A huge bellow of elderly boos greeted his semi-arrival and he was bombarded with hippos and bears and various little stuffed animals – which at first was confusing to him and me both. Then I realized they were the plush toys that some residents put on their walkers to identify them. Before he gained complete cover, he tried to yell: "It's fake news." But the man with the cane angrily rapped on the door. "You liar," he said. "We googled the Web site and saw the ad."

Then the local police were called, presumably by the manager's office requesting urgent rescue from angry 80-year-olds. And when the police came, so did the local TV reporters, who had heard the call go out on the police scanner and realized at once that it doesn't get much better in their business than this – a riot at a retirement community.

At length, Mr. Jones and Mrs. Fothergill were escorted to a squad car by four officers who formed a sort of wedge that gently pushed its way, rather than muscled forward, so as not to further aggravate the outraged seniors. The two of them looked frightened and unnerved, and less like people being rescued than a couple being sent to serve a richly deserved sentence. As it happened, we never saw them again.

The crowd was now left baffled. Residents milled about not knowing what to do. They knew they had won but they did not know what they had won – the last battle or the first skirmish? The TV reporters moved among them and interviewed those they thought were the liveliest characters. Microphone Mike saw his chance and stepped forward to comment but he was so long-winded that the reporter cut him off and went to find someone more succinct.

There were more chants of "No sale, no sale, no way!" but they tailed off. Then Ms. Crocker stepped outside. She did not linger near the door but moved right out in the open until she was close to the nearest of the residents.

She was dressed quite formally, as always, but she had obviously been crying as her makeup was smudged. The boos began again, but she silenced them by saying in a loud clear voice that nevertheless suggested fragility and unease. "Ladies and gentlemen, I want to apologize to all of you." Perhaps it was her quiet courage, perhaps they were curious to see what she would say, but they let her go on.

"I do not support the sale of the Estate. I do not support many of the cost-cutting measures that have been taken. I was the manager's assistant. This was not my plan but it is true that I went along with it. I apologize for that and for not speaking out earlier but I want to stay, if I am allowed, to help make this right."

The old man with the cane interrupted. By now he had given up his plan to beat a manager about the ears – it seemed especially unsporting to do this to a young lady who appeared tearful – but he wasn't going to go easy. "How can you say this? The little rat who made our lives a misery is your fiancé."

"Actually," she said, rather sadly. "I broke up with him two weeks ago. For the last few days I have been living with dear friends I have made here at the Estate." The whole crowd was stunned by this and you could almost feel the general wrath leaving them and being replaced by a great tide of goodwill flowing in her direction. From the back came a woman's voice that seemed to speak for everyone: "You poor dear!"

"All what Miss Crocker has said is true." It was the refined Miss Curtis who now spoke, the former private school principal who was a guest at that long ago ladies tea party where the assistant manager was introduced to a few residents chosen by Betty. On that occasion, Miss Curtis had shocked the younger woman by admitting to having a loving relationship with a woman, not because she frowned upon lesbian relationships – she was young and tolerant – but because Miss Curtis seemed like the least likely person to be in one. In every other aspect she seemed the epitome of old-fashioned behavior.

Miss Curtis was indeed a well-respected figure at the Estate, the gold standard for deportment and manners, and her words carried special weight with the crowd. "Marianne, as I know her as a friend and I hope in time you will too, has gone out of her way to learn about the residents and the workings of the Estate. We all know of the various problems here lately but anything good that was done – that the place kept functioning at all – was due to Marianne. Women end up doing most of the work," she paused as the women in the crowd laughed sympathetically, "and Marianne did it all. So if she now wants to stay and put what she has learned to good use, I say we should let her.

"I have another surprise for you. A secret. I think most of you know that the Estate is a for-profit entity but it is run as a family company as if it were a non-profit, following the wishes of a long deceased family patriarch who had a great sympathy for the elderly and wanted them to be well cared for, even if the businessman in him wanted the enterprise to turn a modest profit for the sake of prudence.

"I am a member of that original family – the Curtises – and I am the older sister of the new board chairman, Eric Curtis. I don't take much interest in the family business, so it is not surprising that Mr. Jones and his father, from another branch of the extended family, had forgotten I lived here. I also didn't know anything about what they were up to until I read The Pine Nut."

At this I beamed even if she had forgotten the new name of our little paper.

"This afternoon I am going to call my brother and suggest that Marianne be retained to fill in as manager. I can't guarantee this will happen but we ladies have our powers of persuasion." This was greeted with more laughter and even a chorus of "For She's a Jolly Good Fellow," which seemed to be honoring Marianne and Miss Curtis both.

Betty winked at me. This was the back story she was going to tell me before it told itself. Apparently she and Miss Curtis had kept seeing Ms. Crocker discreetly after the tea party.

All the while the TV reporters kept filming and it was the perfect ending to the perfect story for them. It also apparently impressed family members on the Board of Trustees when the news clip was later shown to them.

*   *   *   *   *

It all came to pass. Ms. Crocker became the new manager after a trial period of six months, lived in her own cottage on campus and thrived in the job. All plans to sell the Estate were dropped. She hired back Pedro Rodriguez and the Estate was never short of a dessert again. The owners' dues had to stay up to cover inflation but the increase was halved after amicable negotiations with the residents' committee. Pickleballs became free once more and Billy Franks was allowed to have another concert. The Fine Mutt became a joint project of the management and residents and reverted to its old name. Everybody was happy except Minnie who was only happy when she wasn't.

As for Mr. Jones, he went back home, so I am told, to the waste management business, with perhaps a new respect for old people. Nobody knows what happened to Mrs. Fothergill but I suspect she became a prison guard to better perfect her gift for surly behavior. With more back-up, she would never have to back down again. But all this happened in the future.

For the moment I was the only one at the Estate left unhappy, because despite the incredible success of the newsletter's scoop, Linda had disappeared and all my efforts to find her had failed. I called, I emailed, I texted, I knocked on her door. Nothing. The library stayed close without explanation. Maybe she was away but I was left friendless, actually something more than that. I couldn't put my finger on why I missed her so much. I did feel that I had offended her in some way and that gave me real pain. There were times I knocked on her cottage door and I thought she might be there but she never answered.

I ran into Bill Gibson at breakfast. "Hey, buddy," I said. "Do you happen to have seen Linda?"

"Not in the last few days. Not since I waved to you at that restaurant in Carmelito. She happened to be there too with a girlfriend."

"Really? I didn't see her."

"She saw you. She asked me who you were with and I told her that gal from the print shop – what's her name, the account manager? – Sharon Price."

"Brian, I wasn't with Sharon Price. That was my daughter, Roberta, I was with."

"Oh," he said. "Sorry. I never dreamed she was your daughter. I thought you had a hot lunchtime date."

We both laughed in a forced way to cover any embarrassment over the mix-up. Sharon Price did look a bit like Roberta, though she looked more like Susan, so I could see how Bill might have become confused.

But this silliness brought me no closer to finding Linda.

39 - THE MISUNDERSTANDING

Will you still need me,
will you still feed me,
when I'm 64?
– The Beatles, 1967

That afternoon I finally did find Linda. I came over from my cottage for lunch a little late and there she was in the dining hall at one of the back tables with – of all people – Romeo Rawlings. Worse yet, he was holding her left hand and stroking it and all the while he was looking into her eyes with an expression that I suppose was meant to be soulful but looked to me like a severe case of constipation. Linda was staring back at him and I wondered how in the world she managed not to laugh.

As for me, I wanted to cry. It was sickening. I know she saw me out of the corner of her eye but she kept on staring at him. I didn't know what to do. I thought of sitting down with them but that seemed more than awkward. I thought of passing by and saying: "Your fritas will get cold if you ignore them like that." But that line wasn't exactly Oscar Wilde in the cafeteria. I thought of coming over and punching Romeo in the snoot but I had seen enough elderly guys fighting at the Estate to know that would be a farce. Besides, Linda was within her rights to have lunch with any smarmy guy with gold jewelry she wanted to. I had no call on her affections. I just thought her behavior was extremely rude.

So, in the end, I sat down with a group of other people at another table in direct line of sight to Linda. She did not look up and I sat there hopelessly staring and not enjoying my sandwich. When she got up to leave, thankfully not with him, I waited 10 minutes more, so as not to look anxious, and walked over to her cottage and knocked on the door.

I knocked twice and on the second knock she shouted: "Go away."

"Linda, it is Alistair."

"I know who it is. Go away."

"What have I done?"

"You know what you have done."

"No, I don't."

"Well, go ask your girlfriend."

"What girlfriend?"

"That attractive woman you were holding hands with at Hernando's the other day, the one who was looking at you with those big adoring eyes."

"What?" My mind was reeling and I was sputtering. "But Linda..." Then it suddenly dawned on me.

"Linda, that was my daughter, Roberta."

"A likely story," she said. But she opened the door a crack and looked at me uncertainly. "Your daughter? Bill Gibson told me that it was that woman from the print shop – Sharon something or other."

"Bill has never met my daughter but she does look a little like that lady. It's all a big mistake."

She still wasn't completely persuaded that I was telling the truth. Maybe I was the world's most brazen liar. "Then how come you were looking at each other like a man and woman sharing a sad secret of lost love together?"

"Because we were. I had just reminded Roberta that this was the second anniversary of her mother's death. Her mother, my wife.

She had forgotten the date."

All at once, Linda looked emotionally devastated. As her emotions flooded her face, I had just time to ask: "Did you see me cry?" Please, God, spare me that.

"No," she managed to say. "I was looking at your reflection in a mirror. I missed that. You cried?"

Then she burst into tears herself, flung the door wide open and fell into my arms sobbing. "I feel such a fool. Forgive me, forgive me, please. The last few days have been horrible."

"Of course." I stayed silent for a while, waiting out the monsoon of tears flooding my chest. Then I said in a kind voice: "It was a terrible time for me too. It is just an awful misunderstanding."

As emotionally clueless as I was, I thought that we needed to go somewhere else rather than me holding up her limp form. I was oblivious to what passersby might think but this scene needed to be cheered up.

"Linda, it's a Saturday, you don't have a shift in the library this afternoon, right?" She nodded.

"OK, then let's drive down to the ocean – maybe the Carmelito Nature Park so we can talk."

"Yes," she said. "We need to talk."

The nature park did have a sedative effect on our senses, as I hoped it would. Linda had stopped crying and now was approaching her old self. On a bench overlooking a big surf rhythmically beating against the rocks, I asked the question that was most on my mind. Why?

"Linda, please explain something. What is the greater meaning of all this? Even if I were having an affair with that Sharon woman, whom, by the way, I have never seen outside the print shop, why would that matter to you?"

She though this over for maybe half a minute. "Alistair, you said back at the Estate that you had a terrible time this past week, presumably because I was avoiding you."

"Yes, that was it, and what made it worse was that the newsletter had struck a great blow for its readers and you weren't there to share the victory with me. And I had this nameless guilt that I had done some mysterious thing to offend you and I couldn't stand that idea."

"Yes," she said. "So I think there is the answer to the question you asked me and it would be the same answer if I had asked the question of you."

"OK," I said with the look of the classic uncomprehending man. "So....?"

"So...unbeknownst to both of us, we have formed a great affection for each other, something beyond friendship. It has crept up on us when we least expected it."

"This great affection... do you mean, love?" I asked.

"If you like."

"I do like. I like very much." And I leaned over in that lonely spot and kissed her gently on the cheek and everything felt less lonely. She smiled for the first time that day.

"I must say, though, I had only just gotten comfortable with the idea that we were friends. Actually, Roberta at the luncheon asked me if I had any lady friends and it got me thinking."

"You mentioned me in your conversation? That makes me feel doubly bad for the misunderstanding."

"I think that misunderstanding was sent to remind us that we are really back in high school when it comes to romantic failures."

"Yes, we are," she said.

"Now, I have to get my mind around the fact that I am in love with you and we haven't even had a date."

"Yes, we have," she said. "After Gavin's funeral."

"But you promised to tell me if we were on a real date."

"I don't believe in stating the obvious. Did you put on fresh underwear before we went out?"

"I think I did. Surely I did."

"Then it was officially a date."

As we walked back on the trail through the forest to the parking lot, I asked about her absence.

"Why didn't you answer my emails, messages, calls, knocks on the door?"

"I wanted to punish you and I didn't want to see you."

"Why did you show up with Romeo in the dining hall?"

"To get your goat. That's why I took his hand. I was using the presence of an old goat to get your goat. I wanted to punish you and also talk to you, because by then, even though I hated you, I wanted to talk to you and see if you'd grovel. I knew you'd follow me. It all went entirely to plan, except the farcical ending."

"I would have groveled if I'd been guilty. I would have done anything. But I think that Romeo touch was just too cruel."

"I agree. I went too far. I feel really stupid. Sorry."

"No one has been more stupid than me. Forgive me," I said, adding by way of explanation, "I am a man."

It was fairly late in the afternoon when we got back to the Estate and, without discussion, we walked hand-in-hand back to my place and I opened a bottle of red wine and made a cozy fire.

In the hope of amusing her and keeping further tears at bay, I told her a story from my past, a story about another misidentification involving a woman I loved.

"Before you tell it, do you have the makings of dinner? I'd be happy to make it for us while you tell your story. It would be the least I can do."

Sure. No man in his right mind refuses the offer of a hot dinner. As it happened, I did have some hamburger frozen in the fridge and pasta in the pantry and she set about putting a meal together. My cottage was small so it was easy for her to listen as I told my story from a living room chair not six feet from outside the kitchen.

"This is a story about how I accidentally jumped on a woman while she was taking a nap in bed."

"What?" Linda said. "Accidently?" Her astonishment moved her to put down the ladle she was using to look at me.

"Yes. It was a mistake, believe me, but an honest one."

"It was back when Susan and I were first living in Pittsburgh in a little apartment, not long married, and I was working at the paper. I came home early one day and there was Susan on the top of our bed, in her nightie, taking a nap. It was still light but fairly late in the afternoon, maybe five. This was a bit strange because she usually didn't take naps and I usually didn't get back from work so early.

"But, being an affectionate fellow, I thought I'd surprise her and so I took off my shoes, bounded over to the bed and launched myself in the air. As I came down, I realized that the sleeping woman in the bed in Susan's nightie was not, in fact, Susan. It was her sister Margaret, one year older and close in appearance. What she was doing in Susan's nightie I don't know to this day.

"Anyway, when to my horror I realized my mistake, I gave out a little yell. She woke up to find her brother-in-law descending through space above her and she shrieked. And, bang, down I came in a pile on top of her with terror written on my face — and she realized immediately then that my intent was innocent, although thank goodness I was fully clothed."

Linda howled with laughter. "Remind me to tell my sister if she ever comes down here never to take a nap," she said.

"And you tell her not to wear your nightgown. I also learned another lesson that day. In the old cartoons, Wile E. Coyote would fall over the cliff while pursuing the Road Runner and desperately scratch the air to delay his fall. In real life, that doesn't work so well. It gives you only one or two seconds extra before the inevitable crash."

After her expertly improvised Italian meal, with plenty of laughs and affection as side dishes, we were fairly exhausted, having experienced almost the whole range of human emotions in a single day. Linda said to me: "May I stay with you tonight?" And after I said, "Of course!" – and she started to ready herself for bed – a moment of panic overcame me.

"Linda, I don't know how to put this delicately, but..."

"But what, Alistair?"

"Well, I was thinking about those romantic bodice-ripper type books back in the library...."

"Not my usual fare, Alistair, but go on..."

"Well, I was just hoping that you weren't hoping for a master lover raging with virility that I believe are the heroes of such novels, because my libido these days is not so much raging as slumbering. It may have withered on the vine, for all I know. It's certainly not going to win any prizes in the county fair."

"I wonder where county fairs exhibit champion specimens of virility these days," she said. "With the gourds, squashes, maybe with the jellies? But seriously, Alistair, don't worry. It will be lovely enough just to lie with you if that is all that happens."

Having no expectations, we exceeded the ambitions of our mildest dreams. I will spare you the details. Gentlemen never tell and, besides, my kids might read this journal and I don't want them to die of embarrassment.

Our first night together was tender and loving. She didn't have a nightgown that night so there was no chance of leaping on the wrong woman. We found our long lost sparks, our senses awoke from their hibernation and, while I was no hero out of the pages of a romance novel, I think I was worth at least an honorable mention in any county fair.

After our breath slowed and our pulses gently beat back to normal, I asked: "Linda, were you completely surprised by your feelings for me or did you have an early hint that you might love me?"

"Actually, I did. It was at that meeting after we decided to print our own newsletter. The newsletter is your baby and it has been your almost total focus. Yet you still had the thoughtfulness to think of me and worry that I might lose my job if we were to keep meeting in the library. Wow, I thought, that's special. And you, Alistair, did you have a hint?"

"No. Although I knew I was fond of you, I did not know how much and was uncomprehending to the last."

"Sometimes truth is more impressive when it comes as a thunderbolt out of a blue sky," she said.

We lay peacefully in each other's arms for a long time, prolonging this beautiful moment, just looking at each other like two travelers who had reached an unexpected destination.

Finally, I broke the spell and asked a question: "Linda, what is a bodice anyway?"

"Go to sleep, darling, I'll tell you in the morning."

Darling. The endearment that bridges all loneliness.

40 - THE FATEFUL WORDS

Oh honeycomb won't you be my baby
– Jimmie Rodgers, 1957

At any age, the morning after a first awkward embrace can be an occasion for regrets. But we got up and went to breakfast in the dining hall with no regrets and flush with the novelty of our situation. (Actually, I had one regret. I had forgotten to check out the little tattoo on Linda's inner thigh and now she was fully dressed. Darn those senior moments!)

On the way over, I remembered the offer Roberta had made. I asked Linda: "Would you like to come and meet my family at Thanksgiving? When we had lunch at Hernando's, Roberta asked me if I wanted to bring my lady friend to her place for Thanksgiving dinner. But I wasn't even sure that you were my friend and the sleeping arrangements would have been awkward. I mean, what if she gave us a double bed."

"Ah, yes," Linda said, "the horror."

"You know what I mean."

"Of course – I am just giving you a hard time, which is what friends in close relationships do, something I need to practice. Yes, I would love to come. It's been years since I've been to a family Thanksgiving and I am dying to meet your daughter and son. And I need to tell your daughter to stop looking like other people."

After a quick call to Roberta to confirm that the invitation still stood, the plan was set. Two weeks later, we drove up to Palo Alto the night before Thanksgiving and found the whole family was staying in Roberta's big house. True to her word, Roberta and her family were very welcoming, as were my son Sean, his wife Celia and their two boys, Chris and Travis, who had just arrived on a flight from New York City.

Linda was an object of natural curiosity but her kindness, her willingness to pitch in and help and her ready smile put everybody at ease. She was unstintingly embraced as the lady who had made Dad happy again. She took pleasure in their company too, especially Roberta but also the kids. For a person who had no children, Linda turned out to have a natural rapport with kids, although as a librarian before she came to the Estate she probably had more experience interacting with them than I imagined.

She played Monopoly with Kyle, Erica, Chris and Travis and also read to them. As Sean's children were a little younger than Roberta's, she chose something to read that might appeal to the imagination of all ages, a magical classic poem, Samuel Taylor Coleridge's The Rime of the Ancient Mariner, with its extraordinary tale of phantom ships, flying souls, and wedding guests held in thrall, happenings more strange than any Marvel comic.

The mention of wedding guests shortly became more relevant. We had not talked of marriage but Linda's enthusiastic and whole-hearted acceptance by my family perhaps implied that the subject might be raised. As it happened, Roberta was the one who brought it into the open on the evening after Thanksgiving dinner. We were settled in front of the fire in her living room. It was just the three of us by then, the kids having gone to bed after a long day, and we were enjoying a nightcap as the last logs burned low.

"So, Dad, what now? Are you guys going to stay in your own cottages or move in together as domestic partners? Or will you get married so as not to live in sin?" Roberta had a way of being direct. She would have made a good reporter.

"Well, Roberta, if we did anything that could qualify as an actual sin we might both be very proud. But we really haven't had time to discuss that. If we do share a cottage, we will probably just be domestic partners, because it seems silly to me to get married at our age, I mean, why bother?" And then I added the fateful words: "Unless, of course, if the lady were single, never been married, never had experienced being a bride." I thought this was a sensible answer to a difficult question and I was pleased with myself for coming up with it on the spur of the moment.

Linda simply and quietly said: "I was never married." No one said anything more, but Linda looked over at Roberta and smiled and Roberta knowingly smiled back at her. In that instant, I realized that, just as the turkey had been cooked, my goose was cooked, too. And for the moment I would have to simmer in my own juices.

On the drive home the next day, as we were stopped momentarily in the heavy holiday traffic, I looked over at Linda and said: "I wish there was a better moment for this but will you take my hand and the rest of my wreck of a body in marriage?"

"Alistair, I think your romantic language needs a little work. Aren't you supposed to get down on one knee? I have never been proposed to but I read in a book somewhere that's how it is supposed to go down."

"Arthritis won't allow it and there's no room in the car. Besides, old people should at all times resist the temptation to be cornballs."

"You are right there. But a ring and a bottle of Champagne might be helpful."

"You'll get those later. I promise."

"You really don't have to do this on my account."

"I really need to do this on your account. Looking back over the last few years, I reckon I have misread every woman I have met. I thought Betty was a female Romeo. I thought Martha was too straight to be useful, ditto Deidre. I didn't recognize that you and

I were friends and then something beyond friends. And after what you said last night, my intuition is yelling at me not to be so obtuse."

"We could just be girlfriend and boyfriend or else live together as domestic partners," she said.

"We could. But I have decided I want to seal the deal. I don't want Romeo or some other flash Harry luring you away by promising a date at a restaurant offering a 5 pm senior special. Besides, I have always thought that elderly people who call themselves boyfriend and girlfriend are abusing the language. The term partners is equally absurd. When they wake up in the morning do they look over in bed and say: 'Howdy partner! How are you today?' "

"But are you sure, Alistair, that I am the one for you now."

"Absolutely. A wise person once said to me that one test of true love is the sense that you have known the person you love forever, even if you have spent little time with them and know next to nothing about their history. That is how I feel about you, Linda. You are a new acquaintance to my senses but my soul recognized you before my brain did as a familiar spirit who hadn't been properly introduced in the conventional sequence of time but who could fill a space left vacant in my heart."

The traffic had started moving again so I could not look directly at her as she replied. "Well, Alistair, if you put it like that...."

I snuck a glance over. "You mean that you will marry me?"

"Yes, I will say I do, because I feel like that, too. And also because you have promised Champagne and a ring." This was her little joke to break the somberness of the moment, although in truth I was looking forward to some Champagne.

"Hurrah for us!" I said.

"By the way, who was that wise person who taught you about

love?"

"Actually, it was Susan."

"I can see she was a wise person – and with good taste in men too. I couldn't say that about my own life."

"Well, I hope you can now."

We stopped talking for a minute or so to ponder the serious step we had made.

"You know what is amazing? " I said at last.

She didn't offer an immediate reply so I went on.

"When people fall in love they are usually much younger than we are, and they are usually carried away on a hormonal tide that often doesn't immediately engage the mind or the spirit, although that may soon follow. With us, it was the reverse. We had to make our own chemistry. We had to surf a different sort of tide, all mind and spirit."

"What are you saying?"

"That our sort of love is more remarkable, coming deeper from the soul, although the love of the young is probably better suited to torrid honeymoons."

"Oh, I don't know, Alistair, we did alright the other night for older people."

"Yes, but I think we should not wait too long before we get married. Those in a sunset romance need to act fairly quickly while there is still some warmth and light left in their lives. I don't want to leave you a widow before you officially become a bride."

"Cheery thought but you are right," she said. "No long engagement. But if we are to invite out-of-towners like your kids, we need to give them some notice. We should plan something in a couple of months, maybe the spring."

"Ah, spring, when a young man's fancy turns lightly to thoughts of love."

"And an old man's fancy?"

"Heavily to thoughts of rheumatism, I think. But, seriously, we need to get going on this. I suspect that all the usual reception venues in Carmelito have been booked out for months. Where could we go?"

"How about the Estate?"

"Do they have weddings there?" I asked.

"I don't know," Linda said, "but I don't see why not. They have funeral remembrances there so I am sure they can fit in a jollier event."

"Other than my kids and your sister, who would we invite?"

"Everybody," she said.

"Everybody?"

"Yes. Everybody at the Estate," she said. "That place needs an event to bring it back together. Let everybody come together and help put on a wedding like nothing seen at any other place at any other time."

41- WEDDING BELLS AND BAGPIPES

You can't hurry love
– The Supremes, 1966

So everybody was invited, even those across the street in assisted living. The invitation for Saturday April the 7th at 4 pm specified no wedding gifts. "Your present will be your presence and participation," it said. That last was a little redundant – because if those invited were present they would, in fact, be participating, if you stopped to think about it. Few did stop to think about it. They had every intention of participating, and their participation would indeed amount to gifts in kind.

The invitation also mentioned that any lady who wanted to be a bridesmaid could sign up at the library. Almost 100 of them did, ladies who had never been married, ones who had been divorced or widowed (the biggest group of all), and ones still married but who wanted to be part of the retinue. Even Minnie the Moaner signed up to be a bridesmaid, perhaps fearful that she would lose her standing to criticize the dresses if she did not.

This throng of bridal supporters would be preceded down the aisle by the maids of honor, Roberta, and my daughter-in-law, Celia, and the grandchildren, Kyle, Erica, Chris and Travis, who would be flower boys or girls or apprentice grooms or some-thing, the older ones assisting the younger ones.

The same offer was made to men who wanted to have a role. The best man was still to be announced – Gavin would have got the nod if only he had not died – but my son Sean would definitely be the assistant best man, as I was pretty sure he didn't want to run the show. After that, any man with a dark blazer, a blue shirt and a pair of slacks was welcome to be an usher, groomsman, bouncer or whatever. Perhaps not surprisingly, the men did not show as much enthusiasm as the women for being in the bridal party. Only a dozen or so signed up. If minding and tending the beer keg were an official duty, I am thinking the sign-ups would have been more.

All this was Linda's doing. Her kind heart did not want to leave anyone out in a community of many lonely people. She didn't expect so many to take up the bridesmaid offer but she was happy nevertheless. I warned her that it would look strange to have more people in the bridal party than there were regular guests. It helped that the wedding was scheduled to be held outside on the lawn where plenty of space was available, though to my mind the guests in their motley array would look like Farmer Brown's cows trotting over in a great mob across the pasture.

But on the question of how to get some uniformity to the bridal party, the Sewing Club came to the rescue. I confess I had never heard of the Sewing Club before but those sewing ladies turned out to be the biggest participants. With Linda's suggestions, they came up with a plan for more than 100 bridesmaids' dresses in a shade of light blue. They took measurements of each lady and each lady would have to pay a modest sum, nothing more than the cost of the materials, for the privilege. The work was done by several teams of amateur dressmakers working over a couple of weeks, their sewing machines buzzing all afternoon and into the night. They turned out dresses as if they were so many Rosie the Riveters producing Liberty Ships for World War II.

In the meantime, the Gardening Club was making plans for the flowers. Bouquets, boutonnieres, all was in hand. Diane Gibson would take care of the wedding photography (with a few shots reserved for The Pine Nut). The Catering Committee, which until recently had been busy complaining about the great dessert shortage, now worked hand-in-hand with the staff at the dining hall, where Pedro Rodriguez was back on the job and taking a personal interest in the wedding arrangements. Salmon and artichokes, the classic Carmelito dinner, was to be served as the main course. The entertainment would be provided by Billy Franks and The Hot-Water Bottles. Who else? As well as all these contributions, many residents donated food and drink. Miss Curtis ordered cases of French Champagne as well as white and red wine grown locally.

This would not only be the most unusual wedding seen at the Estate or anywhere else but also one of the cheapest for its size. As for the rehearsal dinner, Linda took the view that while she was never a bride, she had seen enough weddings to consider herself fully rehearsed. So the night before we simply had a family dinner with my children and their families at Hernando's in Carmelito, the very restaurant that was the scene of the great misunderstanding that in the end brought us together. Trish Halsey, the widow of Gavin, also attended because on the morrow she would be the best man. We figured that in a wedding with more than 100 bridesmaids a woman as best man would not seem out of place.

That night Linda and I slept in separate quarters. She went back to her cottage one last time and I stayed in mine. This was not only a curtsy to tradition but also a recognition that a man's cave was no place for women to gather for the hairstyle-doing, makeup-preparing, dress-adjusting routine that is part of the traditional bride beautification project before a wedding.

For my part on the morning of the ceremony, I went off to play golf with Sean, returning at 2 pm in time to shower and put on my wedding apparel, which might be called office casual if I were still going to the office – basically the same rig as the groomsmen, dark blazer, slacks, loafers, blue shirt but no tie.

The day was picture perfect and by 3:30 the sky was still cloudless and the afternoon breeze came on cue to take the edge off the heat. Behind the dining hall, just out of sight of the space on the lawn where the chairs had been arranged for the ceremony, the many volunteers in the wedding party assembled.

At 3:50 pm, Sean and I and Trish and the groomsmen took our places front and center in the little bower, where we were met by the ceremony's officiant, Marianne Crocker, acting manager of the Estate, who had obtained a temporary license to perform her matrimonial duties. She has been thrilled to be asked and nothing on that day of the Estate coming together did more to suggest peace than the young manager standing up before the guests. For once, she did not even wear her long gloves, but was simply dressed in the bridesmaid uniform of the day.

No sooner had we taken our places than a swirl of bagpipes sounded behind the dining hall. This was a surprise. Nobody had said anything about bagpipes but a bagpiper now appeared from around the corner leading the great mass of bridesmaids to the ceremony. First came those in wheelchairs and their assistants from across the street, followed by the bridesmaids who needed walkers. The maids of honor, Roberta and Celia, and the flower boys and girls, my grandchildren, followed closely behind. Then came the volunteer bridesmaids who could walk under their own steam. In leading the way, the piper tread with very slow and deliberate steps, careful not to get too far ahead, marking time if he had to. As he came closer, the piper was revealed to be Bobby, normally the sax player in Billy Franks' band but now kitted out in kilt and sporran and playing a mean bagpipes, as if to confirm that the age of wonders is not dead.

They did not look like Farmer Brown's cows being led to the shed, because cows are not rounded up by bagpipers, not even in Scotland. The mass procession looked like an amazing, joyful event, and clearly everybody participating thought it was. The regular guests cheered wildly when the piper and the battalion of bridesmaids and others finally made it to the place where the ceremony would be performed. By the time the ushers had impersonated valet parking attendants at a country club to seat everybody, it was already ten minutes past four. Five minutes later, another roar went up. "Here comes the bride," several dozen bridesmaids said at once.

Some 50 yards to the rear, Linda appeared on the arm of Jimmy Devine, a friend to all as the former residents' committee chairman who had always thought the world of her. With her own father long deceased, she could not think of anyone better to give her away. She and her father figure were led by a troubadour with a ukulele, sweetly singing "Somewhere Over the Rainbow." If this were not eccentric enough, the singer turned out to be Billy Franks broadening his usual repertoire.

Unlike the other women in the wedding party in their long dresses, Linda wore a short, knee-length dress, not quite white but cream, that allowed her long runner's legs to defy the years beautifully. She wore a little hat, also cream, with a small veil.

And so we were wed. The vows were the traditional ones, slightly adapted for the modern age, so no requirement to obey me, but also none of that "I promise to be your soulmate" nonsense either. Marianne Crocker, radiating joy, performed flawlessly, and in the great power invested in her by the state of California for the day, she pronounced us man and wife. I lifted Linda's veil and kissed her.

The reception was in the dining hall, which was decorated grandly by the decoration committee with the help of the garden committee and perhaps other committees unknown to me. For richer or poorer, the Estate remained the land of a thousand mustaches (goatees optional) and a thousand committees.

There were speeches, of course. One advantage of having a rehearsal dinner is that most of the speechmakers get toasts out of their system before the main event, leaving the best man and a few others to say some words without everybody else imitating long-winded members of Congress. We didn't have that advantage but Trish, our best man, was able to deter the few notorious gasbags in the crowd from going on too long.

Trish herself made some good remarks and Sean and Roberta did too. When it came to my turn, I said, "I know we at the Estate love a good rumor, and this wedding has been rushed, so I just wanted to make quite clear that the reason is not because the bride is expecting a baby."

Having got my cheap laugh, I went on to the important thing I really wanted to say. "Linda and I are so happy to have found each other. We are writing the last chapter of our lives, like all of us here, and there is a temptation to think that nothing else good or meaningful can happen. Yet I found a new purpose in working for the newsletter, and Linda did too, and at the time I thought it would just be a way of keeping busy. And together we found love again when we were not looking for it. And if it can happen to us, it can happen to anyone here today. Thank you for celebrating our marriage, but celebrate also the greater truth revealed by our unlikely union – that a meaning and purpose in life can be found by anyone at any time. As long as we breathe, life is there to surprise and sustain us."

Trust me to try and make a serious point to a crowd of Champagne-addled elderly people, and trust kind and considerate Linda to take care of the things that had to be said and that I had forgotten – the long thank-you list of those who helped make the wedding happen, from Marianne Crocker, Pedro Rodriguez, the many bridesmaids, Jimmy Devine, Billy Franks; and individuals like Miss Curtis and the numerous committees with their dress making and flower arranging. "Thank you, thank you, everybody. I have waited a long time for a wedding and I could not have dreamed of a better one or a better husband."

Linda and I danced the first dance – a waltz, the one dance for which we were prepared – and later Linda threw her corsage into the vast sea of bridesmaids. But, of course, the fix was in, as it often is at weddings, and she threw it directly to Marianne Crocker, who needed a better fiancé than the one she had the last time. Nobody minded.

The highlight of the evening's musical entertainment was Bobby, who discarded his bagpipes but retained his kilt to play the sax, so that his sporran was rocking to the beat laid down by Billy Franks and The Hot-Water Bottles. We left at about 8:30 as the party was more or less breaking up, it being a fairly late hour by Estate standards. A limousine had been arranged to take us down to a rustic inn at Big Sur for a one night honeymoon and we were there shortly after nine. We were in bed not long after we arrived at our cabin

Outside the fog was creeping through the tops of the redwoods. Inside it was cozy with a fire lit in the room and the glow from the fireplace keeping the darkness at bay. Linda climbed under the blankets first and in a very drowsy voice said, "Are you coming to bed, darling?"

"I'll be right there," I said. "There's just one thing I need to do."

42 - GOODBYE, MY LOVE

Until the 12th of Never,
I'll still be loving you
– Johnny Mathis, 1957

Dear Susan,

I am writing to ask for your blessing. When we were together, we always agreed that if one of us died the other should feel free to find love again with someone else. I never thought that circumstance would arise, in part because I always assumed you, being younger than me, would live longer. But in a cruel trick of fate that was not to be.

Even when I was suddenly left alone, I never thought that another loving relationship would be in my future. I loved you forever – that is what I always said. And that is as true tonight as it ever was.

But the promise we made on our wedding day was to have and to hold, from this day forward, until death do us part. The poetic soul who came up with those words put a sting in their tail, a reminder of our mortality but one that allows those of us who still live to get on with the business of living, which includes loving another person to help lift our loneliness and despair, if we happen to be so lucky.

Quite unexpectedly, I found that person. I did not seek her. I just went through the motions of living until I actually started to live again and there she was. In no way is she a replacement for you as you cannot be replaced. But she is a comfort and, yes, a joy. Her name is Linda and, as I sense you somehow know and approve, I ask your blessing anyway. We were married this afternoon in a ceremony that no way resembled our own but had its own charm.

Roberta and Sean took part in the ceremony and are grateful that I found her because the alternative for me was to stay lost. Linda honors you, too, and understands that I must go on loving you even as I love her.

But I have not shown her this letter. These little notes are our own thing and I won't be writing to Linda like this (she thinks I am weird enough already). And from now on my wishes and prayers will be my only communication to you. Until we meet again.

In a moment, I will put this letter on the fire and it will go up the chimney as smoke, there to join the fog outside but also the fog that separates the living and the dead. In that shadowland, I trust you may glimpse it.

Rest in peace, Susan.

Love always, Alistair xxxx.

Love in the Late Edition

ABOUT THE AUTHOR

Reg Henry, who grew up in Australia, spent 45 years as a journalist for newspapers in Australia, Britain, and the United States. Early in his career, after service with the Australian army in Vietnam, he worked five years on the sports desk of The Times of London and later spent most of his career at The Pittsburgh (Pennsylvania) Post-Gazette, where he was the deputy editorial page editor. In addition to his other duties, he wrote a weekly humor column, which was nationally syndicated and became the basis of a book of columns The Wry World of Reg Henry. He also spent five years as the editor of The Monterey (California) Herald, a paper then owned by the same family that held the Post-Gazette.

He and his wife, Priscilla, are retired and have a home between Salinas and the Monterey Peninsula. They keep busy playing tennis and biking and participating in volunteer activities. They are also long-distance grandparents as their two children have grown up and live far away with their own families. Their daughter, Allison Gilpin, is in Sydney, Australia, and their son, Jim Henry, lives in Ipswich, Massachusetts.

SETON
PUBLISHING

CPSIA information can be obtained
at www.ICGtesting.com
Printed in the USA
LVHW021742250121
677443LV00015B/2270